## LOVE BITES

### *A Sofie Metropolis Paranormal Mystery*

Sofie Metropolis is back and in the deep end of the coffee pot when she's retained by the neighbourhood vampire to prove he isn't responsible for a recent string of grisly murders, and her mother also talks her into looking for a missing woman neither of them knows, but Thalia has adopted in absentia nonetheless. And if her plate isn't full enough, things heat up on the romantic front when 'bounty hunter' Jake Porter and yummy Greek baker Dino both decide to vie for her undivided attention. What's a good Greek girl with a gun to do...?

# LOVE BITES

*A Sofie Metropolis Novel*

Tori Carrington

**Severn House Large Print**
London & New York

This first large print edition published 2011
in Great Britain and the USA by
SEVERN HOUSE PUBLISHERS LTD of
9-15 High Street, Sutton, Surrey, SM1 1DF.
First world regular print edition published 2010 by
Severn House Publishers Ltd., London and New York.



British Library Cataloguing in Publication Data

Carrington, Tori.
Love bites.
1. Metropolis, Sofie (Fictitious character)--Fiction.
2. Women private investigators--New York (State)--New
York--Fiction. 3. Greek Americans--New York (State)--New
York--Fiction. 4. Missing persons--Investigation--
Fiction. 5. Detective and mystery stories. 6. Large type
books.
I. Title
813.6-dc22

ISBN-13: 978-0-7278-7963-9

Printed and bound in Great Britain by the
MPG Books Group, Bodmin, Cornwall.

As always, for our remarkable sons
Tony and Tim.

# Acknowledgements

When it comes to acknowledging those important in the creation of any of our novels, the first to come to mind are our sons Tony and Tim. Aside from their being the most talented, intelligent and perfect children in the world – said with complete objectivity, of course – they serve as living, breathing reminders of what life was like at their age so we might view the experiences through an objective lens. Well, most of the time. A shame the act of acquiring said insight comes with the reminder of how old that makes us...

Like many siblings, my (Lori) brother Carl J. Schlachter, Jr. and I haven't always been close, but recently have claimed a patch of common ground on which we're both enjoying building. He along with his beautiful wife Sabrina and children Dallas, Charles and Jaelynn – as well as Sabrina's parents Gene and Diane – are a precious source of history, love and laughter, further enriching our lives in a way that can't help but carry over into Sofie's...

'The Man' our agent Robert Gottlieb, and everyone else who works behind the scenes at Trident Media Group, including Alanna Ramirez and Lara Allen: Continued thanks for covering the business angle of our lives with brilliant aplomb so we may focus on the creative end.

Dr. Segunda Eudela and Nurse Gloria of the Toledo-Lucas County Health Department: they know why. Thank you, thank you, a thousand times thank you for your patience, wisdom and unparalleled kindness!

Indy booksellers everywhere: You guys rock! We'd especially like to show appreciation for darling Annette and Mike Fitzgerald of The Book Exchange in Port Clinton, Ohio, fantastic Gay Orr and Annie McGee of The Paperback Outlet in Warren, MI, and marvelous Mary Alice Gorman (aka ma) and Richard Goldman of Mystery Lovers Bookshop in Oakmont, PA. Thank you for ... well, everything should just about cover it.

And, ultimately, we'd like to acknowledge our new publishers Edwin Buckhalter, Rachel Simpson Hutchens and Michelle Duff of Severn House: our girl Sofie is in very good hands, indeed. We raise our own coffee cups in salute to you and look forward to doing the same in person with perhaps something a little stronger very soon. Cheers!

# ONE

Call me picky, but goat doesn't do it for me. The tough, gamey meat doesn't even rate a spot on my Top One Hundred Favorite Foods List, much less come anywhere near the top.

And goat is exactly what my mother fixed for Sunday dinner.

Greeks. Most times, I didn't have a problem with them. Which was a good thing since as a full-fledged Greek-American living in the Greek enclave of Astoria, Queens, New York, I'd be in trouble if I did.

Not that my life wasn't already full of that. Trouble, I mean. While things had definitely settled down from the chaos of a few weeks ago, I had the feeling it was going to be a while before I felt normal again. Normal being a relative term. Because, let's face it, nothing has been 'normal' in my life since I signed on at my uncle Spyros' Private Investigation Agency over six months ago. At least not 'normal' in the way to which I'd previously subscribed. But even that was a damn sight better than stumbling across a serial killer with a twisted fascination for wood-chippers. Hell, anything had to be better than that.

What was of immediate concern as I stood on

the front steps of my parents' house was what I going to do to satisfy my own ballooning hunger. Not just for food, but ... Well, didn't I have enough on my hands without bringing other unsatisfied cravings of a personal nature into the mix? I was in no mindset to think about anything beyond my growling stomach. Even if certain other areas of my anatomy were also feeling a bit neglected.

I looked over my shoulder at the house I'd grown up in and which I usually left satisfied. Today, not only had I not eaten where I usually gorge myself at Sunday dinner, I had no left-overs. Well, not anything I was going to touch, anyway.

Goat. Ugh. What was my mother thinking?

I pulled my black leather jacket closer to ward off the mid-November chill and moved toward my 1965 Mustang parked at the curb. I only lived down the street, but in this cold I didn't walk anywhere unless the destination involved something sweet or involved saving my life. Which inevitably meant hunting for parking spots, no matter what time of day or day of the week it was, but, hey, I'm spoiled that way.

A gust of wintry wind blew straight through me and I shivered, hurrying to get inside my car where it wouldn't be any warmer but at least I'd be out of the elements. The wind and cold I could handle; it was the darkness of this time of year that bothered me most. Take now, for instance. My body told me it should be some-where around eight or nine o'clock at night. Instead it was six. It felt strange.

Stranger still was the conversation I'd left still going on inside the house.

'I don't understand why you can't look for the girl.' My mother kept bringing the conversation back to me while I tried to salvage something from the inedible meal. Mostly, I'd eaten bread and feta and olives and salad. 'It's what you do, isn't it? Find people?'

I suppose I should have been happy that she didn't substitute 'pets' for 'people', since there have been times over the course of my short detective career that the only clients interested in hiring my services were those looking for their lost chihuahuas.

But I wasn't.

OK, so Roula Kalomoira was from the neighborhood. In a manner of speaking. Hey, Queens is a big neighborhood. And I didn't know her. Neither did my mother or the rest of my family, for that matter. None of them had probably even heard her name until she'd gone missing a week ago. But all too readily my mother and her St Demetrios' church friends had lit up the call tree and made the needed connections until Roula was now a relative instead of a relative stranger.

'Mom,' I'd said countless times during dinner. 'I'm sure she's fine. You, yourself, said that she's nineteen. Not exactly a minor. Nine times out of ten missing women pop back up with a story about having met someone. She's probably feathering a love nest or something.'

'Not Roula,' Thalia was adamant. 'She didn't have a boyfriend.'

I'd raised a finger. 'So, see. She could have

met someone...'

'And not tell her mother?'

I'd stared at her, no words necessary.

Rule Number One: Never take on a case until after the money hits your hand.

My uncle Spyros, the owner of the detective agency for which I worked, was fond of rules. Or had been. I hadn't seen him myself for months. But it was a reasonable guess that he still lived his life by the rules where he was currently staying in Greece.

Anyway, I'd learned the reason for this particular rule first-hand and I wasn't about to go looking for a girl I didn't know just because my mother had convinced herself that she was lying dead in a ditch somewhere.

And if she was lying in a ditch?

I got into my car and put the bag of useless leftovers on the passenger's seat. Well, then, someone would find her soon enough. And the mystery would be solved. Without my involvement.

I grabbed the steering wheel with my left hand, immediately regretting the move when my palm nearly froze to the worn leather. I shook it off and blew on the burned skin even as I inserted the key in the ignition. Probably I could have walked home by now.

The old Mustang gave a cough and sputtered reluctantly to life.

'I hear you, girl. I hear you.'

I'd named my car Lucille. She looked like a Lucille. But the name seemed somehow more suited for summer drives to the shore than winter dashes to the store. Apparently Lucille felt the same and was letting me know about it.

I scanned the street in front of me, adjusting my sight to the darkness. A task that would be much easier if halfway up the block red and white strobes weren't bouncing off neighboring houses.

Police cars.

I looked back toward my parents' closed door, surprised they weren't already outside to see what was going on. Probably they were all still at the dining room table talking about poor Roula and what could possibly have happened to her.

I smiled. Thalia was going to hate that real drama was unfolding outside her house while she was inside worrying about a non-drama. Of course, I'd probably get an earful for not running in to tell her. Or at least calling. But I'd just made it to my car and there was no way I was getting out in that wind again. Or getting my cell phone out.

Pulling the sleeves of my jacket down around the heels of my palms before touching the steering wheel again, I pulled away from the curb and drove slowly down the street, trying to figure out which house the police were in front of.

My heart did a double dip as I realized it was Ivan Romanoff's place.

Hunh.

The neighborhood vampire.

Memories of my last encounter with Romanoff and his creepy nephew emerged from the shadows. They included, but certainly weren't limited to, my falling into a cello shipping case – coffin – in the basement (I'd been doing some detecting, not snooping, no matter what my assistant Rosie says), and the lid had closed on top of me.

I gave an eye roll. There was no such thing as vampires.

Oh, yeah? If that were true, then why did I still get the willies every time I drove by the house?

I spotted a familiar figure. Forgetting about the cold, I hand rolled the window down.

'Pino!'

Pino Karras and I went back to St D's elementary. Of course, back then he'd been Pimply Pino, and had hated me with a passion – sometimes I got the feeling he still did – but we'd more or less made peace with each other in recent months. Which was a nice change of pace seeing as he usually threatened to haul me in for being somewhere I wasn't supposed to be.

'Hey, Metro,' he said, coming to stand next to my car, his hand forever resting on his Billy club. But at least he no longer hiked his uniform pants up so high they made me hurt. Oh, wait. Scratch that. He appeared to have lengthened the hem, making it look like he no longer hiked his pants up.

'What's up?' I asked, switching my attention back to the three officers who milled around in front of the house. Curiously, none of them had gone up to the door yet.

'Dunno,' Pino admitted. 'Homicide asked for assistance. Only the dicks have yet to show.' He stood straighter. 'There they are now.'

Homicide? What would homicide want with Romanoff?

Then it occurred to me. Occasionally when dealing with the undead, a person or two were known to show up dead.

Had Romanoff or his creepy nephew finally made a fatal mistake?

I watched as a dark, unmarked sedan pulled up behind me. A blonde woman who couldn't be that much older than me got out from behind the wheel and an older man from the passenger's side. They looked all business.

'Move along, ma'am,' Pino suddenly said, producing a flashlight and waving at me.

I squinted at him. Did he just call me 'ma'am'?

'Nothing to see here,' he continued as if he didn't know me. 'Keep rolling.'

Oh. I got it. He was back into official mode. Probably showing off for the detectives.

I grimaced and reluctantly rolled up the window and put the car back into gear. I mimicked a telephone with my hand, indicating Pino should call me after. He ignored me. And I knew he wouldn't call.

I inched along as slow as I could, watching as Romanoff himself opened the front door to the two detectives standing on his porch. Whatever was up, I'd find out soon enough. While Astoria was large, it wasn't large enough to keep the reason behind the neighborhood vampire being visited by New York's finest under wraps.

Besides, the presence of the police escort meant that this was more than merely a friendly 'hey, we were in the neighborhood and thought we'd stop by' visit.

I craned my neck to continue watching, nearly hitting a parked car in the process. I stepped on the brake.

The detectives had turned Romanoff around and were cuffing him.

Hunh. The neighborhood vampire was being arrested.

The implications of that left me deaf to the blast of a car horn behind me.

'OK, OK.' I fished my cell phone out of my purse and dialed my mother's number. If I couldn't find anything out, she could. And that, I was finding out, was one of the benefits of having a lot of family and friends; wittingly or otherwise, they all were sources.

My mother picked up on the second ring and I smiled. Oh, Rosie was going to love this...

# TWO

I spent what time I could spare at the agency the next day trying to scare up what I could on Romanoff's arrest. Only no official arrest report existed, a morning call to Pino told me, who might now have earned an upgrade to Pissed Pino for not having been let into the loop after providing backup to the arresting detectives the night before.

So, essentially, Romanoff hadn't been arrested; he'd merely been detained. For what, nobody knew.

Oh, I'm sure everyone guessed. And probably those guesses were very similar, all of them beginning and ending with the reasons why he was called 'The Neighborhood Vampire'. But none of us was willing to share those thoughts just yet.

I considered calling my mother to see what she'd found out, then nixed the idea lest she hound me about looking for that long lost cousin Roula. Besides, I was still upset about the goat incident. At around eleven last night I'd gotten my usual case of the munchies ... and the only thing in the house had been the container of goat and lemon potatoes. Even Muffy had turned his furry little snout up at the offering. And while I normally loved my mom's lemon potatoes, these had goat yuk all over them, making them inedible.

The leftovers had become throwaways – container and all – just like that.

I sighed and considered the work in front of me. Trust me, while the idea of being a P.I. usually inspired thoughts of excitement and danger in the minds of others, mostly it involved endless reams of paperwork. Keeping track of every notation, each mile driven, every expense that could be laid out in front of the client to prove I'd lived up to the fees I charged. Mostly, they didn't complain. But here and there I ran into those who wanted every nickel and dime accounted for. Interesting that money was usually no object when they initially came in.

I found that the cheating spouse cases accounted for a large percentage of dissatisfied clientele. I decided it was because the 'dissatisfaction' they were experiencing in their unions bled into every other area of their lives.

Once a suspicious spouse made her or his way to the agency doorstep it was pretty much a given that her or his spouse was doing the tube snake boogie with someone other than them. All that remained was the proof. Sometimes for clarity's sake. More often for leverage in coming divorce proceedings.

More and more often we were seeing unmarried couples looking for proof of infidelity. And from what I understood from my cousin, Nia-the-lawyer, cases of cohabiting couples suing each other could be just as messy as those of the traditional married variety. Nia-the-lawyer's hyphenated status was one she would enjoy for the rest of her life since she was the first in the family to achieve a law degree, no matter that she hadn't really tried any cases outside my Grandpa Kosmos'. It seemed more people were choosing living together; joining their lives without the formality of a court document. Not that this was shocking to me. But I did find it interesting given the many gay friends I had who would give their eye-teeth for the privilege of that piece of paper.

Me, I'd come a little too close for comfort to being legally bound to a man that wanted all the comforts of marriage, and all the freedoms of a single guy on the make.

But we weren't talking about me. We were talking about my clients.

Anyway, office manager and Puerto Rican dynamo Rosie Rodriguez handled most of the bill collecting. Which was a good thing, because after an hour spent explaining why it cost two hundred dollars for me to sit outside a motel waiting for a cheating spouse to zip up, I was just as likely to cut the fee in half than spend another minute playing victim to a hurt spouse who would probably be better off taking it out on a punching bag.

Rosie, on the other hand, was much more likely to threaten to bill for the additional hour the client was taking in order to contest a fee. Probably I should take lessons.

A string of profanity assaulted my ears compliments of the tiny dynamo in question, lending an odd counterpoint to the cheery holiday decorations she'd brought in. I glanced at where she sat across from me. She was alternately filing one of her long nails and nodding as she read something, causing a jolly Santa Claus on her desk to jiggle. It was near the end of a long Monday that had been filled with ranting people that had been served with eviction notices, missing process servers, an angry spouse who had been caught in all his digital Full Monty glory dancing the aforementioned tube snake boogie, all events unfolding while under the unusually watchful eye of my uncle's silent partner Lenny Nash, who was typically so silent we didn't even notice he was there unless he was coming in, or going out. And barely even then.

At any rate, Rosie and I were at the point where we were just pushing papers around waiting until we could close up shop and go home.

'You need help?' I asked.

Her head of dark curls popped up, her mouth working on the gum she forever seemed to be chewing, pop-popping away, causing her dimples to look deeper yet. 'What?' she asked, seeming surprised to find me still there.

I sat back in my chair, causing it to squeak. 'Whatever you're working on. You need help?'

'I ain't working on nothing.' Pop-pop. She lifted the item in question to show she was reading one of the tabloid rags. 'You seen this?'

I gave an eye roll and rocked, sliding a longing gaze toward my uncle's empty office. I'd taken it over for a while a couple of weeks back, but the other day I'd come in to find my cousin Pete working in there so I'd slunk back out to my original desk.

Of course, he hadn't been in since. I could easily go back in. And as a result avoid things like, oh, say the coming conversation.

'How can you read that crap?' I asked.

'It ain't crap. It's the honest to God truth.' Rosie crossed herself and tsked in that way only she knew how. 'Yeah, OK, so maybe I don't buy into all of it – I mean that story about the baby with two heads has got to be a lie – but the rest ... I believe one hundred and ten percent.'

I bit my tongue to prevent myself from pointing out that the baby with the two heads story was probably the truest out of them.

'Have you seen this?'

She held the paper up so I could view the cover. A blurry photo of a sixty-something man in a suit was splashed across the front page along with the word in all caps: CAUGHT!

'Yeah, so?'

Rosie dropped the paper back down in exasperation. 'Yeah, so, what? Have you read what these guys are saying?'

'No. I've read what the more mainstream and trustworthy press is saying.'

'Well, then, you don't know nothing.'

I found it fascinating that when it came to dealing with telephone calls and the public at large, Rosie had perfect grammatical pitch. But when she talked to her family or me, she fell back on street talk.

'Take, for example, this,' she flipped through

the paper, still holding her ever-present nail file. 'Did you know that he worked on Jane Creek?' She stared at me. 'I bet you didn't know that, did you?'

No, I hadn't known that. But it would explain a lot. The New York fixture had been a hot screen actress back in the day, and lately her face was a presence in nearly every newspaper and magazine because of what was obviously her obsession with plastic surgery.

'It says here that she was a patient of Dr Westervelt.'

Dr Westervelt, the current tabloid cover man in a suit, was a prominent plastic surgeon that had recently branched out in the services he offered his patients. From what I gathered, going under the knife and having poison and fat injections were no longer enough for the average, everyday wealthy housewife who had nothing better to do with her time or money but find ways to push back the hands of time. In this particular case, Dr W had slid into the illegal side of the business by offering a broad range of growth hormone replacement therapies, among other things.

'It's a wonder her whole face doesn't fall off,' Rosie commented.

'Probably the doctors would just find a way to glue it back on.'

This earned me a full, silver dollar dimpled grin from her. 'Probably. Like that rubber cement stuff. Or that movie!' She snapped her fingers several times, causing me to cringe. 'What's the name of that movie? You know the one. Ten years ago? Goldie Hawn and Meryl

Streep. Oh! And that *Die Hard* guy. What's his name?'

I knew better than to participate in any Rosie name games. They tended to snowball into even longer games. And I always came out the other side feeling like the loser. Not because I hadn't played well – I was amazed by how much trivia I seemed to accumulate – but because while Rosie seemed to get a great deal out of the exercise, I usually felt like someone had chiseled a hole in the side of my head and let my brains ooze out.

'Bruce Willis!'

I turned to look toward the door. 'Where?'

She tsked in good humor. 'No, silly. It's the name of that actor guy in that movie. You know. The one I forget the title of.'

'*Death Becomes Her*.'

I winced even as I said it. Much to my chagrin, Rosie shook her head. 'Nah, that's not it.'

I refused to argue with her even though I knew that was the name of the movie. It had been one of those flicks for which I'd wished I could demand back my DVD rental fee, along with the hour and a half of my life I'd never get back.

'You know,' I said, deciding it was better to change the subject, 'I should think you'd be more concerned with the unsolved murders that have been piling up lately.'

She gave me a long look, her gum chewing ceasing.

'What?'

'Oh no you di'n't.'

'Oh, yes I did. I mean, five dead bodies in two

weeks. All of them drained of blood...'

'Oh! Look at the time.'

Rosie jumped up, telling me it must be five ... and that she had zero interest in discussing the topic of blood-drained bodies and unsolved murders. Which wasn't like her at all. Usually she was all over anything remotely to do with the occult.

'I have that ... thing tonight,' she said by way of explanation.

I didn't bother asking her what 'thing'. To do so would only be asking for trouble. And I didn't have any more room for that just now.

'Don't stay too late,' Rosie said, shrugging into her short black leather coat, pulling on a multicolored hat and scarf, then shoving her hands into mittens.

'I'm leaving right after you.'

She leaned forward and stage-whispered, 'Has Lenny left yet?'

I looked toward the closed door to the office of my uncle's silent partner. I hadn't seen him leave. But in my experience, that meant little. 'I don't know.'

She frowned. 'You want I should look? You don't want to shut off the lights and lock him up in here like last time.'

'No, I'll check first,' I told her.

'OK. Good night. I'll see you in the morning.'

'Bright-eyed and bushy-tailed.'

She stared at me. 'What does that even mean?'

I shrugged and gave her a final wave, watching as she grabbed her suitcase of a purse and went outside.

God. It was already dark. I blinked, taking in the shadowy scene on Steinway Street. White headlights followed by red tail lights. Occasional foot traffic as people either went home from work, or out for some holiday shopping or perhaps even dinner.

My stomach gave a growl at the mention of food.

Rosie had gone to Phoebe Hall's diner up the street for lunch and brought me back a hefty bowl of lentil soup with thick slices of fresh bread, but I'd only gotten halfway through it when one of our recent hires (who had started out as an evicted tenant in one of my few process-serving jobs), had come in with a cheating spouse horror story that included the destruction of agency equipment.

'Son of a bitch grabbed the damn thing out of my hands and smashed it to the ground,' Eugene Waters had related, his Afro shooting out wildly from his small head. 'And if that weren't enough, he stomped on it for good measure.'

Rosie had tsked loudly. 'That's coming out of your paycheck, I hope you know.'

'Ain't nothing coming out of my paycheck. I'll replace it by tomorrow. With a better model. This damn thing didn't have no zoom anyway.'

I'd learned over the past few weeks that Eugene had resources I couldn't begin to comprehend. Most of them having to do with five-finger discounts and all things shady. What I'd feared would be a drawback when I originally hired him was actually turning out to be a huge benefit whenever I needed assistance that would not come through more conventional channels.

By the time I'd returned to my soup, however, it had grown cold, and my appetite had fled.

Now it returned full force.

I reached for my travel cup of Nescafé frappé, only to find it empty.

I sighed; maybe it was time for me to go home, as well.

I stared at Nash's closed door. I supposed I should make sure he wasn't in there. Last week I'd shut everything off and essentially locked him inside. He hadn't been very pleased. Not that there was much physical difference between his normal expression and his pissed-off one. But I could feel it.

I rapped lightly on the door, waited for a response and received none. I knocked again and called out, turning the handle. Locked.

That meant he'd already left.

I grimaced. I'd been in the office pretty much all day. I'd seen him come in at nine on the button. When had he left?

The bell announcing a customer rang.

'We're closed,' I said as I turned around.

Standing just inside the door had to be the biggest, palest guy I'd ever seen dressed all in black. He was also vaguely familiar. I watched as he took off a short-billed cap and tucked it under his arm.

'Sorry, sir, but we're closed for the day. We open again at nine tomorrow morning.'

He glanced over his shoulder at a spot I couldn't see through the windows which were throwing the interior lights back at me. 'It is not

I who wishes to speak to you, madam.'

I cocked a brow. When was the last time anyone had addressed me with such formality?

Never, I decided. I normally had to watch PBS's Masterpiece Theatre to experience such speech.

Curiosity got the better of me as I stepped closer, trying to get a look around him.

He turned and opened the door. And standing on the sidewalk outside I found none other than the neighborhood vampire himself, Ivan Romanoff.

'May I come in, Sofie...?'

# THREE

Could he come in...?

Romanoff's question spun around in my vaporous brain. If I thought his driver was pale, Ivan was downright ghostlike.

Or, worse, vampire-like.

I swallowed hard, my hand automatically moving to the side of my neck. Had I really just been thinking about how hungry I was?

Now I was more concerned with how hungry Romanoff was.

The topic of conversation around the dinner table yesterday sprang to mind. Missing girl Roula Kalomoira.

'Madam,' the driver prompted.

I was surprised Romanoff still stood outside.

'Yes, sure. Come in,' I said absently, taking a step back.

He seemed to glide inside rather than walk, which sent my creep-o-meter needle off the chart.

'How are you doing?' I asked, remembering my manners. OK, maybe it wasn't exactly that. Truth was, I wanted to know what had gone down the night before. Why he had been handcuffed and taken in.

And how he had gotten back out.

'Very well, thank you,' he said in his accented voice.

Being a Queens girl, I understood that how long a person lived in America had absolutely nothing to do with the thickness of their foreign accent. I knew Greeks who had been here for fifty years, far longer than any time they might have spent in Greece, yet it was sometimes difficult to make out what they were trying to say in English. Of course, it didn't help that since there were so many Greeks in Queens, a body could go their entire lives without learning to speak English.

Ivan Romanoff's accent wasn't quite that bad. But he did give Christopher Lee's rendition of Dracula a run for his money, making me wonder how many Romanians lived in Queens.

So much for getting any information on the day before the easy way...

The agency didn't offer much by the way of comfortable seating unless I invited him back to my uncle's office. And since I wasn't about to do that, I leaned against my desk and crossed my arms to both give the impression of being in control, and to quell the chill that was running up and down my spine at having the neighborhood vampire so close.

'As I was explaining to Mr...' I looked at the driver, expecting him to supply me with his name. He didn't. 'Anyway, we're closed for the day.'

'Day,' Romanoff repeated. 'Yes.' He joined his hands in front of his slender body. I noticed they were gloved. Did vampires register the cold?

'Thank you for inviting me in. I shall not consume much of your time.'

Consume.

The word lodged in my head.

'I'm sorry, but I have this ... condition that compels me to conduct my business only at night.'

Hunh. What condition might that be?

'So I hope you'll forgive my late visit. I was hoping to ... what is the word? Contract for your time.'

I raised a brow and tightened my crossed arms. 'Excuse me?'

'I wish to hire you.'

The neighborhood vampire wanted to hire me.

That was a first.

And hopefully the last.

It was joked by those outside the borough that only the dead know Queens. I was pretty sure that they weren't referring to the undead. But you could never be too careful...

'Sorry?' I asked.

He didn't answer.

'This, um, wouldn't have anything to do with the police being at your place last night, would it?' I should have gone direct straight out of the gate.

He nodded once. 'Yes. Yes, it does.'

I didn't answer this time. Instead, I waited for him to explain and tried my best not to look like I anxiously wanted him out of the agency far more than I wanted to know the information.

'They questioned me well into the evening.'

'The police?'

'Yes.'

'About?'

He looked down at his hands. 'About a police matter.'

'Hmm. Well, you see, Mr Romanoff, you're going to have to be a little more specific.'

Or, rather, I wanted him to be a lot more specific.

Instead, he said, 'It is of little consequence. Nothing to do with what I'd like to hire you for.'

I was disappointed. And doubtful. I indicated for him to continue.

'I would like for you to find out who it is that is killing these young people.'

OK.

Or, rather, not OK.

I was reminded of my pointless conversation with my mother and the rest of my family the day before when they'd tried to convince me to look into Roula's missing person status.

I was also reminded of my last large case, when Little Johnny Laughton's sister had hired me to find the real killer of Little Johnny's girlfriend even as he stood trial for the crime.

Mostly, I was thinking about what happened as a result of my accepting that case and my too close call with a wood-chipper.

Had I just been thinking about how routine my cases had gotten lately? Complained about the paperwork?

Silly me.

I lifted my right hand palm out. 'Whoa. This is more a matter for the police, Mr Romanoff. Not for a private investigator.'

His frown seemed three faces deep. 'It is very unfortunate, but the police think I may be the one responsible.'

OK.

Not.

I squinted at him, working it through in my head.

So that's why he'd been hauled in last night for questioning. Five bodies, drained of blood, and the neighborhood vampire was Suspect Number One.

Made sense to me.

Then why was he in my office asking me to find the real killer?

Or could he really be asking me to pin it on somebody else?

'I see,' I said, although I clearly didn't.

He coughed into his gloved hand and I was reminded that mind reading was supposed be one of the gifts possessed by his kind. If there was such a thing as his kind. Something of which I wasn't completely convinced despite the mounting pile of evidence.

'You see,' he said quietly. 'This matter is not good for business.'

'Yes ... I can see where that would be bad for business...' I said half to myself.

Romanoff was in the blood bank business. Dead bodies popping up without blood ... well, that would look bad on anybody's résumé. But especially on his.

'I will reward you handsomely for this job,' he said.

The cadaverous driver moved and I jumped,

nearly forgetting his presence even though he loomed over Romanoff and was kind of hard to overlook. He took an envelope from his inside jacket pocket and crossed to hand it to me.

'I haven't agreed to take on the case yet.'

'But you must,' Romanoff insisted. 'I have nowhere else left to turn.'

Well, that was a vote of confidence.

'Besides, I understand that you have become quite good at what you do, Sofie. And we have been neighbors for a long, long time...'

Surely he didn't think that earned him points?

The driver remained standing with the envelope outstretched.

'You don't even know what price I'm going to quote you,' I told him, hoping it would buy me time.

'I'm sure you'll find the amount sufficient to cover whatever number you might come up with.'

I sighed and took the envelope. So my curiosity was getting the better of me. The last time I was offered a sufficient amount, it had been very sufficient indeed.

Hey, everyone has their price.

Of course, I was hoping that our idea of sufficient didn't mesh. That I'd peer into the envelope and find the amount an easy one to refuse.

Truth was, I wasn't up for another major case. Not one on this scale. I'd just advanced to the point where I felt competent in my job. And my confidence was growing. But this case, that involved not one, not two, but five dead bodies, and was being actively investigated by the NYPD and followed by every media outlet ... well, that would put me solidly back into unfamiliar territory.

And I was enjoying feeling like an honest to God P.I. rather than an amateur sleuth/pet detective. Even if I was bored more often than not lately.

I dropped the envelope to my side, not looking at the amount, yet not giving it back to Igor. 'I'm sorry, Mr Romanoff, but perhaps this might be more of a job for someone ... in house?'

He blinked at me. 'Pardon?'

Even I knew that people came and went from his place all the time. At night. And he never traveled alone. I'd reluctantly come to the conclusion that he was a part of a larger flock or group, and that he was one of the elders, if not the leader of the clan.

Yeesh, I was losing it.

'You know, maybe someone from within your ... family would be the better one to handle this,' I said, 'Like your nephew Vladimir.'

In case the offender was someone within his family.

'You believe my nephew might be committing these crimes?' he asked with some incredulity.

OK, breakdown in mind-reading communication. 'No, no. I'm not saying that at all.' I swallowed hard. Was I? 'Hey, look. If the police are looking at you, who's to say that a member of your extended ... family isn't the true culprit?' And I was not at all interested in confronting that particular killer. I had trouble enough with the regular kind.

His expression grew grave. 'It is not a member of my family.'

'Are you sure about that?'

'Of course I am sure.'

'Oh, because you've already investigated.'

'No, because no one I know is capable of such a hideous crime.'

'Ah.'

I gripped the envelope tighter. Not because I was considering taking the case on, but because the prospect of stumbling across a rogue vampire was even more unappealing to me than meeting up with a murderous landscaper with a thing for feeding his victims to a wood-chipper.

'Look, Mr Romanoff—'

'Ivan, please.'

I couldn't quite bring myself to call him by his Christian name, mostly because the very word 'Christian' didn't belong anywhere near him or his name.

'I don't think this is a good idea...'

'Please, don't make your decision now. Sleep on it, Sofie. Please. Give me your decision tomorrow.'

I figured there was nothing wrong with the suggestion. While I'd prefer to hand him back the envelope and be done with the entire thing now, especially since I couldn't imagine anything happening to change my mind, I found I couldn't bring myself to be rude to him. There was that whole neighbor thing,

'I suppose this can wait till tomorrow.' I pushed off my desk and looked around the top. 'Let me just give you a receipt for this...'

I opened the envelope to find it packed with hundred-dollar bills. A lot of them. I counted them out and wrote the amount on the receipt, half regretting that I'd have to give it back to him tomorrow.

'Here...'

I turned around, receipt in hand, only to find Romanoff and Igor gone.

I froze. That wasn't possible. Not only had I not heard the cowbell, I hadn't felt the cold draught that usually accompanied the opening of the door.

Receipt still in hand, I pushed the door in question open and stood outside on the sidewalk, a spine-long chill running through me; and not merely because of the cold, either.

Romanoff's car was nowhere to be seen.

Another familiar vehicle, however, was parked right across the street. More specifically, a black, pimped out truck. But not just any black, pimped out truck, but the one belonging to a certain tall, blonde and handsome Australian who might or might not be a bounty hunter.

Jake Porter.

I squinted in the darkness, watching as he took a drag off the cigarette he was smoking where he leaned against the front fender. He tossed the butt. But rather than walking toward me as I hoped, he instead got into the truck cab, started the engine, and drove away.

Hunh...

# FOUR

That was odd. I hadn't seen Jake in a couple of weeks. What had he been doing sitting outside the office? And why had he left instead of coming to talk to me?

The questions remained with me well after I locked up the office for the night, picked up dinner at my favorite souvlaki stand on Broadway at 34th, and made my way home to my apartment, all the time looking over my shoulder for shadows I cared not to identify. Not even Muffy was capable of distracting me. And that was saying a lot, because as I took his favorite snack food out of its bag, the Jack Russell Terrier did his bouncing trick, where he launched himself three feet straight into the air, landed and then bounced again, as if on some sort of invisible trampoline or bungee cord, his pink tongue hanging out of his mouth the entire way.

'You're going to hurt yourself,' I told him.

Like either one of us needed a reminder that just a short time ago he'd suffered a leg fracture in the process of saving my life.

Last Friday, the vet and I were forced to admit that the cast on Muffy's back leg was doing more harm than good, and she'd removed it and recommended I pray that the fracture had healed enough that he wouldn't do any major damage. Because the next step would be knocking him out with doggie downers for the duration if another cast had to be set.

'OK, OK,' I said to him, anything to stop his bouncing.

I fished a bit of grilled meat from inside the pita that wasn't soaked with tzatziki sauce and tossed it to him. One flap of his mouth and the morsel was history. I fed him two more, knowing I was tempting fate by giving him pork, but it had been a while since either of us had enjoyed a good souvlaki and I figured I'd just have to suffer through any noxious clouds that were sure to awake me in the middle of the night.

I put the foil-wrapped souvlaki on the coffee table and brushed my hands together, remembering I needed a nice, cold Coke to go along with my meal. I got halfway to the kitchen when I heard a sound outside. My feet took me to the window. Ignoring the cold draught that caught me around the knees where the sash was open just enough for Muffy to get in and out for his rooftop visits to see to his business, I pushed the sheers aside and looked down at the street three floors below. There didn't appear to be anything going on. Maybe a neighborhood cat getting into trouble. Maybe Tee the Cat, who had taken up residence inside my apartment a few weeks before, much to Muffy's chagrin, and then disappeared as mysteriously as he'd appeared.

I was about to close the sheers again when a brief flash of light pulled my attention to the right. There. Just under the bare elm. Was that ...

I craned my neck. Yes, it was. Jake's truck. And there was Jake again, leaning against the front fender, looking up at my window.

A shiver caressed my skin from shoulder to ankle.

After long months of trying to back the sexy Australian into my bed, and having him reject my attempts, he'd finally introduced me to his waterbed ... as well as all sorts of interesting new sensations I'd had no idea existed.

Then a gunman had chased us both out of the bedroom with a barrage of bullets, Jake's truck blew up, and I was left wondering how wise it had been to sleep with a man I barely knew; no matter how much I wanted to know him better.

Not that I would change anything, mind you...

I grimaced and closed the curtains. What was he doing? He'd barely spoken to me since the incident outside his Astoria Park apartment. I sensed he was distancing himself to protect me from whatever mess he was in the middle of, and a part of me was thankful for that, especially since I seemed to be getting into enough of my own trouble lately, thank you very much.

But a bigger part ached to know what spending the entire night with the hot bounty hunter would be like...

I released a long, wistful sigh.

To say that my love life could use a good P.I. to figure out what was going on would be an understatement. Of course, I'd never seek one out. First, I'd be afraid of what they might find. Second ... well, I wasn't in the market for the truth. It was easier to let things run their course and see where they took me.

Of course, finding Porter hanging around outside wasn't helping with that tack.

Some would argue that I didn't have problems. My mother, for example. As far as she was concerned, she'd found the perfect man for me – by pretending she hadn't. Dino Antonopoulos was a good Greek boy directly from Greece, with a hot accent, who knew his way around a bakery (because he owned one) as well as my body (which I leased to him every now and again).

But even that had cooled down recently, the bucket of ice-cold water my mother had thrown on it effectively taking all the fun out of what I thought was a secret affair.

I got the Coke and went to reclaim my souvlaki only to find Muffy had been busy while I was otherwise occupied. He sat next to the table sporting his most innocent look, the telltale lick of his chops giving him away ... along with the opened pita that was now minus all pieces of grilled pork.

'Bad dog. Bad, bad dog,' I scolded him under my breath.

He barked once, shifted on his paws and then licked his chops again as if to ask if I had another.

I gathered the destroyed meal together, shoved it back into the bag and threw it in the kitchen garbage can. I couldn't seem to catch a decent, full meal lately. I didn't even bother looking into the fridge or cupboards, because I already knew nothing was there.

Instead, my gaze caught on the flyer fastened on the refrigerator by a magnet: The Chirping Chicken.

I took the flyer down and went to retrieve my cell phone.

Fifteen minutes later, the doorbell rang. I shook my finger at Muffy. 'Behave or I'll lock you in the bathroom.'

He barked and ran around and around the couch. I gave an eye roll and went to open the door.

I paid the delivery kid and accepted the bag, just about to close the door again when the one across the hall opened.

'Sofie! I wondered who could be coming to your door so late.'

I refrained from telling her it was only six p.m. 'I'm sorry if I disturbed you, Mrs Nebitz.'

The old Jewish woman had lived in the building for longer than I'd been alive ... and thanks to New York rent control laws, was essentially paying the same as she did when she first moved in.

But that was OK. She was a great neighbor. Quiet. Paid her rent on time every month. And even did a little rent collecting for me on the side. Something I had yet to prove myself any good at since moving into the building my parents had meant as a wedding gift – and that my ex had threatened to sue for half interest in.

'No, no, that's all right. You didn't disturb me.'

Which meant that I had.

'What do you have there?'

I lifted the bag. 'Delivery from the Chirping

Chicken. Have you tried them?'

'Oh, heavens, no. Don't you think it's a little late to be eating, Sofie?'

That made me feel bad. At least slightly. It was, after all, only six. Probably Mrs Nebitz ate her dinner at four thirty. Probably she was settled in front of her television and would be in bed by nine.

'Unfortunately this is the only time all day I've had to eat.'

'Well, be careful that you don't eat too much. You'll have nightmares.'

I smiled. 'I will, Mrs Nebitz. Good night.'

'Good night, dear.'

She closed her door and I followed suit, staring at where Muffy sat at my feet panting up at me.

'You have had your dinner,' I told him. 'This is mine.'

He cocked his head to the side and whined.

I sighed. 'Oh, all right. I ordered a half chicken, so there's plenty for both of us...'

Welcome to my life as a single, professional New York female with a dog...

The following morning, my eyelids flew open long before I was ready. More specifically, at five thirty I was wide awake, promising God and the Fates and the blanket powers-that-be that I'd never feed Muffy another piece of pork again so long as they spared me from lethal doggy clouds for the rest of my natural existence. Considering my previous experience, I should have known better. I'd moved him from where he was curled up on the empty pillow next to mine, his furry butt aimed in my direction, and rolled over ... only to find myself staring at the towering pile of wedding gifts that still sat wrapped and untouched, the dim light from the street outside making them loom like something out of a Dr Seuss book. Which left me something akin to the Grinch. Only it was a pretty good guess that my heart wasn't going to grow anytime soon and I'd give the presents back.

I was assaulted by memories of the wedding that wasn't six months ago. Annoyed, I threw the covers over where Muffy had resettled himself, giving up any chance of more sleep.

Hours later, I reclaimed my uncle's office at the agency, sipping my third frappé of the morning, and considered closing the door. Partly because I didn't want to hear Rosie's play-by-play rundown of her activities last night. Mostly because I didn't want her to see what I was doing.

Still, even though roughly seven yards and an office wall separated us, I leaned in closer to the screen, squinting at the results of my search on all articles related to the bodies that had popped up recently. I scanned *Reuters* pieces that stuck to the facts – which weren't many – and the tabloid type of which Rosie seemed overly fond.

One headline caught my eye: QUEENS' SECRET VAMPIRE SOCIETY.

I jerked back and blinked hard.

OK ... that was one road I wasn't willing to go down just now.

I entered a new search for blood uses. I was surprised that one of the results that came up featured the same picture of the plastic surgeon recently arrested for performing illegal procedures on his patients; one of those patients was the screen legend Jane Creek, who had to be eighty-something if she was a day.

I clicked on the piece.

'What?' Rosie's voice raised an octave higher than its usual high-pitched timbre. 'Oh, no. I know you didn't just say what I think you did.'

I drew in a deep breath and gave an eye roll. Both at my own reaction to the tabloid piece and Rosie's drama queen antics in the next room. I leaned back farther in the chair to see who she was talking to. I vaguely recognized the Korean woman who worked at the restaurant next door.

As if in unison, both she and Rosie turned to stare at me.

I widened my eyes. What did I do?

I turned away and leaned back in toward the computer. I heard Rosie's popping gum before I saw her. I clicked the mouse so the screen flicked to correspondence I was working on.

'Uh uh. You did not let that vampire in here last night.'

I squinted at her. 'What?'

She planted her hands on her narrow, black polyester covered hips even as I looked around her at where the gossipy Korean next door stretched her neck to see inside.

She looked quickly away.

'You know they can't come in a place unless you invite them in,' Rosie said.

I considered her.

Few were the times when I'd seen her

genuinely upset. Oh, I'd witnessed her in various stages of feigned upset. And then there was the whole lovesick episode with Mrs Nebitz's grandson Seth that we'd both agreed never to discuss. But upset ... angry. This was as close as I'd seen her.

'That's a myth,' I told her, pretending to be busy.

'Yeah. Just like you said vampires are a myth.' She reached around me. 'You ain't typing nothin' anyhow, so you might as well face me.'

I sighed and did as she requested, crossing my arms over my own less than ample chest.

'Did you or did you not let that vampire in here last night after I left?'

'I'm sure I don't know to whom you're referring.'

Her carefully plucked brows shot upward. 'Oh, no? Which other vampire to whom would I be referring? That stupid old bloodsucker that lives up the street from you, that's who.'

'Mr Romanoff?'

She drew her head back as if to ask if I was insulting her intelligence.

'OK, OK. He stopped by ... we talked.'

'You invited him in...'

I nodded. 'I invited him in.'

She groaned and stepped backward until she could sink into one of the two visitor chairs positioned in front of the desk. 'You know what that means, don't you?'

'That he came in, I'm still alive with no visible bite marks and life continues on as usual.'

Her gaze went to my neck. I refrained from

pulling my black turtleneck back to offer visible proof.

'What did he want?'

I said something under my breath and went back to pretend work on the computer.

'What was that? I didn't hear you.'

'That's because you weren't meant to hear me.'

She got to her feet again. 'Say it again.'

'I said, he wants to hire me ... us ... the agency...'

'And you accepted?'

'Of course, I didn't accept...'

The envelope of fresh bills that his driver had handed me was locked in my desk drawer in the other room. Probably it wasn't a good idea to keep it there. Probably my cousin Pete knew how to get into it. Probably I should put it in the safe behind me.

'Say that again. And this time, you need to be a hell of a lot more convincing.'

'I didn't accept,' I repeated, my jaw setting in much the same way as Rosie's was. 'Yet...'

# FIVE

The way Rosie gaped at me, you'd have thought I'd put my hand in front of her mouth and asked her to spit out her gum.

'What? You can't seriously be considering taking the case? Nuh uh. No way. No how. There's not a chance in hell I'll ever be associated with a known vampire. Not in this lifetime ... or the next.'

'You wouldn't be associated with him; I would.'

The cowbell on the door rang in the other room as we stared each other down.

'Customer,' I said.

'Forget them.' I got the distinct impression that she would have preferred the other 'f' word. 'I'm not leaving this room until you promise me you aren't taking that case.'

Talk about effective threats.

'Promise!'

'What's up, boss?' The sound of Eugene Waters' voice from the doorway inspired a sigh of relief.

'Promise!' Rosie said again, paying him no mind.

The telephone began ringing in the other room.

I crossed my arms and refused to answer her or

the silent extension on my desk.

Rosie turned to stare at Eugene whose response was a humorous, 'What did I do?' expression.

'You had better have that replacement camera in that box. I'm just saying.'

Then, muttering a string of inventive Spanish curse words under her breath, she finally stalked into the other room on her too-high heels to answer the phone.

Waters gave a low whistle and stepped farther into the room. 'What was that all about?'

'Nothing.' I stretched my neck to ease my tight muscles.

'Ah. OK. I know that type of nothing.'

I smiled at him. 'What you got?'

He placed a medium-sized box on the desk and opened the flaps, looking like a wild-haired, African-American Santa Claus come early.

It was difficult to believe it was only last summer that he and I had been enemies, me the inexperienced process server, he the pink-robed and mule-clad target determined not to be served. He'd been so successful in his attempt to avoid me that once the deed was done, I knew I had to hire him. And he had yet to disappoint. He was Johnny-on-the-spot whenever I needed something. And he not only performed well on assigned task – which began with process serving since he knew so much about his adversaries, but had grown to include cheating spouse cases – but surpassed expectations.

'As promised,' he said now, taking out a camera that was at least four rungs up the ladder quality-wise than the one an angry husband had broken yesterday. I examined it and then handed it back since he was the one who would be using it anyway. 'I also took the liberty of doing a little shopping for the agency.'

'Oh? How much is it going to set me back?'

He beamed. 'Nothing.'

'Well, then, that's a price not even I can argue with.'

I suspected Eugene's favorite shopping place was the back of a truck and consisted of a five-finger-discount inventory, but in this case I subscribed to the 'don't ask, don't tell' school of thinking.

He took out two boxes still bearing price tags. 'I got one for you and one for the sexy little Latina in the other room.'

I accepted the one he held out, staring at the picture on the outside. 'A walkie-talkie?'

God, that's all I needed. I could hear Rosie from fifty feet away; why would I want an instrument that would make her louder?

'No, silly, it's a police scanner.'

Hunh.

I opened the package and slid out the contents. Looked like a walkie-talkie to me. Maybe a little bigger.

I knew that Rosie had a scanner, although since I'd gotten her a new laptop computer,she seemed to listen via the Internet more often than not lately, and frequently filled my ears with her inventive curses when the signal cut out during the best parts.

I put the batteries in and a loud screech

assaulted my ears. Eugene pressed the appropriate button to get it to stop.

'I know why you might need something like this,' I said, taking in his wide grin. 'But I need this because...' I prompted.

He blinked at me. 'I'll take it back then.' He reached for it.

I moved it outside his reach.

'I mean if you don't want it.'

'I want it. I just don't know what I'm going to do with it.'

'Listen for what the police are up to.'

I didn't say anything.

He heaved a sigh. 'Here, look.'

He reached in again and this time I let him. He worked a couple of switches, then turned down the volume.

'Car 56, 10-53 at the corner of Broadway and 27th. Respond.'

My eyes widened. 'That's just down the street from my parents' place.'

Eugene looked smug. 'See.'

'What's a Code 10-53?'

Rosie entered the room. 'It's an accident, stupid.' I squinted at her, watching as she picked up the other box. 'About time you did something useful around here,' she shot in Eugene's direction as she walked back out.

Eugene openly watched her ass as she left. 'She's got the hots for me. I know she does.'

I gave an eye roll. If Rosie's response was meant to portray attraction, I'd hate to see what he thought rejection looked like.

'How did she know what the code meant?'

'There's a list you can get.'
'Do you have one I can copy?'
'Already have them burned into the ole noggin',' he said, tapping a manicured index finger against his temple. 'Important in my line of work.'
I bet. 'Are there many codes, I mean?'
He shrugged as he put the empty packaging back into the box. 'Not too many. The hot Latina can probably print something up for you.'
'The hot Latina is busy,' Rosie said from the other room. 'She can print up her own.'
'And how, exactly, am I supposed to do that?' I shot back.
Eugene gestured toward my computer as he picked up the box. 'Shouldn't be too difficult to find one online.'
'You mean anyone can just get one?'
Seemed wrong to me somehow. What was the point of talking in code if everyone could access the decoder?
'Yep. Catch you later. I've got a cheating spouse to catch with his pants down.'
'Thanks.' I stared at the scanner in my hand. 'Oh, and remember: no shots featuring the guy's Johnson. I got complaints last time.'
Eugene shot me a grin over his shoulder. 'Cover it with magic marker. How else you going to prove he had it out?'
I sat back heavily in my chair, half listening to a final saucy exchange between him and Rosie, and then looked at my computer screen. This could be interesting...

* * *

After that, there was no suffering Rosie for at least the remainder of the morning. I even contemplated avoiding going into the office altogether for the week, but decided against that; to do so would mean time spent in my car. My cold, draughty car. In the frigid, November temperatures.

No thank you.

I coaxed Lucille on, fiddling with the switches on the heater to get her to put out more. I'd learned if you moved the temperature lever just so, and quickly pushed up the fan, it got warmer faster. Or else my movements were responsible. Either way, I felt more comfortable, so did it really matter?

While winter in Manhattan was idealized and captured on postcards and attracted tourists, there was little romance connected to the season in Queens. Especially on an overcast day like today. I looked for pockets of color on the gray street and found little. It didn't help that fashion had taken a black-and-white turn.

There. An older woman wearing a bright red scarf. Probably handmade.

I smiled. Maybe I'd have to get something red to wear around my neck.

The smile disappeared as I put 'red' and 'neck' together with Romanoff and vampires.

Then again, no.

I focused on Steinway, heading south. I could stop by my mother's, see what she was cooking for dinner, which was still served early in the afternoon at the Metropolis household. It was a pretty safe bet that, since she'd already done the goat thing, good eating should be on the menu for the next month, at least. I glanced at my cell phone for the time. No, too early. To go there now would only set the scene for a long coffee and unwelcome questions.

Or, worse, a continued appeal for me to look for my newly adopted cousin, poor Roula Kalomoira.

I shuddered and looked over to the passenger's seat. I'd left Muffy at home. Something I was doing more and more lately now that it had gotten cold. I couldn't just leave him in the car when I did my running around. Not with a canvas top that leaked cold air and rain. And not with an office manager who claimed that half Muffy's hair ended up on her pants whenever he came into the office.

At any rate, he was probably better off at home where it was warm.

I reached for the police scanner on the seat and switched it on, and then picked up the long list of codes I'd found and printed up. How did they remember all this? How did Waters remember all this?

A horn beeped and I realized I'd drifted slightly into the oncoming lane. I grimaced and righted the car, putting the radio and connected codes back on the seat before I was the one at the other end of the next code.

I didn't realize I was heading to the 114th Precinct until I was parking at the curb and considering the patrol car in front of me that spilled two uniformed officers on to the street. I watched as they walked toward the squat, one-story brick building and then fished out my cell and pressed autodial.

'Officer Pino Karras,' he answered on the second ring.

'Good morning, Pino. It's Sofie.'

A heartbeat of silence, then, 'What did you do now?'

'Nothing. Hey, where are you? Because I'm sitting outside the station right now.'

'The precinct?'

'Yes.'

A sigh. 'So question number two is what do you want?'

'I just thought we might grab a coffee together. You know, on your break.'

'Coffee...'

'Mmm-hmm.'

I wasn't sure if my ruse was working.

You see, among my peers, I'd figured out there were those who knew me; those who thought they knew me; and those who perpetually expected the worst from me. Pino fell solidly into the last category.

'Come on inside the precinct. I'm in the conference room straight off the lobby to the right.'

She shoots, she scores!

I rang off, debated shutting off the car engine (hey, only an imbecile would be stupid enough to steal a car outside a police station), and then did it anyway, if only because the way my luck was running, I'd get a ticket for leaving it running.

Pulling my black leather jacket closer, I ran

across the street to the precinct just in time for a uniform to open the door for me as he was coming out.

'Hey, Metro. How goes it?'

I vaguely recognized him, but couldn't tell if his smile was friendly or chiding. I'd amassed quite a reputation in the past six months, and not all of it was good.

'Fine.' I ducked inside. 'Thanks.'

The door closed behind me, shutting out the traffic noises and the cold and replacing them with ringing phones and chatter and a blast of heat I realized came from a vent above me. I shrugged my jacket so it fell right and looked toward what I believed was the conference room to which Pino had referred. Sure enough, there he stood in the doorway, hiking up his pants.

I hid my cringe and walked toward him.

'What's up?' he asked.

'You got some coffee?'

'I thought you only drank those frappés?'

'I meant for you.'

A grin. 'I got coffee.'

I looked over his shoulder. 'Are we going to go in, or are you planning on keeping me out here?'

He didn't say anything for a long moment, and then he turned slightly so I could enter.

The room was large and a couple of other officers looked over, giving me little more than a cursory glance or a nod as Pino led me to the corner where a coffee machine sat.

'Why aren't you out on patrol?' I asked, watching him pour a cup.

'I just brought a delinquent in for shoplifting.'

‘Oh?’ I rubbed my hands together and blew on them, asking him to pour me a half a cup if only to warm my frozen fingers.

‘Yeah, stupid idiot thought the roll of toilet paper wouldn’t show through his jacket.’

He handed me a paper cup rather than a Styrofoam and I felt the warmth immediately.

‘Really hated pulling him in, though.’

I eyed him. ‘Just the facts, ma’am, by-the-book Pino?’

He grimaced. ‘Yeah. I mean what kid steals a roll of toilet paper unless he really needs it?’

‘Maybe he planned on papering his buddy’s house.’

He looked at me. OK, so he had a conscience but he still came up short in the humor department.

I stepped away from him and toward a bulletin board. I took in photographs of two girls who might have been the same girl but for a mole on one’s chin.

Pino grasped my arm and led me away from the board. ‘You’re not supposed to be looking at that.’

Which made me crane my neck so I could get a better look before I got too far away. ‘Why? What’s up? Something hush-hush?’

‘Not for long. But you’re going to find out along with everyone else when the deputy inspector gives a press conference in an hour.’

It rated a press conference? I needed to get closer...

‘Where do you think you’re going?’

I raised my coffee cup. ‘I need some sugar and

cream.'

'No, you don't.' Pino planted himself between me and my destination. 'What did you come here for, Metro? And don't try telling me you stopped by to enjoy the pleasure of my company.'

I tried for a smile. 'Why? It could be the truth.'

He didn't blink.

OK, so he both knew me too well *and* expected the worst from me.

'I need to know what you've got on Romanoff's arrest.'

His smile was slow in coming but when it did, it encompassed his entire unattractive face. 'The vampire?'

'Mmm.'

'Are you sure you want to know?'

I tried looking around him and he compensated. 'Yes. Why?'

'Because it has nothing to do with what's on the board over there.'

I looked at him. 'Oh? Then why don't you start with what's on the board and finish with Romanoff and let me be the judge?'

'I'll give you this on Romanoff: he wasn't arrested. Merely questioned.'

'About?'

'That's all I'm giving you.'

'What about the board?'

His eyes narrowed.

'Come on, Pino, what harm can it do? You said yourself that there's going to be a press conference on it in an hour anyway. I'm not exactly going to scoop the information to the press...'

His right hand went to the back of his neck and I knew I had him. He was going to tell me. Maybe not everything – probably not even close to everything – but enough to give me a jumping off point.

# SIX

Back in the car, I took my pocket notepad out to write down what Pino had told me. My cell vibrated in my leather jacket pocket. I extracted it and looked at the display screen.

Rosie.

'Hey.'

'Hey, yourself,' her voice told me she was still upset with me. 'Waters is busy on another case and the Miller client wants results and she wants them now.'

I gave an eye roll. Susan Miller was itching to catch her husband Dan in the act and toss his cheating ass out of the house. I'd listened in on Rosie's initial meeting with the pretty young brunette with two kids that lived out in Bayside and couldn't help getting the impression that she didn't care one way or another what her husband was up to. She just wanted out, preferably with a large divorce settlement.

Rosie popped her gum in my ear. 'She said he just left the office twenty minutes ago.'

'She know where he's going?'

I imagined her returning my eye roll. 'It's in the file. A charge to The Quality Motel popped up on his business charge card a week ago.'

The Quality Motel. Great. I hated the place.

Too many cheating spouses and rent-by-the-hour guests that left me with a bad taste in my mouth.

'You going?' Rosie wanted to know.

'Yeah, yeah, I'm going.'

I closed the cell phone and then got out of the car to open the trunk. I grabbed the spare camera I kept there – my brother Kosmos' camera that I'd borrowed, stolen and then replaced, all without his knowing – and took it up front. It would need at least twenty minutes to warm up. About the time it would take me to get to the motel in question if I took the secondary streets.

I set off in that direction.

I hated working cheating spouse cases. I knew that a lot of that had to do with my yet unresolved issues with my own cheating almost-spouse. But it went deeper than that. Watching people at their worst made me feel uncomfortable. Made it difficult to watch romantic comedies without thinking at some point, 'Yeah, he's going to cheat on her one day.' Or 'Look! She's flirting with his best friend.' Took all the fun out of what had once been one of my favorite film genres. Since passing off the jobs to Waters, who didn't seem to care one way or another at the non-stop glimpse into the seedier side of love and, in fact, took great pleasure in getting what he called 'the primo money shot', I'd felt the knot in my stomach begin to finally unwind.

Which made the thought of tightening it again doubly unnerving.

Strangely, I hadn't thought about the disaster that had been my wedding day even half as much as I used to. That was a good sign, right? That life was moving on and with every second that ticked by, every step I took forward, the pain and the memory was beginning to fade. I didn't expect either ever to disappear completely, but it was nice that it was manageable to some degree.

I pulled into the motel parking lot to find only two spaces left, and both of them were up front and center. For some reason, the clientele seemed to think that the farther away they parked from the actual rooms, the higher the likelihood of their being able to explain that their being there that had nothing to do with naked trysts with those who were not their significant others.

I pulled into one and got out. Since it had been a good forty minutes since the cheating husband had left it was a pretty good bet he was already in one of the rooms. As I walked toward the seedy office that actually bore a window where they did all their business like some sort of fast-food restaurant for cheaters, I folded a twenty-dollar bill in half and then half again, and then did the same with a fifty. Depended on who was working today how much the info was going to set me back. Correction: how much it was going to set the client back.

Joe was on. Good. I pocketed the fifty and slid the twenty across the narrow counter when he opened up with a smile.

'Metallic blue Dodge in the back center,' I said.

'Guy about thirty-five, dark hair, suit?'

I nodded.

'Room Seventeen.'

‘Thanks.’
‘Don’t mention it. Where’s Eugene?’
‘On another case.’
‘Tell him he still owes me ten.’
The window closed and I returned to my car, smiling to myself. Trust Eugene to give the guy half and report to the agency he’d given the full amount.
I got back into Lucille and turned the engine back on to keep warm. I picked up the camera from where I’d put it on the passenger’s seat next to the scanner and checked it out. It still felt cold. With the lens pointed toward the floor, I checked through the viewfinder. It appeared OK, but it was hard telling.
I settled back in the seat and turned on the radio to 104.3, a classic rock station.
How many hours in my short P.I. career span had I sat in parking lots just like this one, waiting for a clean shot? Too many to count, that was for sure. I lifted the camera and focused on Room Seventeen, which was on the first floor some six doors up. I’d have to be careful I wasn’t spotted, but I wasn’t overly concerned. Usually cheating spouses were too fixated on the person they were saying goodbye to, secure in the fact that no one knew where they were. And in those few cases where they seemed nervous, they were probably looking for their spouse or spouse’s car rather than a P.I.
You’d think they’d have picked up a thing or two from TV.
Then again, if they had, a good percentage of the agency’s income might go up in smoke.

Was it just me, or were there far too many businesses and jobs that made a profit out of somebody else's misfortune? From my aunt's funeral home to blood banks there seemed to be a never-ending source of money flowing from events most didn't think twice about. Income that wasn't affected by the state of the economy or impacted by holidays, but was the dark gift that just kept on giving.

I frowned and fiddled with a few of the switches on the camera, looking up just in time to catch the door to Room Seventeen opening.

Good.

I sank down in the seat and pointed the camera as the couple came into view. Click ... click. The dark-haired man in the business suit grinned, pulling a trashy blonde in a short, hot pink mini-skirt close, his hands planted on her ass in a way that pulled the material up to reveal her ass cheeks and no underwear.

Yikes.

Looked like the husband behind Door Number Seventeen wasn't haven't an affair; he was probably paying for it.

Not that that made any difference in a court of law.

Click ... click.

I zoomed in for a closer shot ... and caught sight of something familiar.

I pulled the camera back and squinted at the couple in question, and then looked through the viewfinder again. The blonde had her back to me, but her hands were on the guy's shoulders ... and on her left hand she wore a very expensive wedding band ... and a unique charm bracelet...

Holy shit.

The blonde finally turned a bit as they walked toward the lot and I took care to get close-ups of her face.

Yep. It was the wife, Susan Miller. She was wearing a slutty blonde wig, lots of garish make-up and cheap clothing, but it was definitely her.

Hunh.

Well, this was a first. Hired by a wife to prove that her husband was screwing around on her ... with her.

I watched as they parted and each got into their respective cars, squeezing off a few shots of both, and then sat up. I had little doubt that the wife was trying to set her husband up. 'See your honor, he's meeting with another woman. I want a divorce and all his money.'

The husband pulled out and I stretched my neck, waiting for the wife to leave as well.

But she didn't appear to be in any hurry.

There were a few cars between hers and mine, so I didn't have a clear shot at what she might be doing.

Not that it mattered, because I found out soon enough anyway.

Another car pulled into the lot. An old Chevy that needed a new muffler. Another cheating spouse? Probably.

Then wifey got out of her car again, sans wig and minus some of the make-up, and walked back to Room Seventeen. Had she forgotten something?

Then a young guy in jeans and brown leather

jacket went to the same door. Susan opened it and this time I watched as she planted her hands on his ass as she kissed him, the wedding ring and charm bracelet in clear view.

I slowly lifted the camera and started clicking...

Back at the agency, I handed over the camera for Rosie to see to, trying to banish the image of Susan Miller's double-dealings. Something that proved easier than I would have thought as I disappeared into my uncle's office and wrote out what Pino had told me at the precinct, along with the information I'd scared up on the recent rash of unsolved murders, all in different colored markers on the dry erase board I'd bought a couple of weeks ago. I gave the red marker a sniff. OK, so I'm a freak. I've always enjoyed the smell of a good marker. Didn't make me a glue sniffer.

'What are you doing now?' Rosie demanded from the open doorway.

I wrote two names in the upper right-hand corner of the board: Laylyn and Allyson Piszchala. Twenty-year-old twins that had gone missing three days ago. It had been their pictures pinned to the precinct bulletin board, and while Pino hadn't admitted as much, it was feared they might be the next bodies to turn up. Next to them, I included long lost cousin Roula's name with a big question mark.

'I'm not at the point of sharing yet.'

She popped her gum loudly, broadcasting that she was still upset with me. 'Whatever.'

I stilled the marker from where I'd written the name of the plastic surgeon who had been recently arrested in the other corner of the board, along with the name of the star on whom it was rumored he'd botched a job, and fashioned another big question mark. Then, for good measure, I circled Jane Creek's name several times. 'Was there something you wanted?'

'Who, me? No.' She swiveled on her too-high heels. 'But you might want to take the call on Line Three. I'm just sayin'.'

I gave an eye roll, capped the marker and leaned toward the desk. 'Sofie Metro,' I said.

'Mmm ... Sofie Metro. I like the sound of that...'

The marker slid from suddenly damp fingers; it took all my concentration to make sure the same didn't happen with the phone.

I'd recognize that sexy, Australian accent anywhere.

Jake Porter.

I swallowed hard and rounded the desk, sinking slowly into the office chair before my knees gave out.

What was it with this guy? One minute he was giving me the runaround, hanging outside the office and leaving without saying goodbye or hello for that matter. The next he was tickling my ear with his lips. Er, I mean, voice.

'Hey, Jake. How's it hanging?' I asked, trying for a nonchalant tone as I moved to cross my feet on top of the desk.

I missed and nearly toppled over on to the floor. But he didn't need to know that.

Then why did I feel his little chuckle told me he did?

'*It* referring to...'

'You know ... your tally whacker ... your dingo ... your doodle.'

Another chuckle that touched places hands couldn't reach.

'In other words, "How are you?"' I finally clarified.

'I'd like to see you.'

That's how he was? He wanted to see me?

I succeeded on getting both feet up on to the desk and carefully crossed my legs at the ankle and leaned back in the chair. The new angle gave me a view of Rosie, who showed me her hand as if I was too much even for her.

'Are you asking me out on a date, Jake?' I wanted to know.

'No.' His answer was quick and clear.

'Well, then. Ditto on my answer.'

Much to my astonishment, I hung up the receiver. Then sat for long minutes staring at it, wondering what in the hell I had done.

After Jake's call, I endured more of Rosie's prying and huffy demeanor before finally giving up on my latest project, taking the envelope with Romanoff's money from my desk drawer – something I should have done earlier in case my cousin Pete came in and smelled it right into his pocket – and then drove to my grandfather's café on Broadway.

The place was little more than a narrow, glass-encased room I'd referred to as 'The Aquarium' when I worked there as a teen, and on and off over the years. As recently as this past summer when he'd needed a hand and, well, I'd been handy. Given that my Grandpa Kosmos stayed true to the Greek standard of a café and offered only coffee, some soft drinks, and a limited selection of sweets that were provided by Lefkos Pyrgos (they used to be supplied by Omonia, which was a couple blocks up and much closer, but Kosmos had a falling out with the owner, the likes of which I still didn't understand beyond he now had to battle traffic to complete his menu).

From where I sat at the end of the long counter along one wall, I could see across the street to my father's restaurant, which would be gearing up for the lunch crowd right about now. It was a place where I had also spent a large chunk of my teenage years as a waitress.

'Sofia!'

My grandfather came from the back room and spotted me. I got up and hugged him, kissing him on both cheeks as if we were only just meeting again after years' long separation when in actuality I'd seen him two days ago at Sunday dinner at my parents' house.

But that was the Greeks for you. Especially when it came to gregarious ones like my grandfather, who was a cross between Anthony Quinn's Zorba and a Greek Sean Connery.

'Sit, sit,' he ordered, edging in between two stools and joining his hands together on top of the counter. 'Georgia! See to it that my favorite granddaughter gets whatever she wants.'

This brought a grin to my face, even though I

knew he'd say the same thing had my younger sister Efi been seated there instead of me. Another Greek thing.

Or, rather, a Grandpa Kosmos thing.

'So to what do I owe the pleasure?' he asked, his big, white bushy eyebrows sitting low over his eyes.

Georgia gave me a frappé and I took the paper off the top of the straw and enjoyed a long, fortifying sip. She placed a small plate of a Greek sweet next to it. One I wasn't used to seeing served outside Greece or my mother's kitchen made of grape must and flour and sprinkled with sesame seeds.

'It's not good to drink a cold liquid on a cold day,' Kosmos gently chided.

'Oh? And where is that written?'

'I'm sure you can find it somewhere. Probably on an old marble that has yet to be unearthed.'

I smiled.

My grandfather was fond of connecting the present to the past. And he was also known to sprinkle his conversation with philosophical quotes that probably were etched into marbles somewhere. But it was his unwavering honesty and unconditional love as well as irreverent sense of humor that made him more than just a grandparent to me.

I took a bite of the sweet *moustalevria*. 'Is Lefkos Pyrgos trying something new?'

'Lefkos Pyrgos? Oh. That.' He waved his hand as if to dismiss the question. 'So, have you looked into that whole Roula Kalomoira deal yet?'

I raised my brows and hoped that he couldn't

read my grimace from where I sipped my frappé. I had to get me one of those hand-blenders. Frappés always tasted much better when I ordered them out.

He handed me a napkin and I drew it across my mouth, although I was sure I didn't need it. I was using a straw, so there would be no frappé mustache.

'Nope,' I answered.

'But you will...'

I moved the glass around on the counter, not wanting to tell him about my visit with Pino this morning. I wanted to get information, not share it. Especially considering that within five minutes of telling my grandfather anything I was working on – however loosely – my mother would be calling me, wanting to know everything the instant it happened.

'Hey, how about those Giants?' I said with a big smile.

He stared at me for a couple of seconds, his eyes dancing with light, and then he laughed. He waggled his finger at me. 'You're getting better at this P.I. stuff.'

I straightened my shoulders. 'Thanks.'

Considering that not too long ago my family had considered me completely incapable of keeping a secret, his comment was the ultimate in compliments.

'So,' I began, eyeing him. 'What's the word in your circles on the bodies popping up?'

'The dead ones?'

'We wouldn't be talking about them if they were alive.'

His chuckle made me smile. 'Andreas thinks we have a secret society of vampires working Queens.'

I nodded, agreeing that his old friend Andreas, who was just as old as my grandfather, but not nearly as wise, would probably say that.

'And you?'

'Me?' He slid his wrists from the counter and crossed his arms. 'I don't know. I think maybe there's some sicko out there doing stuff he shouldn't.' He squinted at me. 'Why are you asking?'

I should have known that I wouldn't get away with a simple information extraction with Kosmos, but it had been worth a try. Thankfully, I was saved from answering when the cowbell over the door rang. We both looked in that direction to find none other than my other sometimes love interest, Dino Antonopoulos, coming inside.

First a phone call from Jake, now I was staring at the Greek object of my affection, all in the same morning. I was familiar with the term 'when it rains, it pours', but I wasn't used to a cloud unleashing its torrent directly over me.

I sat across the table from Dino, wondering if I should have refused when he asked to speak to me. My grandfather and the five older men that were always seated in the back were looking at us, making me wonder how long it would take my mother to find out and begin asking my opinion on gold-foil wedding invitations with Greek flags on them.

'So...' I began, shifting under his gaze. 'You supply the sweets to my grandfather now.'

He nodded. 'For a couple of weeks now.'

'I hope you charge him for delivery.'

His smile widened. 'Most of the stock I bring him is second-day so he can get a discount. What do you think?'

'I think he's taking you for a ride.'

'Not if it's one I want to be on.'

I squinted at him.

He shrugged, looking every inch of the Greek god that he was. 'I enjoy visiting with Kosmos. I arrange it so I'm here during my down time. We have coffee. Talk...'

Yikes. No doubt some of that talk concerned me. I could only imagine what stories my grandfather had told him.

'So,' he said, 'how are you?'

I twisted my lips, then remembered I still had my frappé and took a deep sip from it. 'Fine. Did you make this?' I pointed to the *moustalevria*.

'Yes. I wasn't planning on making it a regular selection at the shop, but it was so popular that I may have to. Try it.'

'I will.' I shifted again. 'I just had a big breakfast.'

Liar.

So sue me, the thought of eating the delicious sweet when in his company didn't sit well with me. Especially considering that our first sexual encounter had centered around a chocolate torte he had brought for my Greek Name Day. And we hadn't eaten it the traditional way, but rather used each other as plates ... that we licked clean.

I cleared my throat.

'You OK?' he asked.

'What? Oh, yeah. Fine. I'm fine.'

I had to stop thinking about items of an intimate nature when in his presence. Partly because I was afraid my face gave me away. Mostly because it inspired me to think about what the *moustalevria* might taste like eaten off his skin.

OK, this was getting ridiculous.

I sat up straighter. 'Was there a specific reason you wanted to talk to me, Dino?'

Nothing like cutting to the chase. I was on work time. And I didn't think imagining Dino and me escaping into the small bathroom at the back of the café qualified as work.

He looked down at his hands where they were clasped in front of him on the table. Georgia had brought him a traditional hot Nescafé and the foam was nice and thick on top. Not that he had noticed.

God, he had great hands. And I wasn't merely talking about the thickness of his fingers and the black hair that peppered the backs or his neat, square nails. When he touched me...

I cleared my throat again. He looked up, taking in what I was sure was my flushed appearance. He grinned suggestively.

I glowered.

'Look, I know we said we'd let things cool off a bit...' he said.

Understatement. The moment I figured out that my mother not only knew I was seeing him, but had secretly pulled the strings to make it happen, I had put the brakes on but fast.

'Well, I...' he continued.

This time he cleared his throat.

'I miss you.'

There were a few three-word phrases specifically designed to melt a girl's heart. And that was definitely one of them.

Only I didn't want my heart to melt. Not now. Not anytime in the immediate future.

'Go out on a date with me, Sofie.'

I was sure I was looking at him as if all his hair had just fallen out and landed in his coffee.

'Nothing grand. We could go for dinner. Maybe at Uncle George's. Take in a movie. You know. Something simple.'

When it came to my dating a Greek, 'simple' didn't land anywhere in the vicinity.

'You're joking. Right?'

His handsome expression told me he wasn't.

'I'm not suggesting we sleep together, Sofie.'

I snorted. An inelegant sound that surprised even me. 'Yeah, well, you probably would have gotten much farther if you had.'

He looked back down at his hands.

My grandfather walked up behind Dino and slapped his shoulder. 'How is my favorite young couple doing?'

I shared a meaningful glance with Dino that I hoped told him exactly the reason why I couldn't date him. Couple? We barely knew each other. Well, OK, maybe we did know each other. In the most biblical of senses. But I was nowhere near dating him. Out in public. Where God and all the Greeks could see.

'Actually, Pappou, I have to be going,' I said,

getting up from the table.

'So soon? You just got here.'

I kissed and hugged him. 'Yeah, Rosie just texted me from the office. I have a client waiting.'

'Make him wait.'

I looked at Dino. 'It was nice seeing you again.'

He got to his feet. 'And the answer to my question?'

I squinted at him again. 'I'll think about it.'

I had meant to say 'no', so when the words came out, I had to stop myself from slapping my hand over my mouth.

But the damage was already done.

# SEVEN

So after a quick stop I headed back to the office. I figured the way my luck was going, if I continued my agency avoidance tactics I'd end up running into my ex-fiancé Thomas-the-Toad Chalikis. And that I could do without just now.

The stop I'd made was to Romanoff's house. I'd knocked, but no one answered. Shocker. Not that I had expected anyone to open the door. I'd learned a couple of months back that if you wanted an audience with the old Romanian, then your best bet was at night. If I preferred not to dwell on the reasons for that, well, that was my business.

Still, I'd debated slipping the envelope of retainer money he'd given me under the door along with a note telling him I couldn't accept the case. No reason. Just 'here, take your money back.'

Of course, I was already working the case, in a manner of speaking. But somehow the thought of being associated with someone the police considered a suspect didn't sit well with me. I wanted my investigation to be untainted. Meaning I wanted to consider every angle, even if a particular avenue led directly to the door I'd knocked at.

Even if that meant I was working for no one save myself.

All of my uncle Spyros' blasted rules streamed through my head.

I walked out of my uncle's office with a pad of notes. Rosie was busy at her computer and picked up the phone when it rang, giving the agency hours and telling the caller that, no, he or she didn't need to schedule an appointment.

She hung up but didn't acknowledge my presence, although I was pretty sure she knew I was standing there. She had the police scanner Waters had bought propped on her desk and it was tuned in, voices spouting codes I couldn't make sense of.

It had been like this since my return a half hour earlier. She was miffed and was hell-bent on letting me and everyone else know about it.

'Rosie, I was hoping you could look into a few things for me,' I said by way of gaining her attention.

She ignored me for a good half minute and then turned just her head. 'Hmm? I'm sorry. Were you talking to me?'

I raised a skeptical brow and placed the pad on her desk. 'I'd like you to run these names through the system. See what comes up.'

Her dimples popped along with her chewing gum. 'Sure. I might be able to get to it tomorrow. Or maybe the day after.'

She turned back toward her computer.

'I'd appreciate it if you could get the information to me by close today.'

It wasn't often that I played the boss card. I

usually reserved it for important items. But, damn it, she was pissing me off. And her treating me as if I wasn't worth her time got under my skin somehow.

All right, so I'd invited a suspected vampire into the office. Was that any reason to shut me out?

She swiveled her chair so quickly that I was forced to jerk back or risk physical injury. 'Fine. Good. OK.'

'Fine.'

The cowbell above the door clanged, letting in a cold blast of air. My cousin Pete.

Good. I had a few things I wanted him to look into for me as well.

I opened my mouth to say the same when he issued a brisk 'good morning' to Rosie and me and then walked past us ... and straight into my uncle's office.

I huffed.

Rosie grinned.

'End of the day today,' I told her.

'I'll see to it right away, Miss Metropolis.'

That set my teeth on edge.

I stalked away from her toward my uncle's office. Pete was shrugging out of his coat and then hung it on the coat tree before seating himself behind the desk. It seemed to take him a minute to understand that my notes littered the desktop, the computer was on, and that I was again actively writing on the white board.

'What's this?' he asked.

I squinted at him, feeling slightly like I was being chided for venturing into territory that wasn't mine.

'I'm working a case.'

'Oh.'

He switched his attention toward the computer.

'You need this?' he asked.

I rounded the desk and edged the chair slightly back with my hip. 'Yes, I need this. If you don't mind.'

You see, up until a few weeks ago, Pete was little more than my uncle's estranged son who was only out to take whatever cash he could find and disappear until he needed more. I figured if he was going to be hanging around, he might as well be doing something useful, so I began giving him work. First with painting and updating the agency. Then assigning him cases. Partly because there was no more cash to be had (I suspected my uncle had actually stashed bills just so his wayward son could find them – some twisted way of alleviating his own guilt), and partly because I felt sorry for him.

Of course, I never thought for a moment that he'd take over as if he were the rightful heir returned.

I grimaced. Oh, yeah? Then why had I essentially given over the office without argument until this morning?

Because I needed it now, I reminded myself.

Pete looked up at me and grinned. 'Is this going to be a problem?'

'Is what going to be a problem?'

'Me working my own cases.'

I had no idea he was working his own cases.

Certainly Rosie hadn't said anything to me. And Pete, himself, had been so scarce lately that I hadn't thought he was working at all.

'Why should it be a problem? I'm not your boss.'

His grin widened.

I walked to get his coat and held it out to him. 'Nor are you mine.'

He crossed his arms and refused to budge. 'How do you reason that you're more entitled to my father's office than I am?'

'Do you want a list?'

We stared at each other for long moments.

OK, sure. In recent weeks since I'd been throwing him things – and he had delivered in a roundabout way the Johnny Laughton case – my cousin seemed to have undergone a transformation of sorts. He'd gone from scowling, spiteful son out for all he could get to efficient, focused and friendly. I suspected that my uncle's absence played a large role in that. And the lack of money an even larger one.

Still, a few weeks didn't mean he was in charge of the agency.

Of course, I was fooling myself thinking I was. But my uncle had given me carte blanche on the telephone when I'd begun gaining some skills and attention, leading to a spike in business, so I figured I was well ahead in the game.

'Fine. OK,' Pete echoed Rosie's words of just a few minutes ago as he got up and took his coat. 'Where do you want me to work then?'

'Since I'm not using my desk, you can have that. For now,' I stressed the last two words.

He stalked from the room and I watched him, noticing the way Rosie sat back in her chair taking in the goings on, her mouth working her ever-present gum.

'Bitch,' I heard Pete say under his breath.

I gave a monster eye roll and then slammed the office door on both of them.

For all my maneuvering to establish my superiority at the agency, I found that the next step in my investigation took me out again, leaving the office at risk of being taken over by my cousin, and Rosie to make a voodoo doll to poke full of pins.

I wasn't sure how I finagled it, but I actually got an appointment to meet Jane Creek for tea at a Manhattan restaurant. The conversation had gone something like this:

'Mrs Jane Creek?' I'd asked, surprised to have gotten the screen legend directly. I'd expected to get a publicist or at least a housekeeper when I looked up her number in the private list to which my uncle paid for access.

'Yes. Were you expecting someone else?'

Of course, I had, but that much was obvious. 'Good morning, Mrs Creek—'

'Please, it's Miss now.'

'Yes, Miss Creek...' It seemed odd somehow that I was addressing an eighty-year-old by miss, but, hey, the Greeks did it as well, partly because there was no 'Ms' in the Greek language. Mostly so everyone would know a woman was an old maid/spinster.

Although I don't think Jane's intention was the

same. She apparently wanted to represent herself as Miss to make it clear she was on the market ... and was actively accepting bids.

I'd introduced myself as a P.I. and told her I'd like to meet with her, to ask a few questions if she could spare some time in the next few days. She established that I wasn't working on behalf of the doctor who had butchered her, and then shocked me by suggesting we meet for tea.

Of course, I fully expected that I would be the one to pay for that tea. But, hey, I figured it was worth the investment just to sit across and gawk at her, much less get any solid answers to the questions I had. Especially since I wasn't all that clear on what I was doing. I only knew that my gut was leading me in this direction, and I was following it.

So after stopping at home to change out of my jeans and long sleeved T-shirt, and into a dressier pair of jeans, a proper shirt and blazer, I took the subway into the city and arrived ten minutes before our appointed time, only to be late because there was no outside sign to identify the place, only the address. When I finally figured it out and entered Lady Mendl's, I found the actress already there, seated at what was probably the best table in the house, a pink hat on top of her white hair, and every inch of her teased and powdered and primped, the epitome of the movie star she had once been.

'Mrs ... Miss Creek, I'm sorry if I kept you waiting,' I said, approaching the table.

She gave me a small pout and then waved her hand, flashing fifty carats of diamonds on her skeletal fingers and wrists. ‘Please, please sit. I’ve already ordered.’

The maitre d’ finally accepted that I belonged (he hadn’t been very good at hiding his skepticism when I told him who I was there to meet even though I was wearing my best jeans and blouse), and pulled out a chair for me. I sat down and awkwardly allowed him to push me in.

As soon as he left, I realized where I was and who I was sitting across from and became tongue-tied. An unusual phenomenon for me, since I usually could come up with something to say to everybody.

But this wasn’t just everybody. This was mother-effin’ Jane Creek!

‘So, dear,’ she began, sipping from a large, gold-rimmed teacup that bore lipstick marks, ‘What is it you wanted to talk to me about?’

‘I loved *I’m a Big Girl Now*,’ I blurted.

I winced, unable to believe I’d just said that. OK, so I’d liked the movie. But I’d never considered myself the type that gushed at movie stars. I’d casually exchanged hellos and nods with the likes of Robert De Niro and Billy Crystal when they were at the Kaufman Astoria Studios in Queens.

Yet here I was acting like a cow-eyed teenager.

‘Thank you,’ she said, appearing to fluff feathers I couldn’t see. ‘It was one of my favorite roles.’ A waiter approached and placed an impressive tray of scones in the middle of the table, while two waitresses supplied us both with clotted cream and preserves.

My stomach growled so loudly one of the

waitresses smiled at me.

'Please, do dig in,' Jane said. 'Lady Mendl's makes the best in the city.'

Not that I would know. I didn't get into the city all that often. Home for me was Queens and it was rare for me to cross the East River.

'So,' I said, trying my best to grab hold of my thoughts. 'What I wanted to talk to you about was Dr Westervelt...'

At first Jane appeared not to hear me. She was engrossed in slathering cream over a scone and taking a none too dainty bite of it. Which gave me a moment to consider her face.

She was eighty if she was a day. But despite the reports that the bad doctor had butchered her during her last plastic surgery, she looked fine to me. Better than fine, she looked better than my mother, who was nearly thirty years younger.

'Why do you think I invited you, dear?' she finally said.

'Jane!' A couple of passing women in hats very much like hers stopped where they were passing our table. I felt suddenly way underdressed for the occasion.

The cool actress pretended she didn't see them and kept her gaze on me. And then as slowly as you please, she finally glanced in their direction, a smile crossing her face.

I couldn't help getting the impression that I'd just witnessed a piece of impeccable acting.

I sat patiently as the three women exchanged pleasantries, not expecting to be included as I spread cream on half a blueberry scone.

'Cissy and Cokie ... I'd like to introduce you to

Miss Metropolis. She's a private investigator.'

The small, silver knife slipped out of my fingers and clanked to the plate then did a half-pike off the table. If I didn't know better, I would have thought the nearby waiter had caught the silverware before it hit the floor.

'Oh, a genuine female P.I. How exciting!'

I didn't know whether I should get up or not.

'Cissy and Cokie are two of my oldest and dearest friends,' Jane explained.

Even working-class me was familiar with the two socialite sisters. While I couldn't remember if they were Rockefeller or Vanderbilt, I knew that the family to which they belonged was very wealthy.

'Tell me, dear,' one of them leaned closer to me, the rim of her hat nearly catching me in the eye. 'Do you handle ... matters of a personal nature?'

I smiled. 'My success rate is a solid ninety-nine percent.'

'Oh!' She leaned back toward her sister. 'We should get her business card, Cok. You never know when you need to go outside for good help.'

Cokie gave an eye roll that would have rivaled any of Rosie's. 'Don't be ridiculous, sister. We own an investigative firm.'

'Thus the mention of "outside", dear.'

I noticed that Jane was enjoying the interaction and wondered if that was part of the reason she'd invited me to meet her in such a public place. A star of her stature meeting with a private investigator outside the loop was sure to start some tongues wagging.

'Well, it was very nice to see you both. We really must catch up sometime,' Jane said, cutting the sisters off at the chase.

The two sisters agreed, their heads together as they allowed the maitre d' to continue leading them to their table.

'That should keep them busy for the next five minutes,' Jane confided to me as she took a self-satisfied sip from her cup.

I shook my head. My mother was going to die when I told her about this meeting.

'I'm confused, Miss Creek. Surely you can afford to retain any investigator in Manhattan ... why agree to meet with me?'

'Simple.' She finished off her scone and daintily wiped her hands with a linen napkin. 'You were the first one to call me.'

Direct enough, I suppose.

'So may I ask what, exactly, you'd like me to do for you?'

'Well, that should be obvious, dear. I want you to nail that vampire with a medical degree to the wall.'

# EIGHT

Of course, Jane hadn't meant that the doctor was actually a vampire. No matter my immediate, shocked reaction.

I really needed to get Romanoff his money back.

No, she'd referred to Westervelt as the undead because he couldn't really be human after what he'd done to her, right? She then proceeded to tell me exactly what she wanted me to do: dig up any and all dirt I could on the disgraced physician, find other victims and get her their contact information so that they might file a class action suit against him and his questionable practices.

At the risk of offending her, I'd asked her point blank what he did. She'd stared at me as if I had instantaneously grown a hairy mole on my chin and said: 'He gave me hepatitis C, of course.'

I made a point of not going back to the agency until after everyone else had gone home for the day and the place was closed up tight. I'd turned all the lights back on, made sure the door was locked and then disappeared into my uncle's office where I found the data I had asked Rosie to compile sitting in the middle of the desk.

I was well into researching Jane's fellow victims when my cell phone rang. I blindly reached for it on the desk and answered.

'Sofie?'

My heart skipped a beat. Damn. I should have checked caller ID before picking up. I'd assumed the caller would be my mother because she usually called around this time of night to see if I'd eaten and check on the status of my love life.

If she only knew who I was talking to...

'Hi, Dino,' I said, balancing the cell between my ear and shoulder as I entered another search string into the browser window. I tried to ignore the warmth that spilled through my lower abdomen at being reminded of his existence and our steamy encounters.

'I hope I'm not interrupting anything.'

'No, no,' I assured him, when I would have preferred to say, 'Yes, yes.'

'Good. Look, I ... we didn't get a chance to finish our talk yesterday...'

I stopped what I was doing and swiveled my chair forward, giving him my full attention.

Because what we had been discussing was his asking me out on an official date.

And if I wasn't mistaken, we had finished.

I squinted at nothing in particular, waiting for him to continue.

'Go out with me, Sofie,' he said point blank.

I worked my mouth around my answer, but nothing came out.

Truth was, he sounded good. Too good. And talking to him like this made me realize how much I'd missed him.

And I was reminded that I hadn't stopped seeing him because I wasn't attracted to him; I'd stopped seeing him because of my mother.

'We could go to Agnanti,' he named a popular Greek restaurant that sat alongside Astoria Park near the river. Then quickly said, 'Or not. We could go anywhere. Manhattan. Long Island. Connecticut. Hell, New Jersey, if that's what you want.'

I smiled at that. I had to give the guy credit. He was taking all this in stride.

'Sofie? Are you still there?'

'Hmm? Oh. Yes.'

A pause and then, 'Yes? Is that in answer to my question?'

'Yes. As in "I'm still here".'

'Oh.'

The dejection in his voice made me smile wider.

'And yes to your invitation.'

'Meaning...'

'I'll go out with you.'

I could virtually hear his smile. 'Good! Name the place.'

'Agnanti.'

I knew I should probably be looking for another restaurant. Going to Agnanti would be little better than making reservations at my father's steak house.

But I liked Dino. And I liked the restaurant. So let the chips fall where they may.

We finalized the arrangements for this Friday at seven and then sat for a few moments smiling at each other through the cell phone before hanging up.

Even after that, I stared for long minutes at

nothing until I heard rapping on the glass out front.

I started out of my reverie of all things chocolatey and sweet and Dino and checked my Glock where it rested in my shoulder holster. Then I went to see who it was.

I stopped midway to the door, instantly recognizing Romanoff's cadaverous driver.

Was it me, or was his skin glowing?

I fought off a shiver and unlocked the door, vaguely remembering Rosie's warning about not inviting a vampire on to the premises. I wondered if it were possible to un-invite him.

I wasn't sure, but I figured it was worth a shot.

I halted the counterclockwise motion on the key and left it locked, holding my hand up to indicate I needed a minute. Then I grabbed my coat, and retrieved the envelope I still had in my purse, and let myself outside.

Lurch gave me a long look, but I wasn't saying anything.

Finally he turned toward the car and after looking both ways opened the back suicide door on the old black Lincoln. Romanoff climbed out with more grace and energy than I would have imagined a man of his apparent age could.

'Good evening, Sofie.'

I hated when he began conversations like that. 'Hi,' I returned. I looked over my shoulder. 'Sorry, but I'm going to have to rescind my invitation for you to come inside the office. Hope you don't mind.'

His smile was somehow knowing and more than a bit amused, I thought.

I half expected him to tell me it was too late. As I waited, I cursed myself for trading the warmth of the office for the frigid cold wind because of Rosie's stupid superstitions.

'I understand you visited me at my home today,' Romanoff said.

Oh! 'Oh. Yes. Yes, I did.' I reached inside my jacket, shivering as I let the air in with my hand as I withdrew the envelope. 'I need to return this to you.'

I held it out but he didn't move to take it. Neither did his driver.

'May I inquire as to why?'

I couldn't very well tell him I couldn't work for a vampire, could I? I cleared my throat. 'I just don't feel comfortable accepting the case,' I said honestly enough.

He finally nodded at the driver and he slowly accepted the envelope. I felt like teeth had been removed from my neck and I gave an audible sigh.

'You know, I would repeat my suggestion that you conduct an in-house investigation.' I don't know why I felt compelled to add that. Maybe because now that my relief had passed I was experiencing a bit of guilt.

'Thank you for your thoughts,' he said in a way that told me he was not happy or thankful.

He turned back toward the car. Lurch followed, opening the door for him.

'For what it's worth, I am investigating the ... deaths,' I said for no good reason I could identify.

He looked over his shoulder. 'Will you be

sharing what you find with the authorities?'

'The police?' I fairly squeaked. 'Um, no. I have no plans to.'

Why would he be asking me that?

'Good evening, Sofie.'

He disappeared into the depths of the car and within moments the old Lincoln pulled into traffic, nothing but its red tail lights visible as it drove away.

I shuddered and pulled my coat tighter around my body. He would have to do that 'good evening' bit again, wouldn't he?

I began to turn to go back inside, even though I was doubtful I'd ever feel warm again, when I spotted a familiar truck parked up the street.

Jake...

After locking the agency doors and pocketing the keys, I stalked to the passenger's side window of Jake's truck and rapped on the glass. A moment later, I watched it whirl down. I could barely make him out in the dimness of the cab.

'What are you doing?'

I heard a click. 'Get in, Sofie.'

I made no move to open the door. Instead, I crossed my arms. 'Answer me. What are you doing sitting outside my door? Again?'

The shadow inside moved and the door opened toward me. I caught it to keep it from knocking me over.

I got in. Not because he'd ordered me to, but because I was freezing.

The truck was new and smelled it. I didn't want to think that the reason why I knew it was new was because I'd watched his previous one get blown to bits when I was only a few feet away from it.

'What are you doing?' he asked.

I was searching for an interior light I could switch on. The ceiling ... the dash... 'There has to be a light here somewhere.'

He didn't seem to move, but within a blink, the ceiling light went on.

I settled back into the seat, allowing the heat blower he'd turned up to wash over me. 'Thanks.'

'No problem.'

I sat for a long moment, trying to wrap my head around what I was doing inside Jake's truck and why I suddenly wanted to launch myself at him.

While the ceiling dome wasn't bright, it cast enough light for me to relearn the rugged lines of his face. Damn, but he was hot. Hotter than any one man had the right to be. His sandy blond hair always seemed disheveled. The stubble on his chin artfully shaped. And he always squinted his blue eyes as if he was either gazing directly into the sun, or trying to figure something out.

Trying to figure me out.

And I liked that I was a mystery to him. A puzzle he wanted to piece together. Because he represented the same to me.

'Are you going to answer my question?' I managed to push through my tight throat.

'Which question?'

Right. Which question, indeed. We both knew that I'd asked countless questions that had gone without answers. He seemed to be asking me why this latest one was any different.

'Are you on an official case?' I asked.

He took a deep breath, scratched his head with both hands and then stretched his right arm across the back of the seat. His fingertips brushed my hair.

I was caught between being offended that he'd used the old stretch and touch trick and shocked that I was letting him get away with it.

His fingers tunneled through my hair and touched my nape. I shivered again, this time for an altogether different reason.

Christ. He was going to be the end of me.

# NINE

Summoning every ounce of strength I had, I reached for his wrist and removed his arm from around my shoulders. 'Please ... don't touch me.'

He sat up straighter. 'Why?'

'Because I can't think when you do, that's why.'

'And the problem lies in...'

'The problem lies in that I already know we have chemistry.'

What was I saying? That I wanted more?

Yes, it was exactly what I was saying.

Which made no sense to me at all. How was it I was trying to hold on to casual with Dino, and reaching for something more intimate with Jake? Was the old double standard to blame? Because Dino was offering more, I wanted less? And because Jake was offering less, I wanted more?

Ugh. I hated being a cliché.

More than that, I hated that even recognizing the truth, I was helpless to do anything to change it.

'I'm going out with Dino,' I blurted.

Jake didn't move a muscle. At least not that I could tell. But I could feel his change in demeanor as surely as if he'd crossed his arms and scowled at me.

Not that I'd ever seen him scowl.

Hell, a scowl would mark a major milestone in our relationship.

'Sorry. I don't even know why I said that.' My voice sounded small in the large truck cab.

I did feel apologetic, but I feared not for the right reasons. I wasn't sorry that I'd said it. But sorry that I felt I'd had to say it.

'What are you doing here, Jake?' I whispered.

Please, please, answer this time, my heart silently pleaded with him.

Nothing.

He began leaning toward me and my stomach pitched to my feet. He was going to kiss me. Remind me why I couldn't get him out of my head. Why I didn't want him out, no matter how frustrating he could be.

Instead, he pulled the handle and pushed the door open.

I didn't move as he returned to an upright position and stared straight ahead, his features sheer granite.

'Jake?'

'Go, Sofie. Before I do something both of us will regret.'

Do it, I silently dared him.

I climbed out of the truck.

And, for what I suspected might be the final time, Jake pulled away from the curb, disappearing in the opposite direction from that in which Romanoff had gone.

* * *

I hated that the agency door wasn't the type I could slam. I tried, but the weak whoosh proved hugely anticlimactic.

So instead I went into my uncle's office, slammed that door, and then opened it and slammed it again for good measure. Feeling infinitesimally better I opened it again and took a deep breath. And then paced the length of the agency and back again, aware of my own frenetic reflection in the glass but ignoring it.

What was with Jake?

And why was it that the instant I climbed out of his truck I felt guilty? As if I had in some way betrayed Dino?

Oh, this was so not the way I saw things happening in my life when I walked out of St Demetrios's church wearing my wedding dress but unmarried seven months ago. Call me foolish, but after that day's events, I'd been convinced that I'd not only never marry, but never get involved with another man again. I'd be the *yerotokori* that every Greek family had. The one daughter left unmarried so she could look after her parents when they were older. I'd believed that I'd die alone and would never be able to trust another man again.

Now I had two men I trusted; and who were both openly pursuing me.

And Jake *was* pursuing me, wasn't he? Oh, he didn't do it with the full frontal attack that Dino employed. He was far subtler.

Far more dangerous.

Which made no sense at all. Why should he have an edge over a perfectly hot, nice Greek guy? Because he had bad boy written all over him?

Something sitting on my desk that hadn't been there before caught my attention. I stopped pacing long enough to stare at it. I looked over my shoulder toward the door I was sure was locked and then back again. Then, slowly, warily, I stepped toward the item in question.

All frustrated romantic energy left me, replaced by something ultimately more ominous. Because despite the fact that I clearly remembered handing Romanoff back his money, his driver taking the envelope from me, and how positive I was that I'd locked the door when I'd gone out to confront Jake, sitting there in the middle of my desk was that same envelope as if it had been there all along.

I looked over my shoulder again and then picked up the envelope, checking inside to make sure it was the item in question. Not only was it, something had been added to it.

I slid out a neat piece of notepaper that was folded over once. I opened it and written in what appeared to be fountain ink were the words, 'I implore you to reconsider.' Signed, Ivan Romanoff.

I dropped both the envelope and the note to my desk, backing away from them as if they were capable of inflicting bodily harm.

It was impossible. How could he have? There was no way...

I swallowed hard, the sound loud in the quiet room.

Well. So much for uninviting a vampire once

you had already invited him in. Not only did it appear he could regain access any time he wanted, he could do so without the convenience of an unlocked door.

I had a feeling this was not going to be good...

And knew that whatever happened, I could never breathe a word to Rosie about tonight's unsettling events.

'Sofie ... Sofie...' The disembodied voice came from the direction of the fog that blanketed the north side of the street. I looked around. Odd. What was I doing standing in the middle of Broadway? And where were all the cars?

Cars? Where were the people?

Nothing moved. Scratch that. The hanging sign above an attorney's office swayed slightly back and forth, the hooks squeaking. Paper fluttered near the curb, the wind picking it up and then pushing it farther down the street behind me.

I shivered and reached to pull my coat closer. Only I wasn't wearing my coat. I was in my normal bedtime apparel of ancient Amazing Mets T-shirt and panties. And the cement was cold under my bare feet.

'Sofie...' the vaguely familiar voice called me again, carried on the wind as if traveling a great distance. It seemed to egg me on, to draw me closer to the thick fog.

I shook my head. There was no way I was going anywhere near that fog. Bad things happened in fog. Bad people hid out in there. Besides, while I was pretty sure I knew who was calling, I wasn't positive. And the person in question wasn't worth the risk.

I moved closer to the fog.

Or, rather, the fog moved closer to me. Surrounded me. Pressed up against me like thick cotton I couldn't blink out of my eyes.

'Sofie...'

I wanted to tell the voice to hush. I needed to get home. Put some clothes on.

Instead, I moved forward without any intention of doing so.

People. I craned my neck. There were people ahead. Or, rather, shadowy outlines of people. Grouped together. Their backs to me. The fog's white fingers wove around us all, blocking them from view and then clearing the way again until I was upon them. Faces turned toward me. Dark, expressionless faces. I stepped up next to them and then looked down to see what they'd been staring at; what had made them gather. So still.

My mouth went dry and my hand fluttered to my throat. Lying there in the middle of the street was ... me.

'Sofie...'

I doubled over. But rather than come closer to the asphalt, I instead found myself jackknifed upright in bed, my bed, safe and sound in my own apartment, my breathing ragged, my hand at my throat. Muffy staring at me from the other pillow accusingly.

I stripped the comforter from my legs, half covering the dog, and padded barefoot to the bathroom where I didn't wait for the water to get warm before splashing it over my face again and again. I stared into the mirror. But I didn't see my reflection. I saw myself lying in the middle of the road, wearing my night-time attire, my body twisted in an unnatural position, my neck bearing bite marks, scarlet red blood pooled under my head, the only color in the dream.

Dream? That was a full-blown nightmare!

I found my hand at my throat again. I quickly removed it, and then checked my neck for any telltale marks. None.

Muffy barked. I looked down to find him at my feet, staring up at me in a mixture of concern and reproach.

'I'm sorry. Did I wake you?'

He barked again and then did his little circle thing while maintaining eye contact.

'Ah. Gotcha.' I saw to my own business before crossing the apartment to open the window so he could do his own thing. The frigid winter air hit my naked thighs like an avalanche of ice cubes and I shivered. The glowing microwave clock told me it was just after four a.m. And all was quiet outside. Big, fat snowflakes floated on drafts of air, although I thought I could make out some stars in the sky. I told myself I should move from in front of the window before I caught my death of cold (did your mother's words ever leave you? Worse, were you doomed to repeat them to your own children some day?), but while the air was cold, it felt good. Helped clear my mind of the gruesome images from my nightmare.

I made out Muffy's paw-falls on the fire escape as he made his way back down from the roof, but he didn't immediately appear in the window. Then I heard him bark. Not in curiosity or concern or exasperation, but in full out defense mode, complete with accompanying growl.

My throat choked off air.

'What is it, boy?' I asked, opening the window wider and looking out.

A large, black shadow swooped down and the sound of flapping sent fear slicing through my heart.

I drew back so quickly I nearly fell to my ass.

Muffy's barking continued and then I heard a muffled yelp.

'Muffy!' I scrambled back to the window.

He jumped inside, ran a few feet and then raced back, barking at the window.

I slammed it shut and locked it, drawing the curtains tight even as I backed away.

OK. I was never going to sleep again. Ever.

# TEN

I finally dropped off to sleep at sometime before seven, meaning as soon as I did, it was time to get up. I hated irony. Especially when it left me with circles under my red eyes and a scowl no amount of coffee could remedy.

I drove to the agency under metal gray skies that just seemed to get darker as the morning got slowly brighter. I'm not usually one to allow the weather to affect my mood, but given that my mood was already foul, well, the weather not only contributed to it; I was determined to make it completely to blame.

I lucked out in grabbing a parking spot near the front of the agency. I got out of the car, wondering if it was ever going to get warm again as I made a mad dash for the door. Only to stop dead ten feet away.

Standing on the sidewalk was Rosie (at least I was pretty sure it was Rosie. The figure was the same height, wore the same high heels that did nothing to add to her petite stature) looking like she was ready for an Arctic expedition in a faux fur lined parka, hood up, gloves on. And it appeared she was directing someone in African dress to do something to the windows.

I slowly drew even with Rosie. 'What's up?'

She jumped, her mouth working overtime on her gum. 'Geez, Louise, scare the soul out of a body, already.'

The man who wore traditional African dress and a hat was chanting something and, despite his lack of a coat, didn't appear to be cold. Maybe he had on battery-charged electric long johns or something.

'What's he doing?'

'Shhh,' Rosie hissed in a way that could easily have been confused as connected to the temperature. 'He's casting a spell.'

I raised my brows and stared at her.

'You know,' she continued in a whisper. 'To keep vampires out.'

I gave a monster eye roll and walked to the door and opened it.

'What are you doing?' Rosie shouted. 'Jesus, Joseph and Mary. Now he's going to have to start all over again.'

I ignored her and let the door close behind me. There were three people waiting in the upright chairs. I saw my cousin Pete was continuing his bid for my uncle's office, and even Nash had his door open and was talking on the phone, completely oblivious to me.

'Hey,' one of our best process servers, Pamela Coe, said, shifting through the morning's summonses on Rosie's desk.

'Hey, yourself.' I shrugged out of my coat and put it on the back of my chair. I was going to have to get a warmer coat. Oh, I had one of those violet quilted numbers that I think moms everywhere felt compelled to give to their daughters for Christmas. The hideous thing stretched to my knees and made me look like a shapeless blob. Didn't matter how warm it was, I wouldn't be caught dead wearing it.

'What's going on out there?' Pamela interrupted my thoughts as they veered to the image in my nightmare.

'Don't ask.'

She took the summonses she wanted and put the rest back on the desk. 'The guy looks familiar. I think I saw him on the news last week. Some sort of witch doctor. Been getting a lot of business lately.'

'Yeah. Rosie's having him protect the agency against vampires.'

Pamela stared at me. I shrugged.

Hey, I wasn't going to argue with the superstitious Puerto Rican too loudly. After all, that envelope had found its way back inside the agency after I'd uninvited Romanoff and locked the door.

'Do African witch doctors even believe in vampires?' Pamela asked.

'I guess so.' I looked over my shoulder where Rosie was now bouncing up and down in an effort to keep warm while the guy chanted. 'Either that, or he needs the money.'

One of the waiting customers said, 'If it's a general spell, it won't work.'

Pamela and I looked at the woman who was about thirty-ish and I guessed was there for a cheating spouse case.

'I'm just sayin'. My sister had a guy like that come over the other day and I grilled him about the extent of his powers. He admitted that all he was capable of performing was a general protection spell; it might not work against specific threats.'

'Sounds like a crock to me,' another customer said, this one a forty-something male who looked like his scowl was permanently attached.

My gaze drifted to the third customer. An elderly woman with ... did she have pink hair?

I nearly groaned aloud. Definitely a missing pet case.

'Whatever floats your boat,' Pamela said under her breath. 'See you at the gun range later?'

'What? Oh, yeah.'

Every Wednesday night I headed over to practice shooting and since I'd begun running into Pamela there, we'd begun synchronizing our visits. Not that we talked much during the sessions (sometimes it was little more than 'hello' and 'see you at the office'), but it was a nice, semi girls' event out since I didn't seem to experience many of those lately. Not since my wedding-day-gone-wrong. Partly because my friends had also been Thomas's friends so I'd given them up. Mostly because it had been my best friend I caught squeezing my groom between her thighs.

Rumor had it Kati and Thomas were still a couple, and I'd seen the ring she donned on her left-hand finger. A ring that might or might not hold the diamond that had been missing from my own ring – a ring made from a family one my grandfather had given Thomas to propose to me with – and replaced by CZ.

Pamela left and on the rush of cold air I heard Rosie cuss her out. I smiled. Probably the process had to start all over again.

'How long am I going to have to wait?' the male customer wanted to know.

I gestured a hand toward Rosie. 'As long as it takes her to finish what she's doing.'

'You can't handle me?'

I gave him a long look. 'No.'

I grabbed my coat and went into my uncle's office. My cousin Pete didn't even bother to look up from the computer. Probably he thought if he ignored me, I'd leave again.

Probably he needed to have his head examined.

'Up,' I said.

He scowled at me.

Seemed to be a lot of scowling going on this morning.

'What, you want to have this discussion again?' I asked.

He muttered something, striking the keyboard harder than necessary as he exited out of whatever he was doing.

'Fine.'

He got up, gathered his things, and left the office.

I gave him a little salute as he left, wondering when the last time was he'd spoken to his father – my uncle – and whether or not I was going to have to forfeit my squatter's rights soon. I glanced at my watch. Actually, today being Wednesday, Uncle Spyros should be making his weekly call later this afternoon. I made a mental note to be there when it came in.

My uncle, you see, was on extended vacation on a Greek island. He'd left for the indefinite trip a few weeks into my employment and had been gone for six months now. My mother liked to say that her brother-in-law must have met a woman while over there, and that's the reason he had yet to return.

My father, his brother, always said under his breath that probably my uncle was in trouble and that's why he was absent.

I didn't care one way or the other so long as I was left to my own devices. In the beginning, the prospect had scared that hell out of me. I mean, aside from a few dozen of the rules Spyros spouted as easily as the day's horse racing line-up, I'd been given very little mentoring. Instead, I'd been forced to go the trial-and-error route. And if my trail of errors meant that I'd learned a lot ... well, that's the way I preferred to look at it.

I glanced down at the morning newspapers Rosie had piled on the desk for me. I didn't think it was a mistake that she'd folded one open on a particular story: SUSPECTED VAMPIRE TAKEN IN FOR QUESTIONING.

A photo of Ivan Romanoff took up a good quarter of the page. It had been taken while he was being led into the precinct in handcuffs. I fished the police scanner I'd been carrying around from my coat pocket and put it on the desk, switching it on to low, and then unfolded the list of codes I had yet to memorize and put it next to the scanner before sitting down.

I turned toward the computer, determined to do some snooping into Romanoff's 'family'. More specifically, I wanted to look into what his nephew Vlad was up to. I hadn't seen him recently, but the sound of his voice in my dream last night was something I was sure never to forget.

I clicked for the browser and a site Pete must have been reading popped up. I moved to clear it until I realized the news piece was on the missing twins.

Hunh. I hadn't thought to ask my cousin what he was working on when he'd told me he was taking on his own cases. I guess I'd automatically assumed he was seeing to cheating spouse cases, which accounted for a good percentage of agency business.

Of course, the piece might have been one I'd pulled up yesterday. I scanned the page again. Nope. This article was posted today.

I turned to look for Pete, only to find him exiting the front door. Another, much louder and explicit blast from Rosie and he was gone.

The police scanner was a low hum of voices as I entered in Vladimir Romanoff's name into the search box. A series of links popped up on a musical conductor born in Toronto of Ukrainian parents. I typed in New York City and there on the second page was a photo of the man who just a few short months earlier had opened the coffin (I don't care how many times I was told it was a cello shipping box) I'd fallen into in his uncle's basement.

The man whose voice had beckoned me into

the fog in my nightmare.

I pulled a post-it notepad closer and copied down his name along with the name of a woman he'd been pictured with at an art gallery event last week. I looked closer, a chill running the length of my back. He looked good. Too good, actually.

I accessed the agency's search database and entered his name and city and then copied down the Upper West Side address.

'Moving up in the world, aren't you, Vlad?' I whispered under my breath.

The female dispatcher's voice on the police scanner sounded more serious than it usually did. I reached out and slightly turned up the volume.

'All units, Code 10-56, Ditmars and River. Verify condition.'

I looked up the code. Outstretched person. Which I took to mean body.

That would be my cue. I got up and shrugged into my coat. I almost ran straight into Rosie where she was entering the office. She slapped something on the desk and then exited again.

'What's this?' I asked, picking up the slip of paper.

'An agency expense.'

I realized it was for the witch doctor.

# ELEVEN

I should have known the first person I would run into was Pino. And there was absolutely no way I could avoid him as I drove down Ditmars. There were cars behind me, and a roadblock ahead of me redirecting traffic. And Pino was the one doing the redirecting.

Crap.

The sky was an ominous gray, giving the flashing lights of the swarm of parked patrol cars even greater urgency somehow. As I drew near the turn-off, Pino bent down as if to verify it was indeed me in the beat up old Mustang – as if it could have been anyone else – and then motioned with his hand for me to roll down the passenger's side window.

I did.

'What's going on?' I asked.

He hiked a brow. Which was much more preferable than his pants. 'Don't tell me you were just out cruising around and happened upon this by accident.'

'Why not? It's the truth.'

He waved the driver behind me to pass.

'So ... who is it?'

'What are you talking about?'

'The dead body.'

Cripes. So much for not blurting things out. There was no possible way I could have information like that so soon unless I'd been tipped off.

'Is it ... has it ... been drained of blood?'

The blare of a horn behind me. I spotted a car pulling out of a parking spot a couple spaces up and sent a silent prayer of thanks above.

I expected Pino's frown to be his answer, but he added, 'That's not for public consumption.'

'Since when am I the public?'

The dispatcher on the police scanner drew both our attention to where it sat on the passenger's seat. I reached for it at the same time he did, snatching it up and placing it between my legs where I shut it off.

'That's illegal, you know,' he said.

'What's illegal?'

'The scanner you're trying to hide.'

I remembered Waters' warning yesterday. 'What are you going to do? Write me a ticket?'

'No. I'm going to confiscate it.'

'Do you know how much I paid for it?' Well, he didn't have to know it was nothing. Speaking of which, was it possible to find out I'd gotten it via the black market? Could I be charged with that, as well?

'I don't care how much you paid for it. It's contraband.'

'It's a hobby,' I countered. 'Now move before I hit you.'

He drew back more out of shock, I think, than any true fear that I'd hit him. Then again, you never know.

I pulled into the vacated parking spot, shut off the engine and got out.

A coroner's van rolled by, directed through the barricade by Pino who had returned to work at the appearance of an official vehicle. Good. Maybe I could get a little closer.

Gathered at the end of the street were at least a half dozen uniformed officers, along with the female detective I'd seen take Romanoff in. Yellow police tape blocked off the sidewalk and a plastic tarp had been placed over what I suspected was the body. I shivered and walked closer, getting to about ten yards away before stopping. A hand peeked out from the tarp, palm up, as white as the random snowflakes that floated on the cold air.

'What do you think you're doing, Metro?'

Pino. Of course. Who else could it be?

'Aren't you supposed to be directing traffic?' My gaze was nailed to the too still hand.

'I've been relieved of duty.'

I glanced at where another, younger uniformed officer had taken over and then looked at him. 'What do you know?'

His jaw set in hard lines and then he sighed. 'Call came in about fifteen minutes ago.'

'Name?'

'Jane Doe.'

'No ID then.'

'No.'

'Stats?'

'Female, late teens, early twenties. Dark hair, dark eyes.'

The description didn't fit the twins that were

missing. But they could fit Roula.

I shuddered. 'And ... the blood?'

He absently rubbed his chin. 'Hard telling. The coroner will have to issue a ruling on that.'

'But—'

'But it looks the same as the other bodies.'

I looked around warily, as if half expecting the flapping wings I'd heard outside my apartment window to come down on me.

'I take it you were first on the scene?' I asked.

'Second. But that's my tarp covering her.'

'You're slipping.'

That earned me a grin.

'Witnesses?'

He looked away just a tad too quickly.

'There are! Who? What did they see?'

He stared at me.

'Come on, Pino. I want to help ... not hurt.'

'Where have I heard that before?'

'Yeah, but the only one I usually end up hurting is myself.'

'Good point.'

'So?'

'Neighbor saw a white van stopped near where the body was eventually discovered.'

'White van?'

'Yeah. Like one of those delivery types. Maybe ten years old. The word "Flow" was written in faded pink on the side.'

I cringed.

'Tell me about it.'

'Could it be short for "Flowers", maybe?'

'Could be.'

That was something.

'Are you going to hand over that scanner?' he asked.

'Are you going to call me when you have the name?'

'You call that negotiating? The way I see it, your volunteering an illegal item is not a bargaining chip.'

I smiled. 'Then you need to take a closer look. Because unless you want to run into me every time you turn around...'

Of course, I had no intention of handing over my new toy. But he didn't have to know that.

The sickening crunch of metal and glass interrupted his attempt to form a response. We turned to find a minor accident as two cars sat pointed at odd angles.

'Are you kidding me?' Pino said. 'How difficult is it?'

He sighed and left me standing alone.

I eyed where my car was now blocked in. Figured...

Since it was close enough to walk, I headed in the direction of my parents' house a few blocks away. I debated going to my place first and taking Muffy with me, but the last time he'd accompanied me, my paternal grandmother, Yiayia, had locked him in the downstairs closet. By the time I'd figured out what she'd done (refusing even now to consider what she'd had in mind for him because it might involve her sharpening her knives and a stockpot), he'd torn down every coat from the hangers, including my mother's prized fox fur of which he had a mouthful as he stared at me curiously from the depths.

Anyway, it would mean adding a few extra blocks to my walk, and I wasn't up to that just then.

While it was still morning, my hopes were high that I'd catch my mother Thalia and Yiayia cooking today's dinner. As in most Greek homes, I'd come to learn, most housewives prepared the meal early in the day, leaving it to further marinate before serving at one or two in the afternoon. If I was in luck, I might be able to get a modified lunch even at this time of the morning.

Of course, out of this little scenario, I'd conveniently left out how cold it was outside. And how vain I was for steadfastly refusing to wear anything heavier than my black leather jacket without any sort of cold-weather lining. Hey, it made me look fat.

Which meant absolutely zilch to me by the time I got to my parents' house, two degrees away from freezing to a solid.

'Hello?' I called out as I entered the house I'd grown up in.

Bingo! I immediately made out the sweet aroma of something cooking.

I shrugged out of my jacket and shoulder holster complete with nine-millimeter and stashed both in the closet where hopefully no one would mess with them.

'In here!' Thalia called out unnecessarily.

I walked through a living room full of reminders of my childhood, plastic on the two decades old furniture, a recliner that bore the permanent imprint of my father's behind and then on through the dining room to the table where we took our Sunday dinners, which was now covered with a handmade lace runner and a large woven basket of fruit. I considered the selection and decided I'd make off with an apple or two on my way back out.

I pushed open the swinging door to the kitchen and whatever residual unease I'd been feeling as a result of my morning run drained away along with the cold.

My mother wore an apron someone had brought her back from Greece that bore a black Greek key design around the edges and vases in the middle. She stood at the sink cleaning eggplant. Yiayia was clad in her traditional widow's black but for her own white apron (interesting that I'd never caught her wearing anything like my mother did) and was at the stove stirring something.

'So was it her?'

I instantly tensed at my mother's question. So much for feeling better.

How was it possible that she knew about the discovery of the latest body already?

Oh, yeah. Right. I'd forgotten that her connections were probably far better than mine were. Who needed a police scanner when you had St Demetrios' phone tree?

I stepped up next to Yiayia to see what she was stirring and to ascertain if it was something I could sample.

'Was who what?' I pretended ignorance.

My mother wiped her hands on a towel and nudged me aside, telling my grandmother that she needed to stop stirring and let the sauce simmer. Yiayia ignored her and kept stirring.

Thalia looked at me. 'Don't play dumb with me, Sofia. You know better.'

'Right.'

Probably Mrs Stefanou had called and told my mother she'd seen me down there. Probably my mother knew my car was still parked there. Probably Mrs Stefanou knew the body had yet to be identified.

'They don't know yet,' I answered honestly enough.

Of course, I didn't have to ask to whom she was referring. Dear missing cousin Roula was now the poster child on flyers being distributed and displayed in Greek-owned businesses all over Queens. I couldn't go anywhere without seeing her senior high school picture smiling at me.

'Was it...' Thalia began.

I gave her a long look. 'Is it all right if I make myself a frappé first?'

Five minutes later I sat at the kitchen table fingering the handmade doily there on top of which sat another, smaller basket of fruit, taking a fortifying sip of my frappé while my mother put a plate of *koulourakia* down beside me. While not the full dinner I had hoped for, the Greek sugar cookies would do in a bind.

I reached for one and she slapped my hand, asking me if I'd washed up first.

'You have to be careful this time of year,

Sofia,' she told me as I stepped to the sink. 'Viruses everywhere. And that damn pig flu has everyone scared.'

'Swine flu.'

She waved her hand. 'Same difference. So, tell me,' she prompted as I sat down and was finally allowed a path to the cookies. 'Was the body ... drained of blood?'

I slowly crunched on the cookie, recalling the lifeless hand sticking out from under the tarp. 'I don't know that either.'

Thalia narrowed her eyes. 'But...'

I made a face and brushed crumbs from my hand onto the napkin before me. 'But Pino was second on the scene and he thinks so.'

She gave a small shiver and picked up her own cup of Greek coffee that she'd probably made first thing that morning and was still nursing.

'Anyway, I was hoping you'd stop by,' she said. 'I wanted to talk to you about Thanksgiving.'

Thanksgiving. I'd almost forgotten the holiday was but a week away.

Despite the cookie I'd fed it, my stomach growled audibly. Food! I was sure to come away from that particular table with at least a week's worth of leftovers.

I picked up another *koulourakia*.

'More specifically I was thinking about who we'd invite this year.'

I raised my brows.

'You know, there's Efi's new boyfriend. What a good boy he is...'

I nodded, keeping my mouth busy with Greek goodness.

'And I thought that if you didn't object, I'd invite Dino over.'

I nearly choked.

# TWELVE

I'd been so surprised by my mother's words that I'd almost forgotten to take a doggy bag with me. Almost.

Still, not even the thought of *koulourakia* was capable of taking my thoughts away from the possibility of being seated next to yummy Dino during the hours long holiday dinner next week.

I stood in front of the white board in my uncle's office, my hand hovering, completely at a loss when it came to what I'd intended to write.

I recapped the marker and scratched my opposite elbow through my sweater.

The fact that my mother was asking my opinion beforehand rather than springing Dino on me the day of the meal was progress. Wasn't it? Still, after she'd uttered the words, it had taken half my frappé to help me swallow the cookie in my mouth whilst I stared at her, searching for clues to ulterior motives.

My cell phone rang on the desk. I crossed to pick it up, careful to check caller ID before answering.

'Sofie?'

My cousin Nia. 'Yes, hi, cuz.' I'd put in a call to her an hour ago and she was just now getting back to me. 'I was hoping to ask you for a favor.'

'Oh?'

I rounded the desk and leafed through the notes there on the victims of Dr Westervelt. 'I was wondering how difficult it would be to gain access to medical records.'

'Impossible. Completely illegal. Unethical.'

I fished one of the papers out. 'And if I had the patient's approval?'

'Well, then. The records are yours.' A heartbeat of silence and then, 'What are you working on?'

'I'm not quite at sharing stage yet,' I admitted, half because I wasn't sure if all this was going to amount to anything; half because I didn't want to take the time to explain it. 'How busy are you?' I asked.

'Pardon me? You want me to, what, like make up the forms?'

'Yes, exactly.'

'They'd have to be signed.'

'Another thing I'd like you to do.'

'And payment?'

Of course, there was that. 'Name a rate.'

She did.

I offered her half.

She accepted.

'How many are there?' she asked.

'A half dozen. But there may be more.' I gathered the notes together and put them in a clean file. 'Oh, and I'll need it all by the end of work day tomorrow.'

'Impossible.'

'Well, then, is there anyone else you could recommend?'
'Email the names to me...'

'Sofie...'
Damn. I wasn't having this dream again, was I?
It was a dream, wasn't it?
The fog pressed in on me from all sides and Vladimir Romanoff's disembodied voice beckoned to me from somewhere within the depths.
Out. I needed to find a way out. If there was a way in, certainly there was a way out.
Even as I tried to reason my way through the fog, I knew a bone deep sense of dread; the fear that there was no way out.
I reached my hands in front of me ever so slowly, afraid of what I might touch, thankful that I didn't feel anything. But it was a pretty good bet that if I moved, I'd hit something.
But which way did I move?
'Sofie...'
In the opposite direction to the voice. I swallowed hard.
I turned around, trying to discern my position, and then tentatively stepped forward, feeling my way around.
A shrill beeping assaulted my ears. I slapped my hands over them and immediately felt myself falling over, images from my previous dream of me lying, bled out on the ground, pushing a scream from my throat.
I blinked open my eyes to find myself on the floor of my apartment between the sofa and the

coffee table. I rubbed my forehead where it must have whacked the table on the way down. The shrill beep, it seemed, was not a part of my dream but had been responsible for pulling me out of it.

I groped around on top of the coffee table for my cell and opened it.

'Hello?'

'Sofie! Christ, woman, where in the hell you been? I've been calling you for the past half hour. You are not going to be—'

I pulled the cell away to look at the time. Near midnight. The last thing I remembered was eating a souvlaki at somewhere around six thirty; a glance at the crumpled wrappings verified that. I must have fallen asleep in front of the television.

'Eugene?' I said into the cell phone. 'Do you have any idea what time it is?'

'Yeah, I freakin' know what time it is! It's half past time I got my black ass out of here and back home, that's what time it is.'

I raised myself up from my awkward position to sit on the sofa, rubbing my forehead with my free hand. That was going to leave a mark.

'Slow down,' I said into the cell. 'What's going on?'

'What's going on? What's going on, she asks!' He sounded out of breath and I blinked several times. 'Where are you? Why are you panting?'

'I'm panting because I'm running as fast as my size ten Pumas will carry my skinny ass, that's why!'

'Why are you running?'

'Hold on...'

I moved the phone away from my ear and stared at it again. Yes, while Eugene was known to be a bit melodramatic, this was an all time high.

'Eugene?' I said after a moment. 'Eugene!'

'Shh! He'll hear you,' his hushed voice filled my ear.

'Who'll hear me?'

No answer.

I gave an eye roll and reached for the remote, shutting off the television. Muffy, who hadn't moved an inch from where he was curled up on his Barcalounger, now looked at me in sleepy reproach.

'Who in the hell is this motherfucker?' Eugene asked.

'Who? Christ, would you take a minute to explain what's going on?'

'That weird Romanoff character.'

A chill rang up my spine and I sat up straighter.

'I don't know, man, but that guy ain't normal, Sof. I mean, he normal. Looks just like everybody else. But...'

'But what?' Now I was whispering.

'But I swear I followed that son-bitch down an alley, you know, all discreet like and all, I know he couldn't have seen me 'cause it's part of my job to know how to blend...'

I wondered if he was going to get to the point anytime soon.

'Anyway, he went around the corner into that skanky alley ... and when I turned into it not three seconds later, he wasn't there.'

'Maybe he went into a door or something,'

I tried.

'They ain't no freakin' doors! I checked. Anyway, that's not what I'm trying to say.'

'Well what are you trying to say then?'

'That he wasn't there ... but this big motherfucking bat was...'

I shuddered and glanced instantly toward the windows. They were closed now, but the curtains were open, reminding me of the other night when Muffy had barked at something flapping what sounded like very large wings.

'If I wasn't a good Christian, I could have sworn that Romanoff guy did some kind of flip-flopping shit ... One minute he was a man – or what looked like one – the next he was a freakin' bat!'

I heard what sounded like a scream.

The sound was so disturbing, I leapt up. 'What? What is it? Who was that?'

Nothing but a panting sound.

'Eugene? Eugene!'

I realized that the scream must have come from him.

'Hold on! I'm coming!' I shouted into the phone. But it had gone dead.

I had only a general idea where I was going as I drove Lucille over Triborough Bridge and into Manhattan. This late on a Wednesday night it should have been a quick ride, and was, but somehow it felt like an eternity to me.

I had my cell phone in one hand, pressing redial continually and being sent directly to Eugene's voicemail; the police scanner sat on the passenger's seat, more silent than active.

Should I call the police? And tell them what, exactly? That one of my more colorful clients, who happened to have a rap sheet as long as my arm, thought he was being chased by a vampire bat?

I stood on the brakes as a homeless woman ventured into the street in front of me. I barely missed the cart she pushed. She glared at me from under five layers of tattered clothing and moved on at a snail's pace. It was all I could do not to beep the horn as I pressed redial again, and again was sent to voicemail.

I swear, if anything happened to him...

I'd what?

The question hung in the air as the woman finally cleared a path and I stepped on the gas.

Well, I'd be pressed to call the police then, wouldn't I? Explain as best I could what had happened.

'I should have called Pino,' I whispered to myself.

And said what? Surely his jurisdiction didn't extend here.

Still, I would have felt better if someone knew where I was.

I was two blocks away from the area Eugene had indicated. I slowed down and scanned both sides of the street, looking for any movement. There was none. Thankfully the street was empty.

Thankfully? Right now I wished there were some sort of rowdy block party going on. This ... deserted look wasn't helping my nerves any.

I drew parallel with an alley entrance. I drew the car to a stop, and stared down into the shadowy depths, then looked across the street to where it continued there.

Which one had he gone down? And had he still been in it when he screamed?

I glanced down at my cell phone and pressed redial again.

There! Something had moved!

I pulled the phone from my face and put the car in park, barely remembering to pull up the emergency brake before getting out. My heart did a triple beat in my chest as I hunkered down further into the hideous winter coat my mother had insisted I take home with me earlier, and that I had automatically grabbed over my leather jacket because it was so cold outside.

'Eugene?'

My voice sounded little better than a low squeak.

I cleared my throat and tried again, this time a little louder.

Nothing but the sound of my tentative footsteps and the din of traffic a few blocks away.

Too dark.

Weren't these alleys supposed to have lights? Where were they?

I ventured ever closer, Eugene's name stuck on the tip of my tongue, my heart pounding like a sledgehammer in my chest. I pulled my cell phone from where I had it clutched close to me and pressed redial. Again, straight through to voicemail.

Damn.

Damn, damn, damn!

Movement.

I jumped, a few feet of sidewalk separating me from the gaping yaw of the alley. A steam grate lay beneath my feet, a faint hissing and white cloud wafting upward. I was reminded of my dream.

I dialed the cell again, but a different number this time. When Rosie's voice sounded on the agency voicemail account, I felt infinitesimally better. 'Rosie, it's Sofie,' I whispered. 'It's twelve thirty Wednesday night and I received a freakish phone call from Eugene.' I gave her my location and told her where my car was parked. 'I just wanted to call and let you know in case something happens.'

I disconnected and tried Eugene's number again with the same result.

Swallowing hard, I moved forward again.

'Eugene?' Little more than a whimper.

The sound of something flapping. I jerked my head up to see a flag stirring in the light night wind.

I took a deep breath and let it out. A bat. Yeah, right.

I turned around to head back to the relative warmth of my car just as something leapt from the shadows and caught me in the back, sending me and my cell phone flying.

# THIRTEEN

In the grand scheme of things, probably I should have been relieved it was an old tomcat that had leapt at me. But from my position with my cheek flush against the cold sidewalk, my knees and the heels of my hands stinging from the fall, all I could do was curse as I watched the gray and white tom stare at me from a few feet away, his fur up, his back arched.

'Shoo! Scram!' I told him as I gingerly lifted myself up.

Damn cats.

My limbs seemed oddly tapped of energy, shaky. Likely the surge of adrenalin when the cat had jumped on my back and I'd feared it was a bat the size of a raptor.

I brushed the front of the coat, frowning at the dirt smears, but thankful to the thick quilting for cushioning my fall. I reached over and picked up my cell, checking to make sure it was all right, and saw another cell phone not too far away, just inside the lip of the alley.

No ... it couldn't be.

I stood for long moments listening to the sound of my own breathing. Then I flipped my cell open and hit redial. The screen of the other cell instantly illuminated.

*'Panayia mou,'* I invoked the name of the Virgin Mary as I picked it up. I put it to my ear for a split second, got nothing but silence, and then pressed disconnect. Then I tried redial on mine again.

The other one lighted up and 'Metro' was featured prominently in the display.

OK, I suddenly had the feeling it was going to take more than the Virgin Mary to help me out with this one.

I peered into the dark alley one last time and then backed up toward my car, one step at a time.

What if Eugene was in there? Lying unconscious and bloody?

Well, he was just going to have to wait until morning and light, because I was too damned afraid of ending up lying right next to him.

I climbed back into my still running car staring at everything; staring at nothing. I'd found myself in my share of sticky situations over recent months. Not the least of them the cement boots I'd been fitted with courtesy of mob wannabe bigwig Tony DiPiazza on top of Hell Gate Bridge. But there had been nothing I could do about that but let things play out.

This situation...

Well, I found myself not just facing a fork in the road, but dead in the middle of a five-point intersection.

I shuddered at my use of the word 'dead' and absently fiddled with the heater levers, although I knew the car was as warm as it was going to get and that my chill came from within, not from without.

There was one thing I could do to verify Eugene's story.

The chill I felt seemed to coalesce around the base of my neck and then snake around it, squeezing with icy fingers.

I eyed the buildings around me. Most had storefronts on the first floor, but doors between led to apartment buildings. But in my research of Vladimir Romanoff's new digs, I knew that his was an actual apartment building complete with front doorman and valet.

I put Lucille in gear and crept farther up the street, keeping an eye out for stray cats, bag ladies and vampire bats alike.

There. An apartment building with an outdoor awning to protect tenants from the elements. I couldn't remember the number of the building, but I remembered the name: and there it was, emblazoned in white against the red canvas: Bates Arms.

I blinked, not making the link to the Bates Motel in *Psycho* until that very moment.

Christ.

I backed Lucille up, blocking what appeared to be a personal garage entrance, and flashed the hazards. Within minutes, I stood in front of the doorman's desk, gazing around at the opulent lobby complete with white marble and antique seating arrangements.

'May I help you, miss?' the tall man who looked more like a bar bouncer than a doorman asked, his expression dubious.

'I'm here to visit Mr Romanoff.'

A smile slowly darkened rather than lightened his face. 'And is he expecting you?'

I fingered my cell phone in my pocket. 'Yes,' I said. 'Yes, I believe he is.'

He lifted a hand and indicated the sitting area. 'Please. I just need to verify your appointment.'

I stepped away, craning my ears to hear what he might be saying on the phone. But I suspected not even the world's most sensitive listening devices could pick up his murmured tone.

I sighed and waited.

'Miss?'

I turned toward him.

'You can go up.'

'Thank you.' I started toward the stairs and then faltered. 'Um, which apartment number? I seem to have forgotten.'

That creepy smile again. 'One-three-one-three.'

Thirteen-thirteen?

OK, maybe this hadn't been the best idea.

'He's waiting for you.'

Yeah, I bet he was. With bared teeth.

I offered a shaky smile of my own and redirected my steps toward the elevator, keenly aware that my hand rested against my neck.

Once the doors closed and I'd pushed the button for the thirteenth floor, I registered how warm it was. I began unbuttoning my coat. On second thought ... I quickly refastened them, including the ones at the neck that left me pretty much covered from chin to knee in bulky lilac quilting.

Finally the doors opened. I stood for a

moment, those icy fingers walking up my spine. I peeked out, looked left, and then right, then drew back again.

Nothing. Just a long, empty hall with white walls and a blood red runner.

I winced. Why did I have to use 'blood' red? Couldn't the carpet have been just red?

The bell dinged indicating the doors were about to close. I reached out a hand to stop them, the thought of facing the doorman again almost worse than the idea of seeing Vlad.

As I ascertained that the thirteenth apartment lay to my right, I headed in that direction. It didn't escape my attention that if Ivan were home to take my call, then it was unlikely he'd been out leading poor Eugene into dark alleyways and turning into a bat. But the fact that my employee and friend was missing was enough for me to battle against my own mounting fears and look into the situation further.

For all I knew, he had Waters trussed up in a dark room in his apartment, readying him for dinner.

I squinted at the ridiculous thought. What prep was needed to empty a thirty-year-old skinny black man for dinner?

Finally, I stood in front of the door. I stared at the polished brass numbers and the lion's head door-knocker and pressed the lighted doorbell to the right instead.

I half expected the door to swing instantly inward. It didn't. Instead, I waited.

Hunh? Could the doorman have called the wrong apartment? Was there more than one

Romanoff in residence?

I looked toward the elevator, considering how rude it would be for me to leave now that he was expecting me. I absently lifted my hand to knock on the door instead of ringing the doorbell ... only to find no door there.

I swung around, my heart nearly leaping clean out of my chest as I stared at another tall, impossibly dark, unsmiling character. Definitely not Vladimir.

How many goons did this guy need?

And how guilty would this one feel about doing away with one too curious Greek girl from Queens?

'That's OK, Simon, I'll take it from here.'

The man stood staring at me for a long moment, as if he wanted to ask, 'Are you sure, boss? I'd be more than happy to see to her for you.'

Finally, he opened the door further. I had to step aside to allow him to leave. I watched as he moved toward the elevator.

'Good evening,' Vladimir said.

I nearly jumped out of my socks. Which was stupid, since I knew he was coming to the door.

'I'm sorry, I didn't mean to startle you.'

I checked to make sure the neck of my coat was secure. 'Um, hi,' I said dumbly.

I looked around him to the apartment beyond. Only one small lamp was lit, barely penetrating the shadows of what appeared to be a cavernous place with an open floor plan. The utter silence was deafening, amplifying the thump of my heartbeat.

'While it is always a pleasure to see you, Miss Metropolis,' he said, bringing my gaze back to his face, 'I feel compelled to ask if there's a specific reason for your visit this late at night.'

I registered that he was dressed in what looked like black silk pajamas. His feet were bare against the black tile, and his dark hair was sexily tousled as if I'd roused him from bed.

I caught myself. Had I just said 'sexily'?

'Um, yes.' I looked back down the hall, wondering if anyone would be able to hear me if I screamed out. These old pre-war buildings had thick walls and doors. Perfect for those who did strange things at night.

'I'm sorry,' I said, regaining a bit of my bearings. 'Did I wake you?'

I cocked a brow, as if daring him to answer, even as I shoved my hands deep into my coat pockets, rubbing the thumb of my right hand over the keypad of my cell. I was good at blind dialing. It's what saved my life on that not so long ago summer day on top of the Hell Gate Bridge.

I half expected him to run his hand through that sexily tousled hair, as a regular guy might, to back up his words. But he merely smiled. 'Yes, in fact, you did.'

I bet.

After my previous encounter with him in the basement of his uncle's house, I wasn't buying that he'd been anywhere near a bed.

Unbidden, an image of a king-size bed, with rumpled silk sheets, sprang to mind and I felt hotter than I did just a moment before.

'I was wondering...' I cleared my throat. 'Were you sleeping alone?'

I watched as this time it was his turn to cock a brow. 'A gentleman never kisses and tells.'

I'd bet dollars to donuts that this man was no gentleman.

'But since you asked, I am alone. This evening...'

His voice seemed to trail off as if in invitation.

I shivered, but this time not because of a chill, but due to a flush of heat.

'Please,' he said. 'Where are my manners? Come in.'

I shook my head. 'No, I don't think that's a good idea.'

'Do not be concerned with waking me. Your visit here at this time of night indicates you have a matter of import on your mind. Allow me to serve you a refreshment while we discuss it.'

The last thing I wanted to do was enter that cave-like apartment without backup.

Why, then, did I suddenly find myself standing inside while he closed the door?

Good Lord in heaven!

'You look ... hot.'

I felt his breath against the back of my neck. Or rather, since my coat covered that part of my body, I felt it stir my hair. The whole of my skin seemed to tingle in response.

'Allow me to take your coat.'

'No, that won't be necessary ... really.'

Even as I tried to hold on to it, he seemed to have an easy time taking it from me. How did the buttons get undone? How had my hands come out of the pocket without my cell phone? Was it possible I was not only standing in his apartment – alone – but without my coat and any way to contact anyone?

'Hold it!'

I grabbed at the hideous garment even as he swept it away. I caught the fabric and tugged, reaching my hand in to grab the phone from the pocket.

I smiled. 'I'm ... expecting a call.'

His expression seemed amused as he hung my coat in a nearby closet.

'Come ... I have an especially excellent bottle of cognac I've been saving for just such an occasion.'

'Just what sort of an occasion? An unwanted visit from your uncle's neighbor?'

I watched as he, indeed, opened a bottle of cognac and poured a finger into each of the two bell-shaped glasses. He handed me one.

'It is, I believe, an expression you Americans are very fond of, no?'

'Greek-American,' I said, without understanding why.

I sipped the liquid, wondering at the golden taste of it on my tongue.

'Aren't you going to drink?' I asked, gesturing to where he swirled his around in the glass.

'I prefer to allow the liquid to ... breathe a bit first.'

Breathe. That's how vampires preferred their victims: breathing.

'Tell me, Vlad,' I said, stepping away from the bar and toward a cold fireplace empty of any family mementos. 'What is it that you do that provides the capital for such an expensive place?'

His chuckle was relaxed. 'Finances are another topic gentlemen do not discuss.'

I turned. 'I think we've already established that you're no gentleman.'

His eyes glistened as he took a small sip of the cognac. 'Mmm. Yes, I suppose we have, haven't we?' He sighed. 'If you must know, a relative deeded me this wonderful place just last month.'

'Let me guess: a distant relative.'

'Very.'

'Was his death ... untimely?'

He smiled. 'No. My uncle lived a long, long ... long life.'

Did even vampires eventually die? While folklore indicated they aged much more slowly than humans, they did age. So did they ultimately share in the same fate as we did?

Or had this particular ... uncle's death been anything but natural?

'So, Miss Metropolis—'

'Sofie, please.' Why had I said that?

He moved closer to me without seeming to do so. 'Very well, then. Sofie. Tell me,' he was beside me, behind me and in front of me all at once. 'What is it that brought you to my door on this cold November evening?'

Suddenly, I seemed incapable of taking the simplest of breaths. I felt him everywhere, both inside and out. I glanced at the glass in my hand, curious to find it empty. Had it been simple cognac? Or something else? I couldn't explain my breathless reaction to his nearness. Was it sexual awareness? Or fear?

'Sofie...'

The voice from my dream.

My knees gave out from under me.

# FOURTEEN

My mouth tasted funny. I moved my tongue around; it seemed enlarged, somehow. And why was it so cold? Did I forget to close the window again after letting Muffy out to do his business?

'Sofie?'

I tried to open my eyes but they felt like they were superglued shut.

Then I remembered the dream. Vladimir ... and the cognac.

I jerked upright, only to find I was already in a seated position. And I wasn't in my bed or Vlad's dark lair, but in my car.

And I wasn't alone.

I automatically fought the shadow sitting in the passenger's seat.

'Christ, woman, easy there, before you put an eye out; namely, mine.'

Jake easily caught my flailing limbs even as I tried to control the erratic beating of my heart.

'Jake.'

His name came out as a shuddering whisper and the heat of his large hands seemed to penetrate the cold quilting of my coat.

My coat...

I looked down to find that it was done up as snugly as it had been when I first entered Vlad's apartment, then I looked around; the car was parked in the spot I'd left it.

'What happened?'

'I was hoping you could tell me.' Jake released my arms; I instantly missed the sensation of his touching me. Somehow it made me feel safe. Like nothing bad could happen so long as he was near.

The night's events slowly returned to me. I remembered Eugene's panicked phone call, my racing into the city to rescue him – for all that was worth – and then my visit to Vlad's apartment.

'What time is it?' I asked.

'Just after two.'

'In the morning?'

He didn't answer. 'Oh.' Of course, in the morning. It was still dark out.

Which meant I'd been out of it for at least an hour.

I took a deep breath and my senses were automatically filled with all things Jake. From his leather jacket, to his lime-scented aftershave, to the manly smell that was all him.

I became aware of how I must look, having zipped out of the house without so much as combing my hair. I'd known I'd run into someone I wouldn't want to in this butt-ugly coat the instant my mother insisted I take it home.

I cleared my throat. 'What are you doing here?'

I caught his grin in the light from a passing car and my stomach pitched to my feet. 'I was in the neighborhood?'

I found myself smiling back. 'Try again.'

He shifted in the seat, making the whole car look smaller by his mere presence.

'Were you following me?'

'Sadly, no. Had I been following you, I would have put a halt to whatever no good you were up to.'

He reached over and I caught my breath. But instead of touching me, he gripped the key in the ignition. 'Be a doll and press the clutch for me.'

I did as asked and Lucille roared to beautiful life ... and then the vents blasted me with cold air. I hurried to turn down the fan until the engine could warm.

'So what are you doing here, then?'

'You might want to check your cell phone messages.'

My cell phone!

I patted the many pockets in the coat and then fished the object in question from the right front. The display indicated no messages from Eugene, but twenty-three from Rosie. The screen lit up again, startling me. Rosie again.

I ignored it for the time being.

'Rosie called you?' I asked.

'She did. Ranted on about some cryptic message you left on the agency voicemail and the coordinates you gave her.'

Trust him to use the word 'coordinates' to describe my hastily said directions. It prompted me to wonder all over again who he was and what he really did for a living.

'So are you going to tell me what happened?' he asked.

I swirled my tongue around in my mouth again, wishing I had thought to make a frappé before storming out of the house. 'I wish I could tell you,' I said honestly enough. 'But I have no idea.'

One minute I'd been wondering where the cognac in my glass had gone, the next I'd woken up to the sound of Jake's voice in my ear.

Had Vlad drugged me? My cottonmouth was a symptom, but otherwise I felt fine. And being that I wasn't normally a big drinker, I couldn't tell you if the liquor alone might be responsible. Especially good liquor, which I supposed his was.

Of course, there was always the possibility that he'd put me under some sort of spell...

I swallowed hard and then quickly undid the catches on my coat, nearly tearing them off in my hurry to check myself.

'Whoa, what's going on?' Jake asked.

With my hands, I checked that all my clothes were where they were supposed to be and that there were no bite marks on my neck or anywhere else on my person.

Jake's chuckle drew my gaze to him.

'What?' I wanted to know.

He shook his head. 'Nothing.'

I shivered and put the coat back on, although I left it open.

'Are you going to be OK driving back home?' he asked.

'And if I said no?'

'Well, then, I'd just have to drive you.'

'And leave my car here?'

'No. I'd drive you in your car and then come back for my truck.'

A naughty part of me wanted to ask him to do exactly that. The idea of being in his company for the half hour it would take to drive me home, combined with the possibility of inviting him up to my place where hopefully no gunmen waited to take one or both of us out, was almost too tempting to resist.

But resist I did.

'I think I'll be OK.'

Was it me, or did he look disappointed?

'Good.' He opened the door. 'I'm glad you're all right, then.'

He climbed out.

'Jake?'

He ducked back down to look inside the open door.

'Um, thanks.'

There was a moment of silence and then, 'You're welcome, Sofie. Just try to stay out of trouble, you hear?'

'You, too.'

I held his gaze until he finally stood back up and quietly closed my door.

I sat watching him walk to his truck parked halfway up the block. Damn, but the man was hot. From the way his faded Levi's hugged his ass and legs, to the drape of black leather across his broad shoulders and down his back, to the self-assured way he carried himself, everything screamed for a closer look.

The problem was a look was all you got. My experience with the hunky Australian had taught me that he might as well be wearing a sign that read, 'You can come this close, but no closer.'

And I wanted closer.

I didn't realize he'd already pulled away until I found myself staring at the empty parking spot.

I sighed, did my coat back up, and fiddled with the heat blower now that the engine had warmed. Then I was on my way.

I wasn't surprised that a half a block up a dark truck that looked awfully similar to Jake's had come up on my rear; and stayed there all the way home.

The next day I caught hell from Rosie for not calling to tell her I was all right. She'd said it was all she could do not to call the police, but thankfully 'that nice Mr Porter' had the common courtesy to let her know I was OK.

That nice Mr Porter had called her? I scratched my head as I stood in front of my white board at around ten a.m. I'd had the same thought at least a dozen times this morning.

I poked my head around the corner. 'You get through to Waters yet?'

Rosie glared at me from where she was typing on her laptop, her police scanner to the right, a portable radio to the left that was playing some sort of hip-hop in Spanish. 'I musta left him a hundred messages. He's sure to get one of them.'

A dig. I got it. And deserved it. Probably I should have called her back. And probably I should be glad that Jake had or else I would have likely awoken to the sound of either the police or

Rosie pounding on my door in the middle of the night.

'Call again,' I told her.

She gave me a monster eye roll and then picked up the phone.

The cowbell above the door rang and I leaned again.

'Waters!'

I put the dry erase marker down and rushed into the other room, giving the short, skinny black man a hug to end all hugs.

'Hey, hey, hey, watch it now; you'll wrinkle the shirt.'

I drew back and looked him over to make sure he was OK, stopping just short of checking his neck for any telltale bite marks.

Rosie popped her gum loudly. 'You two are so much alike it's scary.'

We both looked at her.

She tsked. 'Neither one of you know how to return a call and let a body know you're all right.'

'Sorry,' Eugene said, straightening his knee-length black leather coat from where I must have disturbed it, a plain brown bag in one hand. 'I, um, lost my cell phone last night.'

'You lost it?'

'Yeah. Right after I talked to you.' He grimaced. 'My entire life was on that cell phone. Now I don't have nobody's numbers. Which is part of the reason I came by here.' He whipped out a brand-spanking new cell phone. 'I need your numbers...'

I squinted at him. 'That's it? That's why you

came by here? For numbers?'

He blinked. 'Partly. Yeah. Why?'

I noticed the way Rosie pretended to be busy but was really listening closely to what I was saying.

I took Eugene by the arm and led him toward my uncle's office. She was insufferable enough; the less she knew about what happened last night, the better.

'Hey! I done already told you once to be careful of the clothes.'

I released my grip and held my hand up by way of apology. 'Can we talk in my office, please? Privately?'

His toothy grin was a little too suggestive. 'All you gotta do is ask, baby. Eugene Waters is a man who likes to keep all his ladies happy.'

Rosie and I gave matching eye rolls.

I led the way and he closed the office door after him.

'What in the hell happened last night?' I whispered.

He leaned on one foot as if to ask if I were joking. 'I told you what happened.'

'Yeah, but you don't know that I raced into town in the middle of the night, scared to death something had happened to you...' And was nearly ravaged by a creepy, sexy vampire.

Of course, I kept the second part to myself.

'Hey, I was the one who was nearly scared to death here. Don't forget that.'

'But you could have called to let me know you were OK.'

'I wasn't convinced I was until I woke up in

my own bed this morning and discovered I was still alive.'

I had pretty much the same experience, so I couldn't argue with him there.

He waved the cell phone. 'Besides, didn't you hear what I said? I don't have no one's numbers.'

'Anyone's,' I absently corrected.

'Who died and left you in charge of the grammar police?'

I grimaced.

'Oh. I almost forgot.' He held out the bag in his hand. 'I got the sucker.'

I squinted at him. 'What do you mean you got the sucker?'

His grin was a little too self-satisfied for my tastes after the night I'd had.

'Well, go on; take it.'

'I'm not sure I want to.'

'Don't worry; it's dead.'

What was dead?

I shuddered.

'Here, let me show you...'

He stepped over to the desk. I followed, making sure I was one step behind him and glad he was short enough for me to look over his shoulder. He opened the bag.

I shrieked and jumped back.

The door swung inward. 'What?' Rosie wanted to know. 'What is it? What happened?'

She spotted the item on the desk and edged slightly closer.

'Oh, no you didn't.' She pointed a blood-red nail nearly the length of her finger at the desk.

'Tell me that ain't what I think it is.'
'A bat,' Waters and I said in unison.
Rosie backed up toward the door as if afraid to take her eyes off of it.
'I think it's one of those vampire bats,' Eugene said.
'Don't even say that,' I warned.
'It moved!' Rosie said.
'No it didn't; it's dead,' Eugene reached out a hand and poked it. 'See.'
This time I saw it move.
And I followed in kind, running for the door, hot on Rosie's fleeing heels.
Eugene tsked. 'You guys are afraid of everything. That's why you need a big, strong guy to look out after you.'
Rosie and I stared at each other even as we peeked around the door jamb, viewing things from a safe distance.
The bat not only moved again, it flapped its wings, and then flew straight into Eugene's chest.
He shrieked like a girl and ran toward the door, batting at the bat. 'Get 'im off! Get 'im off!'
So much for his being a big, strong man.
'Open the front door!' I ordered Rosie.
'Forget that!' She ran toward Nash's office and locked herself inside.
Eugene ran around the two desks again and again, the bat now dislodged but seeming to chase him. I reached for my gun, then thought better of it and instead went to the small bathroom and collected the broom, aiming the bristles in the bat's direction.

'Eugene, open the door!'

He apparently couldn't hear me over the sound of his own girlish screams.

Aiming the broom in front of me like a deadly weapon, I edged toward the door, praying the bat wouldn't switch targets and come after me.

I was reaching for the door handle when it swung outward.

My uncle's silent partner Lenny Nash stood staring at the scene, his features changing not one bit.

'Watch out!' I told him, advancing on the bat as Eugene led it back nearer the door.

Cocking the broomstick back like a baseball bat, I gave aim and hit a home run, connecting squarely with the winged creature and sending it soaring outside where Nash leaned slightly sideways to allow it to pass.

Eugene's shrieking was replaced by the bat's cries. I ran outside, shielding my eyes from the sudden, rare spear of sunlight that penetrated the clouds.

I swallowed hard. Was it just me, or was the bat smoking? As if about to catch fire?

It dived between two buildings across the street and disappeared from sight.

I glanced at Nash as if to ask him if he'd seen what I just had. He didn't even blink, merely turned toward the still open door and went inside.

Good God almighty, what had just happened?

# FIFTEEN

I still hadn't completely recovered from 'the bat incident' by the time Friday night and my date with Dino rolled around. Hell, I think everyone present for the experience had been scarred for life.

Eugene had disappeared in the opposite direction to the bat without having gotten the numbers he came for, and without giving me his new one.

If Rosie wasn't ducking from some unseen flying object where she sat at her desk, she was spritzing holy water from an extra-large perfume bottle.

Of course, I wasn't about to admit it to her, but I'd scrounged around for the small bottle she'd given me a couple of months earlier and kept it in my coat pocket, praying there wasn't some sort of expiration date on the stuff. But the thought of asking her to have it re-blessed – or whatever it was that made water holy – stopped me dead in my tracks.

As I made myself a fortifying evening frappé in my apartment kitchen I heard Muffy's nails click against the kitchen tile and turned to look at him as I shook my frappé into a good froth.

'What?' I asked as he plopped his furry butt on

the floor and panted at me.

He seemed to give me a once over and then poked his right front paw at my leg.

'Yeah, so? I'm wearing a dress. Is there something wrong with that?'

His nail caught on my nylons and I felt rather than heard the snag that ran all the way up to my hip.

I clunked my cup down and stared at him. 'Are you serious?'

If I didn't know better, I would say he'd done it on purpose. Or at the very least, was highly amused.

Great. My first time in forever wearing stockings, and now I had to change them. Which reminded me why I never wore them.

Or a dress, for that matter.

I don't know what I was thinking.

I stepped out of my too high heels and shimmied out of my ruined stockings.

Of course, the doorbell would pick then to ring.

Since I hadn't buzzed anyone up, it was a reasonable guess that someone in the building was looking for a word with me. At eight p.m. on a Friday night.

Probably Mrs Nebitz.

I opened the door, trying for a smile.

'Hi,' Dino said.

I blinked. And then blinked again.

'You're early,' I blurted.

'Am I?' he frowned as he looked at his watch. 'Yes. I guess I am. By five minutes.'

We both looked at where I still held the ruined

stockings in my hand and then down to my bare feet.

'Um, come in,' I said, giving a mental eye roll.

It figured that the moment I decided to change into my favorite pair of comfortable jeans and a nice top Dino would show up. Now how could I possibly come out of my bedroom wearing something else?

I closed the door after him and he held out a box.

'I thought you might like this,' he said.

I hid the hose behind my back – like he hadn't already seen them – and accepted the box. 'Thank you. That was thoughtful of you.'

I crossed the room and threw away the ruined nylons into the garbage before opening the box. Sparkling up at me was an assortment of sticky Greek goodies. My mouth watered shamelessly.

Oh, yes. There was a lot to be said for dating a man who owned a bakery.

I picked out a baklava roll and took a bite out of it, only then realizing that Dino stood behind me. I turned, my mouth full of phyllo and honey, and nearly bumped into him.

'Hungry?' he asked.

I ran my tongue over my bottom lip, reminded of the first time he and I had stood in this very kitchen, a box of something sweet between us. We'd ended up eating that sweet off of each other.

The memory shot sparks of awareness through me.

'You missed a spot,' he murmured.

He raised his hand and rubbed his thumb

against my chin.

His gaze rose to mine and I tumbled head first into the dark depths.

I don't know how it is I kept forgetting about the chemistry that existed between him and me whenever we were alone. I felt one way while we were apart; quite another when we were together. It struck me that it was mind over matter. At least so long as I could think.

Because one moment I was fighting to swallow the bite of baklava in my mouth; the next I was trying to swallow him.

Lord, but he felt good. His lips slanted perfectly against mine, his hands touched me in all the right places, his body was hard in all the right places. Oh, boy, was he hard in all the right places.

He pressed against me and I became aware of why a woman might be inclined to wear a dress more often. The light cotton felt like little more than panties between him and me, allowing for an all too intimate feel of his arousal.

Oh, boy...

I backed him up, my intention to make it to the bedroom instead of the kitchen table, where I'd suffered more than one bruise the last time we found ourselves in a similar situation. He must have backed into Muffy because the terrier gave a small yelp. We broke apart just long enough to look down to make sure he was all right, then ignored his barks as we continued re-familiarizing ourselves with the other's tongue.

Before I knew it, I was shoving him to my bed, licking my lips as if he was even more enticing than the Greek sweets he'd brought me.

And he was.

And I was looking forward to devouring every last inch of him.

'I don't know about you, but I'm starving,' Dino said from behind his menu two hours later.

We'd missed our reservation, but thankfully a couple was vacating a primo table at the front when we arrived and we were shown to it. Every inch of me still tingled from our pre-dinner activities and I found myself wanting to ask for the food to go so we could pick up where we left off back at my place.

'Sex will do that to you,' I said.

Dino's menu budged downward and his dark eyes sparkled at me suggestively.

Damn, but he was the epitome of tall, dark and handsome. Everything about him was appealing, from the shape of his almost black brows to the hair that peppered the back of his long, thick fingers where he held the menu. Fingers I'd much rather put in my mouth and suck on just then instead of one of the stuffed grape leaves the waitress had delivered to our table along with a generous slice of feta, drizzled with olive oil and peppered with Greek oregano, and a bread basket.

'Maybe we should have gone with your idea and ordered in,' he said.

'Mmm,' I agreed. 'I definitely think we should have.'

We were seated next to the front window of the restaurant where we could view Broadway and the cars streaming down the narrow street. There was parking at either curb, but Dino had chosen a paid public lot. I sighed, finding my gaze drifting out the window. I caught myself staring at something without realizing it and then blinked. And blinked again.

Dark truck ... parked directly across the street. Cigarette smoke swirling outside the cracked driver's side window.

It couldn't be...

'Is something wrong?' Dino asked.

It took a moment for his words to register. Yes, I silently answered him. Something was very wrong. Jake Porter was sitting outside watching us.

How long had he been there? More importantly, how long had he known Dino and I had been together tonight? Had he been sitting outside my apartment when Dino arrived? Noticed that it had taken us two hours to leave?

Dino put his menu down, his attention homing in on me. 'Sofia?'

I forced my gaze back to him and tried for a smile. 'I suddenly don't feel so well.'

He began to turn his head toward the window, as if to seek out what I'd been looking at. I quickly put my hands on his.

'I'm afraid, you know, that my ... little visitor may be arriving this evening.'

'Little visitor...'

I watched as the meaning of my words dawned on him.

I hated resorting to subterfuge to regain his attention. Hated more falling back on the old female standby of mysterious feminine workings. I'd watched my mother do it a thousand times and had always vowed never to do it myself.

Yet here I was, doing exactly the same thing.

I idly wondered if my mother would be proud.

I rubbed my arms where they were left bare by the dress I had put back on if only because I'd enjoyed Dino's grin when he'd first seen me in it.

'You know, I'm cold sitting here by the window.' I looked around, noticing there was another table free nearer the back, away from prying blue Australian eyes. 'Do you mind if we move to another table?'

'No,' Dino said, already raising his hand to signal the waitress. 'Of course not.'

Within moments we were settled at the other table, but even though I could no longer see Jake, and I knew he couldn't see us, I felt his presence as strongly as if he were standing behind me, his hot breath on the back of my neck.

I shivered.

'Are you still cold?' Dino asked, reaching for where he'd draped his blazer on the chair next to him.

I opened my mouth to protest, but the words died on my lips as he got to his feet and put the warm tweed over my shoulders. I automatically drew it closer, loving that it smelled of him.

'Thanks,' I said, and meant it.

He sat back down and the waitress came then to take our orders. Dino went with the roasted lamb shank and I asked for the *kalamarakia* as a meal instead of an appetizer (that would be *kalamari* or squid to others). As soon as she finished, a male server delivered a small carafe of red wine along with two flat-bottomed Greek wine glasses. I caught his arm before he could pour.

'Do you mind bringing us a bigger carafe?'

Dino raised a brow.

The server immediately complied and I popped a piece of bread into my mouth and then downed the glassful he'd poured, hoping the wine would help me forget about the man sitting in the truck across the street and focus on the one in front of me.

'So,' Dino said, crossing his arms on the table in front of him and leaning forward.

I was afraid he was going to ask me if something were wrong again and shifted in my chair.

'I was hoping this ... dinner would give us a chance to talk.'

I cleared my throat, tamping down the desire to excuse myself and go outside and have a word with Jake. Make him leave. Make him leave me alone.

I smiled. 'We talk all the time.'

One side of Dino's mouth budged upward. 'I wouldn't exactly call what we do when we're alone together talking.'

I warmed up to the conversation and leaned forward as well. 'Oh, no? Tell me, is there a more genuine, primal form of conversation that I don't know about?'

I liked flirting with him. I told myself that even though Jake could no longer see us, I recognized at least a half dozen other diners in the restaurant and at least double that number probably knew me. And all of them knew my mother, which meant that if Thalia didn't already know about my being there with Dino, she very soon would. It also meant that I probably shouldn't give them any more to relate to her than the two of us being seated at the same table together enjoying a meal.

But I couldn't help myself. Watching Dino's pupils widen, turning his dark eyes even darker, turned me on no end.

'No ... no. You're right there.' He cleared his throat and appeared to have a hard time stopping himself from leaning the few more inches needed in order for us to kiss. I silently dared him. 'But I was hoping to actually exchange words.'

'Mmm,' I agreed vocally, even though I was now staring at his full mouth, wishing it on mine.

'You see, there are some things I'd like to know about you,' he said, the lowness of his voice giving away his growing arousal. 'And you should know more about me.'

'Mmm ... have I told you I love your accent?'

He chuckled at that. 'I'm serious, Sofia.'

I also loved the way he called me by my given name. Normally only members of my family did that. But he did it with such ease it was almost easy to imagine that he'd been doing it all my life.

And easy to imagine him doing it for the rest of it.

'OK,' I said. 'What do you want to know?'

He cleared his throat. 'Well, for one thing, how do you feel about children?'

I twisted my lips, drawing his gaze there. 'Children are nice.'

'That's not what I meant.'

'I think we've already well established my interest in the activity that goes into creating them.'

'Yes. That we have. But what I'm asking is, do you have an interest in actually creating them?'

Something skated on the fringes of my mind, but I was so engrossed in detailing the plains of his handsome face, the darkness of his slightly curly hair, and taking in the manly shape of his hands, I couldn't give it much more than a passing note.

'More specifically, I'm asking if you're interested in creating them ... with me?'

# SIXTEEN

The following morning, at the agency by myself before dawn, I was still in a state of emotional shock.

Dino hadn't ... he couldn't have been. There was no way in hell Dino had asked what I thought he had.

I squinted at the white board without really seeing it or the different colored words I'd scrawled on it. Had he?

I drew slowly back, focusing on what I'd just written, even though I still saw Dino as clearly as if I were still sitting across the table from him.

Following my silence, and physical pulling back, he must have caught on that my reaction wasn't exactly positive and he chuckled again, albeit this time with a little hesitation.

'I'm sorry. That didn't come out the way I planned. What I meant was ... are you interested in having children? Some day?'

The rest of the night had taken a nosedive after that. Not only did I have Jake outside watching my every move for reasons I couldn't fathom, I began reading hidden messages in everything that Dino said.

And if that wasn't bad enough, I'd barely tasted the food I ate. The moment I realized that, I'd stopped eating.

I drew a deep breath and stepped back from the board. While I'd come to the office on the weekends on several occasions, the utter silence of the place still unnerved me. I could actually hear the sparse traffic outside on Steinway. I peeked through the door into the empty but brightly lit front, surprised to find it still dark outside. A glance at my watch told me it was almost six thirty.

I sighed, thinking I really should have tried to go back to sleep this morning.

Muffy barked at me from where he sat at my heels. I grimaced at him.

'Better be careful or I'll take you back home.'

He cocked his head at me, his pink tongue lolling out of the side of his mouth.

I put the red marker I held back down and went to sit behind the desk, considering the two piles of items Rosie had left there for me. How was it possible for a night to start so well and then end so badly? From hot, sweaty sex to a perfunctory kiss good night in three hours. Had to qualify for some world record, I thought.

Thankfully, Dino hadn't pressed the issue. He'd obviously understood that something was wrong, but probably put it down to the impending arrival of my 'monthly visitor'. I gave an eye roll. My period wasn't due for another week yet. What would I say if an opportunity to set the sheets on fire with him happened again then? Say it was the longest period in history? Or that I had been off in my original calculations?

Then again, I didn't anticipate facing that

dilemma. Because I'd already deduced that after that surprising first date there wasn't going to be a second.

I pulled an item off the first pile and read Rosie's post-it note, which contained little more than a series of question marks. I looked under it to find the form I'd asked my cousin Nia to put together.

'Yes.'

I gathered the pile closer, finding not only the signed permission forms from all of the patients, but their related medical records as well.

I smiled from ear to ear. Nia, it seemed, was as good as gold. And had yet to learn the finer points of billing by the hour...

I plucked the telephone up and then put it back down, realizing that not only was it Saturday, it was too early to call anyone.

The reality popped my momentary bubble.

Muffy barked again. Once. A sharp, high-pitched bark that was followed by a low growl and a loud sniff.

I just had time to look at where he sat near the office door, looking into the other room, and then he was off like a shot, his little legs nearly a blur as he charged the front door, barking like a dog thirty times his size.

Now what?

I considered letting him do what he would. The front door was locked, so there were no worries that someone would open it and become an unwitting victim.

But his barking was driving me nuts.

I pushed back from the chair and went into the

other room.

'Muffy, come here, boy.' I made the requisite kissing sounds and called again. To no avail.

What was going on?

'All right, that's enough,' I began to lose patience as I neared him.

I'd only seen him this worked up twice before. The last time when he'd rescued me from the wood-chipper.

The memory sent goosebumps running up my arms.

I absently rubbed them, even as I realized that Muffy wasn't barking at a squirrel or stray cat through the door; he was barking at Ivan Romanoff's driver.

The goose bumps multiplied.

Well.

I supposed I should be glad Muffy was barking. Well, he was both barking and leaping in the air and scratching on the glass, as if he'd like nothing better than to sink his sharp little teeth into the man's flesh. Which would be A-OK with me.

'Muffy! Stop!'

He gave me a brief glance over his shoulder even as he continued to jump, then ignored me altogether.

I shrugged at Lurch, both hands up, as if to indicate I wasn't to blame.

Then he stepped aside and Ivan Romanoff stepped up.

Great. He was essentially my client. No matter how many times I tried to give him his money back.

I reached down and caught Muffy by the back of his collar, stopping him mid-air. He gave a yelp as I petted him.

'It's OK, boy. I've got this.'

He looked at me doubtfully as I picked him up and carried him toward the office, him growling over my shoulder as we went.

I put him down and quickly slammed the door, knowing he was going to try to bypass me for another shot at Lurch.

Sure enough, the closed door stopped him and I heard his whimper and the 'bam' as he hit the solid wood.

I cringed, hoping he hadn't done any further damage to his leg.

A moment later, his barking resumed, and judging by his scratching sounds, I gathered so had his leaping, which meant that he was at least well enough to continue that.

I went to the door and unlocked it.

'Good morning,' I said. 'I would never have expected to see you in the daytime.'

I wished I could take back my words the instant they exited my mouth.

All three of us stared up at the sky that was still dark.

I swallowed hard, trying to remember the exact time of sunrise.

Mr Romanoff smiled as he entered, followed by Lurch. 'I hope you don't mind. We were just returning home and I noticed your lights were on and your car was parked outside.'

'No, no. Of course I don't mind.'

There was something about being caught unawares that made me overly polite. I should work on that, I silently told myself.

'I understand that you and my nephew had a visit the other evening.'

'Your nephew?'

Stupid question.

'Oh. Oh, yes! Your nephew.'

Romanoff was unblinking. 'He's what I've come to discuss with you.'

Uh oh. Here it goes. He'd figured out I was having Vladimir followed. Scratch that: I'd been *having* Vladimir followed. Eugene wasn't going anywhere near that guy now. Wasn't enough money in the world, he said.

'I'm going out of town for a couple of days,' he continued. 'And Vladimir will be in charge.'

I was pretty sure I'd swallowed my tongue. 'In charge of what?'

'This ... ongoing matter. Should you find yourself in need of anything, he is the one with whom you'll want to consult.'

Great.

'I trust you already have his contact information?'

I nodded.

'Very good then.'

Somewhere in the back of my mind, I realized I should be trying to return his money again, but my teeth felt superglued together.

Movement behind him startled me. I craned my neck to watch the back door of the scary mobile open, and none other than Vladimir get out.

Oh, boy.

I expected him to advance on me, but instead he turned back toward the car and helped out a very attractive blonde dressed to the nines. She tittered as he helped her into a full-length fur coat. Her perfume was nearly overwhelming as Vlad and she stepped closer.

'Sofie,' Vlad said. 'How very nice to see you again.'

I reluctantly gave up my hand so he could kiss the back of it like some outdated Dracula. I noticed his date wasn't pleased.

'May I present Miss Wendy Newberger.'

I briefly shook – or rather wagged – her hand.

Sheesh. I was just beginning my day; they had yet to end their night.

'Uncle, it's getting early. Miss Newberger and I will catch a taxi back into the city,' Vladimir said.

Early. I looked up at the sky, never wanting the sun to rise more.

The two men spoke in hushed tones in a foreign language I couldn't identify. Romanian? Hell, for all I knew, they could be speaking Chinese.

Then, Vladimir's gaze was on me again, and I was reminded of vampires' reputed ability to read minds.

'Pleasure to see you again, Sofie.'

Then he was hailing a taxi that seemed to be driving by at just the right time and he and his lady friend were gone.

'Is anything the matter, Miss Metropolis?' Ivan asked.

'What?' I dragged my gaze from the taxi that

was swallowed up by the thickening morning traffic. 'No, no. Everything's fine. Just peachy.'

Right. Not even I was buying that one.

'Very well, then. Since my business here is completed, I will bid you a good morning, Miss Metropolis.'

I attempted a smile, then realized it didn't matter. He was already climbing back into the car with a little help from Lurch. And for the second time, I watched a car disappear into traffic, this time in the opposite direction.

I shuddered from head to toe. I was cold, but didn't seem to be overly aware of it.

Still, I was instantly aware of the temperature difference as I stepped back inside the agency. I was also made aware of Muffy's very unhappy state locked in my uncle's office.

# SEVENTEEN

There was a time not so long ago that I thought I lived life skating on the edge of the envelope. Then I hired on at my uncle's agency, and realized that I didn't have the slightest idea what that meant, and was forced to accept I was more of a creature of habit than I might like.

This morning's early visit from the Romanoffs served as an unwelcome reminder of that.

I rubbed the back of my neck as I drove my old Mustang downtown for the second time this week, Muffy happy to drool all over the passenger's window as he occasionally barked at the cars I passed and who knew what else. I was just hoping he'd gotten over the trauma of my locking him in the office for the duration of Ivan's visit.

Were dogs supposed to be afraid of vampires, I idly wondered. No, wait. Werewolves were supposed to be the guardians of the undead, weren't they? And since wolves were a close cousin to dogs...

I shook my head and picked up my frappé where I had it wedged between the emergency brake and the passenger's seat; no convenient cup holders in this old jalopy.

The Mustang coughed and I instantly repented.

'Sorry, Lucille. I love you even without cup holders.'

I was lucky that Jake's warmer weather tinkering with her left me set for the winter months. I'd taken her into a cousin's friend's auto shop for a check up and he'd said nothing needed doing except to top up the windshield wiper fluid. I'd tucked the information in the back of my mind, planning on using it to tease Jake, but so far hadn't come across the opportunity. Which was just as well, because I wasn't sure what I'd say to him the next time our paths crossed. His sitting outside Agnanti while Dino and I were eating had been more than unsettling; it had been weird. He hadn't been there when we left, and I hadn't seen him since, but every now and again I got the feeling that just because I couldn't see him didn't mean he couldn't see me.

At any rate, Lucille's primed running condition meant I didn't have much to worry about as I drove into the city to see if I couldn't catch up with what the press was now calling The Chop Doc.

Dr Westervelt had made the headlines pretty much every day over the past week. Which was saying a lot in a city of 8 million where there was a different scandal or grisly murder or sting to report on nearly every day. Oh, he shared space with the latest on the serial killer they were calling The Bleeder, but they were running pretty much neck and neck.

I didn't fool myself into thinking I could gain an audience with the upscale doctor, no matter how far he'd fallen in the social ranks since butchering Jane Creek and her friends. But 'no guts, no glory' was pretty much my motto of late. And while I failed spectacularly more often than not, my few successes more than made up for it.

Take the old screen legend. Who knew my blind phone call would net me a client? Had I gone with the odds, I never would have dialed that number.

Of course, I still didn't know what I could do for her. But I figured going downtown and doing some snooping around couldn't hurt. And it was a far sight better than doing nothing at all.

Besides, sitting around the quiet office was driving me batty.

I shivered. Wrong choice of adjectives. Way wrong choice.

Muffy turned his head my way and gave a bark, as if he'd known what I was thinking.

As I drove over the Triborough Bridge, I marveled at the Manhattan skyline. It was another cloudy morning, but here and there sunlight seemed to spear through, spotlighting parts of the incredible island.

No matter how long I lived there, I didn't think I'd ever tire of looking at it.

All too soon I was over the bridge and navigating my way through the towering buildings, a modern jungle where swinging vines were replaced by banners promoting one event or another, and fruit by flashing lights. This time I'd been a little more specific in requesting directions from the Internet and even skimmed the street view picture of the building itself.

Of course, now I realized how futile that had been. All the damn buildings in this part of the city looked the same.

I found a parking garage and put Muffy's lead on him, with surprisingly little struggle. Usually I had to wrestle him down for a good ten-minute session before I could get the lead on him. Probably, he had to go the bathroom and had already picked out his fire hydrant.

Of course, when I'd brought him with me, I hadn't thought about taking him into any buildings.

I compared the address in my notes to the ones on the street, finding the building quickly. I wondered if I could get away with pretending Muffy was a Seeing Eye dog. I yanked on his lead when he sniffed the hem of a passing woman's skirt – a very short skirt – and thought the odds of my succeeding in that lay somewhere between zero and nil.

In fact, if I hadn't known his original owner was Bangladeshi and blissfully unaware of the crude reference, I'd think Muffy had earned his name from his insatiable desire to sniff women out.

'Good morning,' the security guard behind the polished black marble lobby desk greeted me. 'Can I help you?'

The place was deserted. As it would be, seeing as it was an office building on a weekend.

I flashed him what I hoped was my most convincing smile. 'Yes, hi. I'm here to see Mr Westervelt.'

I didn't say 'doctor,' for fear that it would indicate I wasn't personally connected to him. Of course, I wasn't, but he didn't have to know that.

I'd considered using my fake press credentials to gain access to the Chop Doc's offices, but since his picture was spread across the front page of every newspaper in the city and her outer boroughs, I didn't think I'd get very far.

So I went with the personal angle.

I yanked on Muffy's leash to no avail. I was ceaselessly surprised of the strength the little dog possessed as he led me instead to the side of the desk. His furry little butt wagged in unison with his tail as he slid under the counter door and sniffed the guard's pants leg.

Great. Now all I needed was for Muffy to relieve himself on him. That would get us both kicked out and fast.

The guard grinned and bent down to pat the Jack Russell. 'Great dogs. I had one years ago. A little high-spirited but fun.'

Fun?

If he said so. Right now, I wasn't having much fun.

The guard murmured some gibberish to Muffy that had the dog wagging his entire body even faster.

Probably he was hungry for affection. Probably I should take him out more.

The guard finally rose back to his feet and straightened his jacket.

'You're in luck,' he said. 'The doc just went up.'

I tried not to show my relief as I finally succeeded in yanking Muffy to the other side of the desk. 'Thanks.'

'And you are?'

'His granddaughter, of course. He asked me to meet him here. We're going for brunch.'

The sign in sheet he'd been pushing in my direction was pulled back.

'Go right on up then.'

I turned toward the elevators.

'Oh, I'm sorry. I forget which floor he's on.'

'Fifteenth.'

'Of course. Thanks again.'

'No problem. I'll see you when you come back through.'

If he wasn't called to haul me out beforehand, I thought, as Muffy trotted next to me.

In the elevator on the way up, I tried to come up with something to say. At best, I'd hoped to gain access to his office, perhaps via a member of his staff. I certainly hadn't expected the doctor himself to be in.

By the time I got off on the fifteenth floor, my palms were damp and I stopped to catch my breath as if I'd just run a marathon. Muffy barked at me, apparently impatient to get on with it.

Probably he wanted to sniff out more people to scratch him behind the ears.

I tried the glass doors bearing the doctor's name, finding the place brightly lit but deserted. I'd read that he'd owned a solo practice, but I thought that most doctor's offices employed others. At the very least, I'd thought a receptionist might be there. I read the hours on the door.

Oh. He was closed on the weekends.

To my relief, the door wasn't locked and I walked right in, a panting Muffy leading the way, the sound of his breathing competing with the quiet muzak pumping through unseen speakers.

'Hello?' I called out tentatively, just in case there was someone else there.

No answer.

I walked around, fingering through the items on the reception's desk – an appointment book with names crossed out – and peered through open doorways. Three examining rooms. Two treatment rooms holding various equipment I didn't care to identify. What looked like a posh recovering room. Then, finally, a large room with a stunning view of the city through the floor-to-ceiling windows, decorated with dark antique furniture including a mammoth desk.

There was an open filing box on that same desk.

Bingo.

I looked around for something to tie Muffy's leash to, finding nothing, so I hooked the end over my hand so it hung on my wrist and went to work on the box.

Patient charts. I flipped through a number of them, reading the names, a lot of which I was familiar with. Holy shit! She came here? Wait until the press get a hold of that.

Of course, there was no reason to think they would. Not unless someone leaked the information.

Muffy fought against the leash. I yanked him

back, inadvertently causing a tug-o-war, with him biting into the leash and pulling with his entire canine might, his growling constant.

I ignored him and held firm.

Out of sheer curiosity, I pulled the performer's file out and flipped it open. She'd had the works.

God, the girl wasn't much older than I was, I thought. I ran my finger to where her birth date was listed and my brows shot up. Wrong. She was fifteen years older than I was.

And probably didn't look it due to the doctor's skilled attention.

I closed the file and slid it back inside. What was I talking about? The guy had done a hatchet job on at least five of his patients and was being brought up on charges. Yes, took a certain kind of skill for that.

Muffy pulled on the lead hard, his growling loud.

'Hush!' I whispered.

'Excuse me. Just what do you think you're doing?'

I whirled around, nearly tangling myself in Muffy's leash. There in an open doorway off to the side stood an elderly looking man in a plaid sweater vest, reading glasses shoved up on to his mop of white hair.

I barely recognized him from all the photographs: Dr Westervelt, I presume.

I pulled Muffy until his leash was no longer wrapped around my legs, actually glad this time when he focused his growling attention on the man.

'Hi,' I was sure I fairly croaked. 'My name's

Sofie Metropolis. I'm a P.I. and I was hoping I might talk to you.'

He stared at me for a long moment, then came farther into the room and put down a small stack of files. 'How did you get up here?'

I considered what to say, then decided to go for the truth: 'I told the guard I was your granddaughter.'

Was that a ghost of a smile? 'Right choice. You actually look like Amanda.'

I released the breath I was holding and pulled Muffy back from where he was straining to get a better sniff of the doc.

'What can I do for you?'

His response was probably a conditioned one, honed over a number of years.

I couldn't help thinking that he looked every one of those eighty-one years now, plus an extra decade to boot. I almost felt sorry for him. Almost.

'I have authorization forms to access some of your patient records,' I said quietly.

He sighed and his shoulders slumped. 'The D.A.'s office took everything. The only thing I have left is what you see here.'

I'd already glimpsed one of the patients in there and my fingers were itching to get a hold of it.

'What?' he asked.

I must have been looking at him curiously. 'Oh, I don't know. I guess I expected you to be a little more difficult. Defensive maybe.'

'Why? My career is over, anyway.' He shrugged. 'What use is there in fighting?' His grimace was bone deep. 'My wife was right; I should have retired years ago.'

'Why didn't you?' I found myself asking.

'I don't know. Once you've been doing something for so long ... well, it becomes like a habit. Some people are addicted to booze or drugs, or both. Me, I was addicted to my job.'

'May I?' I asked, gesturing toward the box.

'Go ahead. Take it all if you want. I no longer have any use for them.'

'I'm only interested in the ones pertaining to my clients.'

Given the congenial quality of our conversation, Muffy had relaxed and had planted his butt on the Persian rug, his head moving back and forth as he looked at us.

The doctor moved to the bookcase and began taking leather bound books off the third shelf, reading the spines of each, then putting his selections into another box.

'Those poor girls...'

My fingers froze where I was going through the files. 'Girls?'

'Those dead bodies...'

The ice washed up from my fingers to encase my entire body.

'In the beginning I thought they couldn't possibly be related.' He shook his head, his voice eerily quiet, as if no one else was in the room. 'I never questioned where he got the blood...'

'Who?' My throat had nearly closed altogether.

'What?' The bad doc appeared out of sorts as he once again brought me into focus.

‘Who supplied the blood?’

His smile held no humor. ‘Well, that’s what should have tipped me off from the beginning: he has no name...’

# EIGHTEEN

I'd returned to the agency with half the files in hand, and was still there hours later, a bored Muffy curled up in the corner issuing an exasperated sigh every now and again while I sat at my uncle's desk poring over what I had while making notes everywhere that would take them.

I'd gotten more than I could have dreamed from the disgraced doctor (I found it curious I no longer thought of him as The Chop Doc or The Butcher of Manhattan, as the papers were fond of calling him).

Hell, I was still buzzing from the adrenalin rush.

I'd been working on sheer gut instinct before, but now I had what might be a link between the doctor and the rash of gruesome, unsolved murders that had taken all Queens women by the throat.

At least I thought I did.

I rubbed my forehead as I stood staring at the notes on the desk and the marks I'd made on the white board. Now I wasn't so sure.

Of course, there was one tidbit that kept screaming in my head. It had come when I'd asked him to describe his blood supplier:

'Tall, dark hair, really pale. Oh, and we only

ever met at night.'

I shuddered as if I were hearing the words for the first time all over again.

The first person that came to mind was Ivan Romanoff...

I rubbed my forehead harder and sighed. 'The description could fit a good number of the male population.'

I plopped down in the desk chair and Muffy lifted his head, sighed, and then lay it back down again.

I'd asked the bad doctor what he'd needed black market blood for and he'd stared at me.

'Don't you read the papers?'

I told him that of course I did.

'Then you know I've been administering highly experimental treatments to my patients.'

'Blood treatments...'

He'd nodded. 'Word gets out in Europe about some new treatment, a new tap for the fountain of youth, and in no time wealthy women of a certain age here are clamoring for it. Don't offer it and they'll find somebody else who will.'

He'd shaken his head.

'I should never have given in this time. I should have retired my shingle and called it a day. I'd had a bad feeling about this since the beginning.'

'And this guy who supplied you the blood; if you didn't know his name, how did you get in contact with him?'

'He got in contact with me. Right after a blood bank I'd been working with had refused to supply me with any more blood because they were concerned about my usage.'

I looked down at the notepad that I'd written BLOOD BANK on in large letters and circled several times.

Muffy lifted his head again, but this time it wasn't me he was interested in: he was looking toward the door.

In the next instant, I heard the cowbell tell me someone with a key had just come in.

Nash? I leaned to the right to get a look.

My cousin Pete.

I frowned.

'Hey,' I called out.

Was it me, or had he just tensed where he was shrugging out of his coat?

'Hey, yourself.'

He came to lean on the door jamb, looking around the office in detached interest.

'Haven't seen you around lately,' I said.

'That's because I haven't been around lately. At least not during the times you're here.'

I squinted at him. 'Why?'

He shrugged, avoiding meeting my gaze.

'Mind telling me what you're working on?'

His attention caught on something on the white board. He stepped inside and tapped on it.

'How do you know about this?' he asked.

I got up and came to stand next to him. He was referring to where I'd written Roula's name. 'Are you kidding? My mother has her picture up on the mantel like she's a long lost cousin. I think every Greek family in Astoria has adopted her since she went missing.' I looked at him. 'Why?'

He finally met my gaze. 'Because that's what I'm working on.'

'You're kidding?'

'Nope. You working it, too?'

I shook my head. 'No. Been busy with other things.'

He took in the rest of the board and then the desk behind us. 'I can see that.'

'So are you making any progress on the case?' I asked.

'I don't know. Are you making any progress on yours?'

A gauntlet had been thrown.

One I was all too happy to pick up after so many hours left alone.

I realized that outside my supply of frappés, I hadn't ingested anything since the night before.

'Why don't I tell you over a late lunch?' I offered. 'My treat?'

'Delivery?'

'Of course. You don't really expect me to leave here, do you?'

He threw his handsome head back and chuckled.

'So, what should we order?'

Much later, with Chinese takeout cartons littering the desk between us, me in my uncle's chair, Pete in mine that he'd pulled into the room, we were both mentally exhausted, but happy to have someone else to bounce ideas off of.

Pete leaned back in his chair and blew out a long breath. 'I don't know. I'm beginning to think the girl did run off somewhere. And it would be just my luck for her to pop up first thing tomorrow morning, married, shouting "surprise".'

I picked up a carton of fried rice and poked at the few remaining grains with my chopsticks. 'Hell, at this point, I'd be the first one to throw her a party.'

Pete grimaced. 'Yeah, that didn't sound right, did it? Like I somehow want her to end up kidnapped or worse, just so I won't feel I've wasted my time.'

'You don't have to explain the process to me. I experience the feeling all the time with the remorse that usually follows on the heels of it.'

He didn't say anything for a long moment and then gestured toward the board. 'I still can't believe how you've gotten around to all this. It's so ... chaotic. Not a linear route to be found.'

I shrugged. 'Welcome to my life.'

My cell phone vibrated on the edge of the desk. I tilted it toward me. My mother.

I ignored it.

'What I can't believe is you got up the nerve to go to Roula's parents and ask them if they wanted to hire you.'

Pete ran his hand through his dark hair. 'Yeah, well, every Greek in town is talking about the case and every time I went anywhere, it's all they wanted to know about. So I figured I should make it official.' He smiled almost sheepishly. 'Turns out they've heard of you and hired me on the spot.'

I slowed my chewing. 'You're kidding me?'

'Nope.'

'And you're just now telling me this?'

'Yeah, well, bruised my ego a bit. They knew who you were, but not me. Not my father, either. Then that whole battle of the office bit started and...'

'And you didn't tell me.'

'I didn't tell you.'

'Fair enough, I guess.'

He looked back over his shoulder at the board again. 'You don't think Roula might be a victim of this killer?'

'It's a possibility. That's why her name is up there. But I figure she's been missing how long now? Shouldn't her body have shown up already?'

He sat up straight. 'That's the thing about this whole serial killer case. I mean, the mode of killing is the same. Or I think it is, since the papers really only mention the bloodletting; not the cause of death. But the places the bodies are left—'

'Are different. I know. If not for the ... blood bit,' I shuddered and put the carton down. I'd stopped being hungry twenty minutes ago anyway and was just eating to be eating. 'They may not even be linked.'

'Exactly.'

My cell phone vibrated again.

I gave an eye roll and checked the display.

Dino...

Something in my stomach twirled around and my thumb caressed the answer button. But I let it go to voicemail.

‘Am I keeping you from something?’ Pete asked.

‘What? Oh. No.’ I got up and gathered the cartons, maneuvering my way around Muffy who had been sitting at my feet accepting scraps of chicken and – Lord help me tonight – pork. I stuffed them into the bag they’d been delivered in and placed it by the door to take with me when I left. Stuff like that had a way of stinking up the place if I left it until Monday.

And Rosie had been difficult enough to handle as it was.

‘So what’s your next step?’ I asked.

‘I don’t know. I was hoping to work that out here.’

‘Yeah, I don’t know what I’m going to do next either.’ I drew in a deep breath and squinted at the front window. Was it really dark already?

I gave a shiver and wrapped my arms around myself.

Pete pushed from his chair. ‘Well, I guess I’m going to head out then. I have a date tonight.’

I quirked a brow. ‘A date?’

‘Mmm. I’ve been seeing this girl from Brooklyn. This will be our third date. Nothing serious yet, but I’m hoping it’s heading in that direction.’

‘Good for you.’

I walked him to the door where we traded a couple more ideas that went nowhere and then finally he put on his coat, collected his notes and was gone. I watched him walk toward the subway station through the windows and then my gaze scanned the street.

Even though I wasn't prepared to admit it to myself, I knew I was hoping to spot Jake's truck parked somewhere, the telltale cigarette smoke curling up toward the sky. But there were no vehicles I recognized.

Muffy barked at my feet.

'You're right. Let's go home. There's that Season 5 *Seinfeld* DVD I've been meaning to watch.'

My partner and room-mate barked and ran around in a circle, apparently in agreement.

# NINETEEN

At this rate, I was never going to get a decent meal.

I'd arrived at my parents' for dinner on Sunday earlier than usual. Where I tended to get there in time to set the table and within ten minutes be elbow deep into whatever feast my mother and Yiayia had spent hours preparing, today I intended to help out. Well, my lifelong version of assistance anyway. Which meant hanging around the kitchen getting in the way, popping whatever goody I could grab into my mouth, and suffering the wrath of Yiayia's wooden spoon.

Problem was there were no true goodies to be had. At least not any I was remotely interested in sampling before dinner.

Trust the Greeks to find a way to inject suffering even into Thanksgiving.

'You'll enjoy Thursday's dinner even more,' my mother told me as I scowled into the mammoth pan of *fasolada* – Greek bean soup.

'Mama, the Pilgrims didn't suffer.'

'Yes, they did! They nearly starved to death before the local Indians helped them learn how to plant and harvest and hunt and cook the indigenous foods. I know more about the observation than you do and you were born and educated here.'

'Yeah, and I celebrate Thanksgiving the way all Americans do: by stuffing myself fuller than the turkey.'

OK, I was used to my mother imposing a fast before Christmas and Easter, and understood that it was part of the tradition. But nowhere had I ever read that before Thanksgiving you were supposed to live as the Pilgrims did. In essence, suffer.

My Yiayia waved her ever present spoon at me as if to say, 'It's good for you.'

Probably she was out of her rye and I should have brought her a fresh bottle.

I put the lid back on the pan and sighed the sigh of the starving daughter who had yet to get into the habit of cooking for herself.

I turned to pick up the frappé I'd brought with me and felt the sting of the spoon on my backside.

'Ow!'

I stared at my grandmother, but she had returned to stirring the contents of the pan, a satisfied smile on her wrinkled mouth.

I sipped my frappé and stepped over to an iron baker's rack where a series of cookbooks lined one shelf. All of them Greek, of course, but one; likely the one my mother referred to when preparing Thanksgiving dinner. I fingered the spine of a Greek one and then pulled it out.

'What are you doing?' Thalia wanted to know.

'I figured if you're not going to feed me, I'd better start feeding myself.'

'Well, you're not going to find any guidance

in there.'

I squinted at her.

'I only buy those to support the local Greeks who either wrote them or used them for fund-raising purposes. You don't think I've ever opened any of them, do you? No. You want to learn how to cook, I'll teach you.'

I suppressed an eye roll at my mother's description of cooking lessons. A 'handful' here, a 'dab' or a 'pinch' there weren't exactly helpful directions. It's why I still didn't know how to cook. And Lord forbid she slow down long enough for me to write anything down.

My day was going from bad to worse faster than I could get a handle on.

It began with my mother grilling me on what I had done or had yet to be doing in the search for Cousin Roula; for reasons I couldn't fathom, my news that Pete was working the case didn't buy me any favor. The downward spiral continued with the discovery that there wasn't going to be any yummy food today. And now she'd told me that if I wanted to learn how to cook, I'd have to spend copious amounts of time with her.

No, thank you.

'Where are you going?'

'To see what Dad and Grandpa are doing.'

I caught something along the lines of, 'They're doing what they're always doing on Sunday: sitting in their recliners reading rival newspapers and giving each other the evil eye.'

The kitchen door swung closed behind me and I crossed the dining room, and I saw first-hand that what she said was true. There they were.

The television was on a Greek satellite station that was broadcasting a show that traveled from Greek town to town and where the local women offered up variants on the same recipes to be featured in all their stomach-growling glory to the camera lens.

No, they didn't have Thanksgiving in Greece; every day was Thanksgiving.

I sipped on my frappé, watching a woman in traditional dress offer up a heaping plate of *karithopita*. I wished I could reach through the television and take one.

My grandfather rustled his paper. My father followed suit. I looked at them both, sighed, and then continued toward the front staircase to go up to my old room.

Out of sheer habit, I took the steps two at a time and then grabbed the end of the railing to swing myself around the corner into the upper hall. Straight off, I saw my sister Efi's door cracked open. As usual, she was lying across her twin bed, her feet swinging back and forth, her earbuds in and her fingers flying across the laptop in front of her. I opened the door a little farther, if only to see what color streak she had in the front of her short, brown hair. Orange. Bright, fluorescent orange.

I smiled fondly. I wouldn't have gotten away with half the stuff she did when I was her age. But I had long accepted that was my lot in life. As the oldest child, I'd been the guinea pig, the one on whom they'd made all their mistakes; and my brother Kosmos and sister Efi had been the ones to reap all the benefits.

I mean, sheesh. Kosmos was only a year younger than I was and was little more than a professional student. But was anyone bugging him to get a job? Get married? And what about Efi? I didn't see Mom making her go to liturgy with her in a skirt!

Something she still managed to talk me into on occasion; usually out of guilt because I'd refused her other ten invitations.

I looked over my shoulder at Kosmos' closed door. Probably he was in there studying some ancient text. My brother, the doctor. Of course, it wasn't a medical distinction, but an academic one. But try explaining that to my mother, who loved calling him her 'doctor' son.

I gave myself an eye roll and moved on to my room. I'd be seeing both my brother and sister at dinner, so there was no hurry.

Besides, I figured as long as I was there, I might as well go through the boxes of my old stuff, see if there wasn't something better there than the violet quilt my mother had given me by way of a warmer coat.

I switched on the light, stepped inside, and immediately stepped back outside again.

What the...

I blinked, looked down the hall and counted the doors, and then stared inside again. What was going on? Where was my flowered wallpaper? My bed with the white chenille bedspread? The cork board that still held my senior prom corsage pinned to it along with photos dating back to high school?

I warily stepped back inside and looked

around. The walls had been painted white. The bed was nowhere to be found. And a sewing machine had been set up in the middle of the room. I fingered a bolt of black fabric. Surely during the many conversations I had with my mom throughout the week, she could have taken the time to tell me she'd stolen my room.

A quiet knock on the door.

I turned, ready to face off with Thalia, only to find Grandpa Kosmos smiling at me.

'Wow. Will you look at this. I'd heard your mom was redecorating, but this is the first I've seen of it.'

'Well, at least she told somebody.' I crossed my arms, feeling a bit like a petulant child. Which was ridiculous, really. After all, I not only had my own apartment, along with the building it was in, my parents had bought it for me. Surely if my mom wanted to make my old room into a sewing room for herself, she was entitled.

Still, there was something about the sneakiness of it that rankled.

'She didn't tell you?'

I shook my head.

His grin widened. 'Probably she didn't want to upset you.'

I went to the closet and opened the door, half afraid to see the boxes missing from in there. Thankfully, she'd left that part alone. Aside from the addition of an ironing board and an iron, along with a couple bolts of fabric, it appeared she hadn't touched anything in there.

Thank God for small favors.

'Whoa! Let me get that for you.'

I shifted to allow my grandfather to help me with the box I was taking from the top shelf. Since there was no other place to put it – say, my bed – we let it drop to the floor.

'What are you looking for?' he asked.

'Oh, nothing. I just wanted to see if maybe I had a warmer coat in here somewhere.'

'Ah. Quality over style.'

'No,' I said slowly. 'Style with quality.'

'No such animal. All good style requires sacrifice.'

I laughed. 'So that means something warm is always hideous?'

'Yes. Or else it wouldn't be warm.'

I thought of the violet quilt I'd thrown into Muffy's room the night I'd gotten home after seeing Jake; he'd readily accepted it as his new bed. Which meant for me it was no longer wearable. Thank God. So long as it was hanging in my apartment closet, I was no longer at risk of being a fashion emergency.

'So,' my grandfather said. 'How did your date go the other night?'

I rifled through the box. 'Date? What date?'

My motions slowed. I was so used to pretending nothing was going on in my private life that it was a hard habit to break.

'Oh,' I said slowly. 'You mean with Dino?'

'Have you gone out with anyone else since then?'

'Um ... no.'

'Then, yes, with Constantino.'

I'd referred to Dino as, well, Dino, for so long, I'd almost forgotten it was a shortened version of Constantine. Or, when said in Greek, Constantino, with the 'nt' pronounced as 'd.'

'It was OK,' I said carefully.

'Oh? He said it was a disaster.'

I snapped upright, aggravated that the box only held summer items I'd never wear again and should have gotten rid of years ago, and that Kosmos had spoken to Dino.

'Why did you ask then?' I wanted to know.

He held up his hands, an amused twinkle in his eyes. 'Don't get angry with me. I just wanted your take on it.'

'Yeah, well, Dino's take was right: it was a disaster. An unqualified one.'

What exactly that meant, I didn't know, but it sounded right.

'What happened?'

'He got serious.'

'Ah. I see.'

He helped me take another box down.

'What do you see, exactly?' I asked.

A mistake: the instant the words were out of my mouth, I knew it. But there you had it.

'Well, Sofie, you guys have been ... dating, for how long now?'

I squinted at him. How much had Dino been telling him? My cheeks suddenly grew hot.

'No, no, he hasn't said anything to me. He doesn't have to. It's written all over both your faces whenever you're in the same room.'

I continued to stare.

'What? You don't think I've walked the earth this long without learning a few things about love, do you?'

'Love?' I nearly choked on the word.

'Mmm. Love.'

My movements were decidedly jerky as I went through the second box, finding nothing of use. At least I think so. After I closed it again, I couldn't remember what was in it.

'I really should label these things,' I muttered. 'Actually...' I picked the box up and put it in his hands, 'I should take them to the church drop off box. Here, you get this one; I'll get the other.'

He put the box down and placed a hand on my arm. I knew this look; he wasn't going anywhere until he'd said what he'd come up to say.

I reluctantly put the box I held back down and took a deep breath. 'What?'

'I hear you've been doing some late night detective work.'

I'd expected to hear some more about Dino, so his words surprised me.

Going way back, I'd always felt closest to my grandfather over anyone else in the family. He was wise and funny and he didn't give a lick what anyone else thought about him. He lived life his way; no regrets, no apologies.

And I liked to think that I was a little bit like him. Or at least moving in that sure-footed direction.

'You don't have to give me the details,' he said. 'But I just wanted to give you something that might come in handy...'

I watched as he took something out of his pants pocket and shook it out. It was a silver chain, on the end of which was an ornate Greek Orthodox cross with a blue 'eye' stone in the middle. Hanging next to it was a delicate gold medallion of St George.

I reached out and fingered the chain. 'I remember this.' I met his eyes. 'This was Yiayia's, wasn't it?'

A shadow of grief passed over his features at the mention of his late wife. It touched me that after so many years, he could still feel such depth of emotion for her.

'Yes. Yes, it was.'

I was hesitant to take the offering, no matter how much I wanted to. 'The last time you gave me something of Yiayia's, it ... well...'

I didn't have to say exactly what had happened to my grandmother's wedding ring. We both knew all too well that when my ex-fiancé had accepted the generous offering and had the ring reset, he'd switched the real diamonds out for CZ.

Grandpa Kosmos had clocked him for it ... and had been arrested for his efforts.

'Turn around,' he told me now.

I did as asked, pulling back my hair so he could drape the chain around my neck and fasten it. I faced him, fingering the cross and medallion, marveling at the way the metal instantly warmed in my hand.

Kosmos chucked me under the chin. 'For those nights when you might need a little extra protection.'

I smiled at him.

'And if that doesn't work ... you have my number.'

I laughed and hugged him hard, amazed by

how easily I could slip back into the shoes of the seven-year-old who'd run away for the first time and had her grandpa talk her into returning home.

*'S'euxaristo*, *Pappou*,' I murmured my thanks in Greek, kissing him soundly on both cheeks. *'S'euxariousto para poli...'*

Even as I showed my appreciation, I hoped in my heart of hearts that I wouldn't need the protection.

# TWENTY

Monday morning dawned with thankfully no need for the extra protection Grandpa Kosmos had given me the night before. Still, when I'd dressed, I'd tucked the chain under my black sweater (most Greek jewelry of this nature was designed to be worn under rather than over – true protection, kept close to the heart – not as a fashion statement).

Things at the agency appeared to be running smoothly. At least as well as could be expected considering there was a madman running loose somewhere out there and everyone seemed to be holding their collective breath, waiting for the next bloodless body to pop up.

Rosie had decked out her desk with even more vampire paraphernalia: she'd hung strings of garlic from the handles of filing cabinets, had a foot-long cross sitting on the corner of her desk and every few minutes spritzed what I gathered was holy water from her perfume mister, you know, just in case there were any more of those bats around.

Of course, I had yet to see Waters, which meant there were some cases backing up; cases I had handled before hiring him and that I was afraid I'd have to see to again if he didn't come back soon.

I'd put Pamela Coe on Vlad; something she wasn't happy with but agreed to do nonetheless ... for double the money I'd have paid someone else.

As for me, being in my uncle's office surrounded by ideas but no solid answers had driven me out nearly as quickly as I'd gone in. I knew I'd hit a wall of sorts, and wasn't going to accomplish anything by looking at the same information until it and I became blurry.

So I placed a call instead and made arrangements that took me outside for coffee mid-morning. As I drove to the agreed meeting place, I listened to the police scanner, still completely clueless as to the codes. For all I knew, they could be broadcasting the end of the world and warning people who wanted to live to jump into the East River, and I would be the only one stupid enough not to know that, and as a result the only one to die.

It would be just my luck, considering how it was running.

I took the last sip from my frappé and put the empty cup back down between the emergency brake and the seat, finding nothing ironic about drinking coffee while on my way to have coffee.

I pulled up outside one of a countless number of diners on Ditmars and assessed the parking situation, which was never good, but was doubly bad around this time of day. But I was lucky in that I was close to St Demetrios Cathedral so I could park in their lot. Everyone in the Greek community knew my Mustang and wouldn't give a second thought to my parking there.

Besides, I could use the opportunity to drop off the boxes I'd brought from my parents' house that I had stowed in the trunk. That qualified as genuine church business, right?

I entered the diner ten minutes early to find Pino already waiting for me at the counter. He was half-sitting on a stool, a coffee cup in hand, looking at his watch.

'You know, one of these days you're going to have to give me your regular schedule,' I said, taking the stool next to him.

He took a sip from his cup. 'Who says I have a regular schedule?'

'Everyone has a regular schedule.'

'Not me.'

'I noticed.'

I accepted the coffee the waitress offered to pour for me even though frappé was my preferred method of caffeine imbibing. Unfortunately, Pino had chosen one of the few diners that wasn't owned by Greeks. Actually, more and more diners were owned by newer, Middle Eastern immigrants than by Greeks, I was finding.

I pointed to a plate of stacked donuts and asked the question voiced by diner patrons everywhere: 'Are those fresh?'

'Of course they are. Made just this morning,' the waitress responded with words uttered by her cohorts worldwide.

I asked her to bring me a bear claw. 'You want one?'

Pino shook his head and then patted his flat stomach. 'Trying to watch the waistline.'

I raised a brow.

'Besides, it's never a good idea for a cop to be enjoying both coffee and a donut while on duty. Feeds into the old stereotype.'

'Ah. And not having them counteracts that?'

I stirred as much sugar and cream into the coffee as I could without causing it to overflow the rim.

'Thanks for doing this,' I told him.

He squared his shoulders and for a moment I was afraid he was going to hike the waist of his pants up; he didn't. 'Yeah, just don't get used to it.'

I smiled.

'Here she is now.'

He stood up, nearly knocking his coffee cup over. I quickly reached to prevent the spillage, my own days as a waitress serving me well.

I turned to acknowledge the female homicide detective Pino had arranged for me to meet with. He introduced us and we shook hands. I noticed this close up that Gina DellaFlora had pretty green eyes which the honey blonde of her hair set off. She couldn't be all that much older than me, but somehow looked older. I wondered if it was the job. Dealing with death day in and day out tended to take its toll on people. Just look at my Aunt Sotiria; she'd looked like a candidate for a customer at her own funeral home for at least the past ten years.

'Well...' Pino said, smiling. 'I guess I'll leave the two of you to talk. If you, um, need anything, I'll be right over there.'

I had to bite my tongue to prevent myself from

asking what we could possibly need, but then I caught the way he gazed lingeringly at the detective, and was surprised by her almost blushing response to it.

Pino finally moved away, but I had to wait until the detective looked at me before I could initiate conversation.

'Thanks for agreeing to meet me,' I said.

'Sure.'

Gina put her hand on the overturned cup in front of her and asked the waitress for tea instead, her mind appearing to be on other things.

I shifted on my chair. 'That Pino, huh? He's something.'

Her immediate smile told me I was right: she was actually attracted to the awkward police officer who took his job seriously enough for ten cops. 'Yeah.'

I wasn't an expert on workplace romances, but I knew enough to know they probably weren't a good idea.

Then again, where else was a guy like Pino, who was married to his job, supposed to meet anyone?

Of course, that didn't explain why a woman as attractive as Detective DellaFlora would be the same.

'So, Pino tells me you might have information on The Bleeder case.'

'Is that what you guys are calling him, too?'

She shrugged. 'It fits.'

Yeah, I supposed it did.

'What do you know about Weston Westervelt?'

She stirred honey into her tea from one of those plastic squeezy bear bottles. 'The Chop Doc?'

'That would be him.'

'Nothing outside the headlines and evening news. Why?'

I settled in a little more comfortably and enjoyed my donut. 'First, let's talk about what you might be able to offer me.'

A half hour later I sat in my car in the church parking lot making notes. I'd considered that it might not be a good idea approaching a new detective for possible insider info. Two greenhorns that didn't know much about the game of 'you scratch my back, I'll scratch yours' was like two blind men feeling their way around in the dark. But even in that case, the men were bound to bump into something sooner or later, find something of use within their grasp.

I wasn't sure if Gina DellaFlora truly didn't have anything additional to offer me or if she was just reluctant to share that info with someone without a badge. I assured her that whatever she told me would go no farther, but it hadn't seemed to chip the wall she'd placed up between us. She had agreed to meet me solely to receive information related to the case; not to give any.

She'd also reminded me that if I didn't share something that would prove useful down the road, I could be charged with obstruction of justice and face jail time.

I'd laughed at that. After all, how could she

prove I knew something unless I told her?

She'd then said, 'Well, if that doesn't affect you, how about this? People are dying out there. And if you hold any information that could prevent the death of one more...' She paused for effect and I questioned just how green she really was at this type of thing, considering the way my stomach tightened. 'I don't know about you, but I wouldn't want that on my conscience.'

Thing is, she did appear to know about me.

Probably it would have been a good idea to pump Pino for more background on her. Probably she had pumped Pino for more about me. Which had left her way ahead of the game.

I sighed and sat back in the seat, barely registering the cold while the police scanner droned on from the passenger's seat.

A rap on the side window caused me to jump.

I looked to find a wall of black and automatically reached for my Glock.

'Sofie? Sofie, is that you?'

Cripes. I just nearly shot the priest.

I secured my gun and rolled down the window. 'Papa Ari? Well, hello. How are you?'

'I thought that might be you.'

He offered his hand and I took it, showing my respect. 'I, um, just dropped off a couple of boxes of old clothes,' I told him.

Yeah, forty-five minutes ago. Didn't explain what I was still doing there now.

'I saw. The girls have already sorted through them. Unfortunately I don't think a lot of it's going to make it to the homeless shelter.'

Papa Ari was the youngest of the four priests at

St D's, having come to the parish maybe a year ago from somewhere in the Midwest. Toledo, I think. He was maybe thirty, thirty-five and had almost startling light brown eyes and his dark hair was neatly cut, no beard marring his chiseled chin.

He was so young, in fact, that a lot of the older women had trouble referring to him as Papa. They said that maybe that would change when he got married and older.

Of course, by then, they'd have probably died off.

I felt instantly guilty.

'I was hoping for a chat,' he said.

My brows shot up. 'With me?'

His grin was probably as close to angelic as they came.

I was reminded that one of the reasons I didn't fight my mother too hard when she pressed me into going to liturgy was because of Papa Ari. In fact, there had been a recent uptick in the number of young, single females attending church since he'd transferred there.

Shocker.

'Now?' I fairly croaked.

You see, Greek Orthodox priests were not only permitted to marry; they were encouraged to. It set a good example for the rest of the families in the parish.

'No. You're probably busy. But if we might schedule something?'

God, he wasn't asking me for a date, was he?

I glanced at my watch, not sure how I felt about that. 'Um, actually I have a few minutes.'

'Great. Do you want to come in for coffee?'
I smiled. 'Depends ... do you have frappé?'
'It's all I drink.'

# TWENTY-ONE

'What do you mean a priest hit on you?' Rosie's neck stuck out so far I half expected her head to pop off and roll across the agency's black-and-white tiled floor, her eyes still staring at me accusingly.

'Not a Catholic priest. A Greek Orthodox one. They're allowed to marry.'

She tsked and returned to her laptop. 'Well, he ain't no priest then.'

'What would you call him?'

'A fake.'

I threw my head back and laughed from where I sat on the edge of my desk across the way from her. 'That's a narrow view to take on life. What about a rabbi?'

'That's different.'

'Oh?'

'He ain't a priest either.'

I shook my head, trying to keep my amusement in check.

In all honesty, I wasn't completely convinced that Papa Ari had been hitting on me. My female intuition told me yes, but my mind told me no. Probably because my love life was complicated enough without throwing a hot priest into the mix.

God, I could only imagine what my mother would make of that! She'd probably view it as the ultimate redemption: of her and me.

'Where you going?' Rosie wanted to know.

'Into the office. Why? You had something else to say?'

'Just that you shouldn't be messing around with any man of the cloth.'

'Who said I was messing around with him?'

She gave an eye roll and popped her gum.

'OK ... maybe I flirted back a little bit. He's hot.'

Her eyes narrowed.

'What? Priests aren't allowed to be hot?'

'Hot like how? Like *Thorn Birds* hot? Or Hugh Jackman hot?'

I continued walking toward the office, not about to engage in this conversation. I knew it could lead to nowhere good. I don't even know why I shared the information in the first place. I guess I'd been both surprised and flattered that Papa Ari had sought me out and looked at me like a woman, not merely a parishioner.

Of course, I didn't share what he'd asked of me; the reason for him approaching the car.

Did he really think I could teach Greek to parish adults?

'I see there's an influx of other women your age,' he'd said, handing me a frappé that was better than any I'd ever made. 'I was thinking there might be something we could do to encourage them to get more involved in the community and the church.'

By teaching them Greek?

I'd told him I'd think about it, but given the nature of my work, my hours weren't regular ones, so I didn't think I'd be able to commit the amount of routine time required of such a position.

He'd nodded his head, as if he'd expected this response, and made me want to give him another one entirely.

I hung my coat up on the rack in my uncle's office, set up my scanner on the desk and then sat down with my fresh notes. At this point, there were so many notes I didn't know where to begin.

I began with the doctor's files.

I'd already done a cursory scan of them. Since the D.A.'s office had confiscated his actual patient records, and these only appeared to be scant duplicates of his own personal notes, there wasn't really much to be gleaned. Aside from that, most of his notations were almost impossible to read.

Sheesh. Did doctors go to school to learn how to write that badly?

I rocked back in the chair, trying to get a handle on his shorthand.

'Test new blood supply. Suspect drugs; STD.'

I squinted at the words. At least I think that's what it said.

I flipped back to the first page in the file. It was on a patient named Augustine Patton. Someone Jane Creek had put me in contact with, but whom I didn't know personally.

Something played around the fringes of my mind.

I put the file aside and picked up the one I'd created on the actress, my gaze also trailing to the board.

'Hepatitis C.'

Her words rolled in my mind, 'He gave me hepatitis.'

At the time I hadn't paid much attention. But now that the blood link was becoming a little clearer, well, it was time to review some earlier information.

I picked up my cell phone, calling a number that I hadn't anticipated calling so soon. I'd only had it for an hour. I hope she didn't think I was setting a dangerous precedent.

She had, however, asked that I call if I came across any helpful information.

'Detective DellaFlora? Hi, it's Sofie.'

Silence.

What had I expected? That she'd act like we were old friends calling to tell the other of a not-to-be-missed sale on leather boots?

'Quick question: were any of the victims diagnosed with hepatitis C?'

'They were all drained of blood. Remember?'

This time I remained silent, refusing to rise to the bait.

'Hold on.'

I heard her rifling through papers on her end. After a minute, she came back.

'Nope.'

Shit.

'OK, thanks.'

'That's it?'

'That's it.'

'All right. Bye.'

'Bye.'

I disconnected the call and sighed. Well, so much for that idea.

I absently chewed on my thumbnail and then opened up a fresh notepad, writing hepatitis C at the top, and then put it aside.

The doctor had also mentioned that he'd initially satisfied his increasing demand for blood through a blood bank. I took my small notepad out and looked through it, noting the name of two. One of them happened to be the one with which Ivan Romanoff was associated.

I shuddered and wrote the names of the banks down under the other notation.

I picked up the agency phone and dialed the other bank.

'Yes, excuse me, I'd like to talk to someone about the screening process your blood goes through?'

'And your name is?'

This time I did use the fake reporter ID. 'Pamela Coe of the *New York Gazette-Times*.'

Turned out blood was screened for liver disease and a host of other diseases, the bank's PR person was happy to inform me. So the blood that had infected Jane Creek hadn't come from there.

Good. Narrowed it down.

But narrowed it down to what? I couldn't be sure.

As for contacting the other blood bank, well, I decided that would have to wait until Ivan

Romanoff's return. There was no way in hell I was going to contact his nephew directly again unless it was absolutely necessary. And this definitely didn't fall into that category.

Anyway, he was only supposed to be gone a couple of days, right? I could wait that long. Couldn't I? Especially since Pamela Coe had called in reporting no unusual night-time activity that she could detect in her tailing of Vladimir.

At any rate, it was lunchtime and I was hungry. Rosie was ordering in from Phoebe Hall's diner, but I felt like something a little more indulgent after yesterday's disappointment. And the bear claw had done little to calm my growling stomach.

I wasn't exactly sure what I wanted, but I wasn't surprised when I found myself on the same block as Dino's sweet shop. I told myself I wasn't there to see him, per se. There was a good Bangladeshi place next door to him and I saw the perfect opportunity to pick up some *kalia* for Muffy, as well as for myself.

I pressed on the brakes, making out a familiar black truck parked right in front of Dino's. I squinted. Was Jake following me again? But that didn't make any sense. He was in front of me, not behind me. And there was no way he could have known I'd be coming this way.

A horn honked and I waved, giving Lucille some gas, but not much. I couldn't go too fast and still try to look inside. It was another cold, cloudy November day, so I didn't have to compete with the sun reflecting off the shop windows.

And right there, at the table to the right, in front, sat none other than Jake Porter. With Dino.

Holy shit!

I was so shocked, I stood on the brakes. Tires squealed behind me and the ruckus caused the two men to look out as I stared at them.

I thought about giving a little wave, but the truth was my hands were frozen to the steering wheel and I was too shocked even to acknowledge the bump to my back bumper.

Both men rose from the table and my heart skipped a beat in my chest. Finally, I pried my foot from the brake and pressed the gas, nearly running the red light in front of me.

I was still in shock that afternoon as I sat at my uncle's desk trying to wrap my head around what I'd seen.

What in the hell did Jake and Dino have in common, other than me? Oh, I didn't buy for a second that Jake had just casually happened upon the bakery and decided to go in for a coffee and a roll. Not when I knew that he knew I'd gone out with Dino the other night.

I groaned and dropped my head into my hands, rubbing vigorously.

'Yeah, must be hard to be you.'

I peeked through my fingers at Rosie. 'What do you want?'

She shrugged in that one-shoulder way that she employed when she knew something I didn't and that I would probably want to know. 'Nothing.'

I sighed and dropped my hands. 'What is it?'
'I finally heard from Waters.'
'Oh, thank God. Where is he?'
'Jail.'
'What?' I got up from my chair.
'You heard me. He got picked up on something about some stuff he was selling.'
The scanners.
Oh, great. Pino was going to have a field day with this one.
'Where they holding him?'
'The 114th.'
'Bail hearing?'
'Yep. Set at twenty-five thousand dollars.'
Yikes. 'The value of the merchandise couldn't be that much.'
'Not his first offense.'
'Of course not.' I knew Waters had a rap sheet as long as my leg. And with each new charge, bail was set higher and higher, in an attempt to teach him a lesson, I guess. At this rate, he was going to get slapped for thirty thousand bail for not paying traffic tickets.
I shrugged into my coat. 'Call Fedor Petenka, have him meet me there.'
Petenka was my uncle's go-to guy for bail bonds, as well as for other mysterious business I didn't have a need for. At least not yet.
'Are you kidding me?'
I stopped halfway to the door. 'Why would I be kidding?'
'The guy is a flight risk if ever there was one. They set the bail that high, then he's practically guaranteed jail time.'

'You don't know that.'

She crossed her arms under her breasts and popped her gum, regarding me as if I was one or two worry beads short of a full *koboloi*.

'What would you have me do? Leave him there?'

'He did the crime.'

'Are you sure of that? Seems you've already tried and convicted him and he's only been arrested.'

She gave me an eye roll. 'Spyros would never approve such an expenditure.'

'Yeah, well, my uncle Spyros isn't exactly around to approve or disapprove of anything right now, is he?'

'I'm going to tell him.'

I twisted my lips. 'Be my guest.'

And I left the agency, feeling better than I had in a while.

# TWENTY-TWO

'Goddamn, mother-fucking sons-a-bitches...' Waters muttered under his breath as I walked with him down the corridor toward the door. What he lacked in volume, he more than made up for in severity. 'Nab a guy when he's making love to his lady...'

I raised my brows, watching as he shrugged into his leather coat and then took a pick to his Afro, which needed the attention.

'They arrested you at home?'

I gave the police kudos: not even I knew where Waters lived.

'Nah, I was in the back of my car.'

Well, that would teach me to ask stupid questions, wouldn't it? The image of the skinny little African-American with his bare ass up in the air while he 'made love' to his lady was enough to scar a body for life.

'What did they catch you with?'

'You mean aside from with my pants down around my ankles?' He sniffed and put his pick away. I told him he missed a spot and he went at it again. 'About eight grand worth of merchandise.'

'Wholesale or retail?'

'Street sale.'

Which meant retail it could go for anywhere between two times the value or ten.

'Not good.'

'You ain't telling me nothing I don't already know. I swear, I was set up. It's a conspiracy.'

I grimaced as I opened the precinct door for him.

'Metro!'

Damn. Almost there.

I'd been hoping to get in and out without running into Pino. I already knew he didn't like my latest hire. This would be just one more thing for him to add to the list.

'Well if it ain't the son-a-bitch that arrested me,' Waters said, looking like a miniature Dobermann about to attack a pit bull.

I held my arm out to stop him from advancing. 'You want to add assaulting a police officer to the charges?' I asked.

'Already on there,' Pino clarified, crossing his arms and appearing to dare Waters to go for count number two.

'Yeah, well, since I'm already being charged with it, I might as well make the most of it.'

I strengthened my hold. 'Go wait for me in the car.'

He appeared not to hear me, he was so fixated on Pino.

'Now.'

Finally, he looked at me. Then he ran his tongue over his teeth with a sucking sound, muttered some more profanity, and pushed the door open as if it was preventing him making a grand exit. I watched his coat fan out after him like he was some sort of pint-sized superhero of pimps everywhere and then turned back to Pino.

'Did you really arrest him?'

His smile grew larger. 'Uh huh.'

'Was he really in the back seat at the time, um...'

'Uh huh.'

'Sheesh.'

'Tell me about it. You weren't there to see it.'

'Thank God for small favors.'

He chuckled. 'Hey, I just wanted to let you know that Gina was impressed with your conversation this morning.'

'Gina?'

His eyes narrowed slightly.

'I'm glad you told me that because I was almost convinced she'd have liked to have arrested me on the spot.'

The sensation wasn't all that unlike how I sometimes felt around Pino. As if he were waiting for me to slip up once, just once, so he could haul my ass in. Collect on some sort of karmic debt for all the times I spread glue on his chair back in third grade at St D's.

'I think it only fair to warn you that if you're withholding information, she will arrest you.'

'Yeah, that came across loud and clear. No warning needed.' I looked around him into the conference room, my gaze zooming in on the bulletin board that appeared to have a couple of added photos. 'I could use a favor from you.'

'And I should honor it because...'

'Because you made me lose an hour of my workday bailing out what amounts to a tiny minnow swimming in a sea of sharks. Not to mention the hassle of arranging for bail money.'

He didn't say anything.

'Hey, I need the guy. So long as he's around working the cheating spouse cases, I don't have to.'

'Yeah, well maybe he should stick to catching others at it rather than indulging in it himself.'

'Who died and left you morality police?'

I didn't much like the look in his eyes.

I sighed. 'Fine. Look, I just need a list of the people that are still missing. Can you get me that?'

He didn't move. Then he leaned back, took something from just inside the door of the conference room, and handed it to me.

It was a flyer with the photos and stats on the missing people. All of them young.

'Thanks,' I said.

'You owe me one.'

'Do I?' I waved the sheet. 'Looks to me that this is for public circulation.' I smiled. 'Now if you want to give me information that isn't, well, then we'd be talking favors.'

His gaze was no longer on me, but rather somewhere over my shoulder toward the door.

'You better get going, Metro. Looks like your employee is about to get arrested again.'

I swiveled around. Sure enough, there was Eugene, kicking the door of my Mustang, two uniformed police officers advancing on him from behind.

Christ.

* * *

‘Don’t this piece of shit on wheels have no heat?’

Somehow just watching Waters trying to keep warm in his leather coat that was high on style, low on substance, made me feel warmer. Could be the laugh I was suppressing, even though he’d just called my Lucille a ‘piece of shit’.

‘Bet it was warmer in jail.’

‘Damn straight it was.’ He stared at me as if to ask what I was implying. ‘Oh, look,’ he said, distracted by the police scanner I had propped between the seats. ‘You’re using it.’

‘That’s the last thing you should be thinking about right now. It’s those scanners that got you into trouble.’

‘Nah. I only had a couple of those left. They’re always fast movers. I got nipped for a bunch of electric shavers.’

‘Electric shavers?’

He rubbed his chin. ‘Yeah. I could use one right now, as a matter of fact.’ He sucked his teeth. ‘Damn, they probably confiscated all my inventory.’

‘Speaking of which, you do know how much the agency put out to spring you, don’t you?’

‘Yeah, I know. Thank you.’ He looked instantly contrite. ‘You know I’m good for it.’

Did I? ‘What about family, Eugene? Isn’t there anyone out there you could have called?’

He looked out the window. ‘Nah. I don’t have much of that. Not any more. My Mama, bless her soul, passed last year. Never knew my daddy. And my sister, well, she live out in Trenton, Jersey somewhere with four kids of her own to look after. She don't need me complicating things.'

It was the most he'd said to me about his personal life since I'd known him.

'And your wife?' I thought of the large-size woman I'd seen him with the first day we met who'd blown my hair back when she shouted at me to leave. The idea of her being stuffed into the back seat of Eugene's Cadillac with her legs up in the air made me feel suddenly nauseous. 'She the lady you got caught with last night?'

'Dolores? Aw, hell no. Dee don't want nothing to do with my black ass any more. Gave all my clothes to The Salvation Army and everything. Said if I even think about showing up on her doorstep she'll have me hauled back to jail.'

'So that means home is...'

He flashed his wide grin at me. 'Home is wherever I am, baby.'

I couldn't imagine not only not having family around, but a place to call home with at least a pillow to lay my head on.

'So where am I taking you then?'

'Where they arrested me. Damn, I hope they didn't impound my goddamn car. Now that would be enough to piss a brother off but good.'

The radio crackled and both of us looked at it.

'What does that code mean?' I asked, listening as cruisers responded. I recognized the cross-streets not that far from the river.

'Aw, nothing. Somebody laying in the street or some such shit. Nothing we have to worry about.'

I looked toward the precinct and sure enough

spotted Pino hauling ass outside, pulling his coat on as he went.

'You going to take me back to my car or what?' Waters wanted to know.

'Where's it at?'

'Corona, near the park.'

I reached across and opened his door. 'Sorry, I'm going in the opposite direction.'

'What?'

'Unless you want to ride along.'

He shook his head. 'Ain't that some shit.' He raised his hands. 'Excuse me, but I've been around cops enough for one day. Hell, a week. A freakin' year.'

He got out. 'Now what am I supposed to do?' he asked.

I hooked thumb over my shoulder. 'Subway's that way.'

I stuck as close to Pino's racing squad car as I dared; I figured they had bigger fish to fry than worrying about issuing me a speeding ticket. Feeding Lucille's engine some gas also revved my adrenalin levels. If this is what being a cop felt like, I could understand the attraction. There was an urgency, an importance in those few minutes it took us all to get to the address in question.

Of course, I pulled off well before the final stop; I didn't want to push my luck too far. Especially considering what Pino had said to me back at the precinct.

At least five squad cars were gathered in front of a vacant lot. I reached for my brother's camera where it still sat in the back seat and pointed it in their direction. I wasn't so much interested in getting a shot as I was in zooming in on the scene unfolding some five hundred feet up the block. I aimed and worked the lens until I could see the backs of the officers' legs, then further still until I could peek through them. An old blue blanket had been placed over the body and one of the officers lifted a corner, giving me a perfect shot of the young woman underneath.

I felt suddenly ill and found myself pressing the shutter button, taking photos.

The possibility that it was Roula surged high in my mind. Dark hair, same bone structure. I lowered the camera and swallowed hard. So pale.

A knock on my window. I jumped.

Jake.

I found myself swallowing again, albeit this time for different reasons.

I thought about rolling down my window but decided to put the camera down and got out instead.

'Hey,' he said as I closed the door behind me, engine still running.

'Hey, yourself.'

His gaze narrowed on my face. 'You OK?'

'Me?' I stared at him. 'Yeah, I'm fine. Much better than that girl over there.' I poked my thumb in that direction.

'Yeah, I'd say we're all doing a far sight better than she is.'

I leaned against the car and wrapped my arms around myself. But my chill had little to do with the bitter cold and more to do with the situation.

'Can I ask what you're doing here?' I asked.

'I heard the call come in.'

I'd never stopped to think that the reason why Jake popped up at so many of the same places at the same time I did was because he had a scanner. Of course, it made perfect sense.

But the romantic in me liked to think about there being some more dreamy meaning. Like fate. Or destiny. Or at least his having followed me.

Speaking of which...

'What were you doing at Dino's place earlier?'

'Dino?'

I grimaced. 'Don't even try playing dumb with me, Jake. We both know I saw you there.'

'Ah. You must be referring to the baker.'

'Mmm.'

He slid his hands into his front jeans pockets, but I knew better than to buy the casual motion. He shrugged. 'Heard the new place served some good coffee and decided to stop by and have a cup.'

'Right. Try again.'

His grin was teasingly suggestive. 'What do you think I was doing there?'

'Truly? I can't figure it out for the life of me.'

'Try again,' he turned my own words against me.

'Well, if I had to venture a guess, I'd say it was to check out the competition.'

His gaze lingered on mine for a long moment and I knew that the shot in the dark had hit its mark.

And the knowledge raced through my veins as heady as a drug.

Oh, sure-fire, burn-it-to-the-ground chemistry had always existed between us. There wasn't a time when we were together that I didn't want to shove the soft cotton of his dark T-shirt up, and his jeans down – including now. The guy did things to me I couldn't begin to explain or battle.

But while our bodies spoke the same language, I couldn't get him to communicate with me verbally to save my life. And it had nothing to do with his sexy Australian accent.

I considered him now. 'Only in order for there to be a competition,' I said softly, 'you have to be in the game.'

'And I'm not in the game?'

I tilted my head, my heart contracting at this new side of Jake I was glimpsing for the first time. 'I don't know. Are you?'

He didn't appear to like the question.

'I think in order for you to be in the game, you have to be willing to share, Jake. And you haven't done much of that. In fact, you haven't done any of that.'

'And this bloke, Dino, did you say his name was? He shares?'

This time I glanced away.

'Look, I didn't rap on your window looking for a row, Sof,' he said quietly. 'I just thought it would be a good idea if you had a closer look at the body.'

'Me?'

'You're working that missing persons case, aren't you?'

'You mean Roula Kalomoira?'

He nodded.

'How did you know ... Oh, never mind. I'm not going to ask another question that's never going to be answered.' I took a deep breath. 'My cousin Pete is actually the one officially working the case.'

'But he's with your agency, right? And you know what she looks like.'

'I've never met her, but yes, I've got a pretty good idea what I'm looking for from photos.'

I thought of the one on the mantel at my parents' place and my skin iced over.

'Well, that's more than what these guys are working with. Go on.'

'Go on?'

He moved his head in that direction.

I turned to see Pino looking at me. He nodded.

Damn. Why did I have the feeling I wasn't going to like what I was about to see?

# TWENTY-THREE

'Was it her?'

Rosie jumped up the instant I entered the agency an hour later. I raised a hand and passed by her on my way to the closet that served as the bathroom, not stopping until I had closed the door and was splashing water over my face again and again. It didn't faze me that the water was running cold. Or that I had just splattered my leather jacket. Or even that I had just messed up my hair. I merely needed to battle back the bile collecting in my throat.

Knocking at the door. 'Sofie? Sof? You OK in there?'

I grabbed a wad of stiff paper towels and mopped at my face, staring at myself in the old mirror. I noticed I looked nearly as pale as the body had lying on the cold, cracked cement of an old driveway.

No, scratch that; at least I still laid claim to my blood.

I opened the door. Rosie jumped back.

'Jesus, you scared me.'

I walked past her toward my uncle's office.

'Well, answer me: was it her?'

I dropped into the desk chair, feeling as if I didn't have the energy even to answer her.

It was amazing how personally everyone had taken this one Astoria girl's disappearance. Six people had died – now seven – in gruesome fashion, and everyone was worried about this one person that no one seemed to know. It was tragic somehow.

Especially considering the outcome.

'Yes,' I finally whispered. 'Yes, it was Roula.'

Rosie gasped and put her hand over her heart.

That had been my initial response when I'd stepped up to the body, everyone around me was still, only the sound of the radios the officers wore breaking the silence, our breath creating a white cloud that disappeared as quickly as it appeared.

Somewhere in the agency a telephone rang. But I couldn't bring myself to find it, much less answer it. And Rosie seemed in the same shocked state.

She finally found her voice again. 'Was she ... I mean did they...'

I squinted at her.

'Did she have her blood?'

I slowly shook my head, although I questioned the logic of sharing the information with her. While she was sure to find out soon anyway by regular channels, I had a feeling that this latest bit of information might make her run for home where she'd lock herself up until the 'killer vampire' was caught.

Hell, it's what I wanted to do. Sort of. Considering the 'wing flapping' incident outside my window, and my vivid dreams, I wasn't so sure my house would be the one to go to.

'Omigawd,' Rosie said in one word. 'I've got to call my sister. I've got to call my brother.'

She hurried to her desk where she began doing all of the above, seemingly at once.

Somehow I'd managed to call my cousin Pete from the crime scene. He'd made it there in record time and confirmed my ID, looking as pale as I'd felt, although he'd been a damn sight more professional, asking questions I couldn't even formulate.

It was Roula.

Oh, shit.

I got back up, reached for my coat, then realized I still had it on.

'Where in the hell you going at such a time?' Rosie asked as I rushed by her.

'The last place in the world I want to be right now, but the one place I should be: my mother's.'

I knew that Thalia would take the news badly. I just hadn't realized how badly.

As I sat across the kitchen table from her, I shifted uncomfortably in my seat, unsure how I could comfort my sobbing mother. Even my grandmother had taken a seat next to me, her silence loud as she fiddled with a handkerchief.

'I'm sorry,' I murmured. 'I hate to be the one to share the news, but I figured it would be better coming from me than somewhere else.'

My mom nodded, accepting the box of tissues I handed her from the baker's rack behind me. She pulled out three or four and then loudly blew her nose. 'Thank you ... I appreciate it.'

I couldn't remember the last time I'd seen my mother such an emotional mess. Especially over someone she hadn't even known. Even when her long-time best friend and next-door neighbor – and incidentally Muffy's former owner – Mrs Kapoor had died suddenly of a heart attack, taking an unscheduled trip to the Hindu heaven in the sky, my mother had been stoic. Oh, she'd cried, but not with the soul-deep sobs I watched rack her body now.

'Have they ... will they tell her parents?' she asked.

I nodded. 'I'm sure they're talking to them now.'

Thalia made a move to get up. 'I have to call them, help them see to funeral arrangements...'

I reached across the table and touched her arm. 'That can wait. Sit here with me for a minute first.'

She stared at me as if it was taking her twice the normal time to hear anything I said. Finally, she nodded and settled back into her chair. 'Of course. You're right. They'll need to absorb the news first.'

I found it interesting that I was thinking the same thing about her.

My grandmother nudged my arm and I looked to find her holding out the tissues to me.

Without my realizing it, I had begun to cry, as well.

Not so much about the loss of Roula's life, as tragic as that was. But that life – and death – in general had the ability to cause so much pain.

I pulled out a Kleenex and wiped my own cheeks as the three of us sat in silence.

Pretty much the whole day went by in the same emotional blur. I'd been so sidetracked by the response to Roula's death that I ended up staying with my Mom for longer than I intended, even helping her fix several casseroles and then going with her to Roula's family house where we both ended up helping out with identification and initial funeral arrangements and taking care of secondary items until other family members arrived to take over.

I hadn't been able to concentrate on anything else and I'm not sure if it was a good or a bad thing that no one else seemed equally distraught. Pete had come to the office and he, Rosie and I essentially went through the motions with no real sense of what we were doing for the remainder of the workday. Sure, we'd all known that the possibility that Roula was dead existed all along. It had been hanging out there like a threatening noose. We just hadn't expected to feel that same noose take us by the throats once her body showed up.

The day seemed to drag by, but at the same time, I was surprised to find myself at home so soon. By ten o'clock, I had no sense of the passage of time at all, or even of what I was doing. I think I ate at some point, but couldn't recall what. And I'd put in my *Seinfeld* DVD only to realize I'd missed four episodes without registering a single one.

The only thing I was sure of was that Muffy

had been fed. He wouldn't be snoozing in his Barcalounger right now if he hadn't; he'd be bugging the hell out of me. Which was just as well, because if he weren't so insistent I stick to some sort of schedule, I probably wouldn't have remembered to feed him at all.

I leaned forward on the couch and propped my elbows on my knees, my face in my hands. A part of me was mildly surprised by my reaction. But another knew there was a very important reason why: Roula had been in exactly the same position on that cold cement as I was in my recurring nightmare.

Since one of the identifying marks on my information sheet had been a small tattoo of the Greek flag on her outer left ankle, the blanket had been entirely lifted for me to view the body. The way she lay wasn't immediately apparent to me, but a bell had run in the deep recesses of my mind as I tried to identify her as emotionally as possible. She'd been so ... colorless. So lifeless. And even though I hadn't known her, she could have easily been any one of a number of kids I'd gone to St D's with, or saw in church, or even just passed in the street any time of day.

Then it had struck me as I asked an officer to tilt her ankle so I could verify the presence of the tat: it hadn't been me I'd seen in my dream: it had been Roula.

I shivered all over again there in the warmth and safety of my living room.

Had my dream been a premonition? I knew of others who read a lot into their own unconscious wanderings. I was even familiar with a few

Greek seers who claimed to be able to interpret your dreams, along with reading your coffee, for one low fee. But I'd always listened to such claims with a dismissive ear and a polite eye roll.

Of course, I knew that I was probably reading too much into this. Making a connection that wasn't there. But damned if I could stop myself from doing it.

Muffy's head shot up from where he lay on the chair. I glanced at him, watching as he growled and then leapt toward the window as if he'd been poised to do so for the past five minutes rather than just awakened from a dead sleep.

I frowned as he jumped up and down in front of the closed window.

'What is it, boy?' I asked, even as icy dread stole up my spine.

While it wasn't entirely impossible that he had to go to the bathroom, this wasn't his usual 'open the window already before I make a mess on the floor' jump.

This was his 'that freakin' flappin' thing is back' jump.

I reached for the remote and pressed the mute button and then slowly got up, turning off lights as I went until the apartment was dark. Muffy momentarily halted his jumping and looked up at me as I leaned to peer through the curtains.

The unmistakable sound of flapping.

I gasped and drew away, my hand slapping against my chest. Muffy resumed his barking with renewed fervor while I backed up, gauging the distance between my gun and me. It, along with its holster, was hanging on the coat tree near the door where I always left it when I came in. I slowly reached for it, my gaze trained on the window and the shadows moving there.

The knock at the door nearly sent me flying from my own skin.

# TWENTY-FOUR

I stood stock-still, sure my fear-paralyzed brain had imagined the sound. Muffy still barked at the window.

What had I been thinking, shutting off all the lights?

I slowly reached for my gun, taking it out of the holster and stepping closer to the door so I could look out the peephole. I didn't expect to see anything, but if I did, I was hoping it was the top of Mrs Nebitz's professionally tended gray hair.

Instead, I saw the last person I expected – or wanted – to see there: Vladimir Romanoff.

Oh, God.

I drew back from the door, holding my breath. There was no way for him to know I was home, right? I'd turned off the television well before he was outside my door. Surely he hadn't heard it.

Another knock.

I closed my eyes, gripping the gun tightly in front of me in full shooting mode, although the muzzle pointed toward the floor.

Go away, go away, go away, I silently prayed.

All too fresh in my memory was the image of Roula lying in the same position as I had been in my dream, along with the memory of waking up in my cold car after drinking a shot of cognac in the man's company, with no knowledge of what had happened between the two events or how I had ended up where I was, my coat securely fastened up to my neck.

'Sofie...' the voice from my dream said, only it was live and in person now. 'I know you're in there. Open up to me.'

My throat choked off air. Open up to him? I knew he meant the door, but I couldn't help thinking there was a double meaning.

'No,' I said, without realizing I'd planned to say anything.

A quiet chuckle.

Behind me, Muffy had stopped barking. I heard his nails click against the bare wood planks between throw rugs as he came to stand by my side, his tongue hanging out of his mouth. He looked from me to the door and back again. I wondered why he wasn't barking now.

'I mean you no harm, Sofie.'

I bet, I said silently. Probably he was going to confess.

'My uncle sends his regards.'

His uncle needed to get his head examined if he thought I was going to deal with this lunatic killer vampire.

'I assure you, my visit is innocent.'

Before I knew it, I'd opened the door, backing up so I had enough room to point the gun straight at his chest. He took in my stance from where he stood spotlighted by the bright hall fixture and smiled.

'There is no need for that.'

'No need or no use?' I asked, holding my ground.

If it were true that vampires were impervious to regular human weapons, then he was right; bullets would be of no use to me.

Two men crowded closer to either side of him. Two of his guards, I gathered. I looked at them, measuring the threat they presented, when my gaze zeroed in on a fresh scar on one of their faces. Was that a burn? It was red and raw and ran the length of his face from forehead to jaw and then disappeared into the black collar of his shirt under his black leather coat.

The sight combined with the flapping sound made me remember the incident at the agency with the bat.

'Please,' Vlad said to his men. 'You may wait out with the car.'

The one with the scar seemed to linger, staring at me with undisguised wrath.

Finally, they disappeared. And when I say disappeared, I mean it. While I was too far back from the door to watch them descend, there was no telltale sound of old stairs squeaking that I was accustomed to hearing, even when petite Mrs Nebitz went down them, much less two grown men who outweighed her by at least a hundred pounds apiece.

'May I come in?' Vlad asked.

I squinted at him. 'Are you serious?'

His smile was wide. 'I see. Very well then. If you wish to conduct business in the hall, then the hall it is.'

I readjusted my grip on the gun.

He merely stood there.

'Well?' I prompted.

'I am sorry ... have I done something to offend you?'

My brows rose. 'Get to the point.'

The gun was starting to feel heavy in my hands.

'My uncle shared that you were concerned it was someone within our family who might be responsible for the rash of recent unfortunate killings.'

Unfortunate? Had he really said unfortunate? As in, 'hey, it was an accident, but an innocent one'?

'I merely want to assure you that I am not the one you're looking for.'

I was rendered speechless.

'Please, in the best interest of all involved, stop having your people follow me.'

Pamela Coe.

My face must have revealed my immediate concern for her well-being.

'Your employee is safe. Sitting outside my apartment building as we speak, unaware of my whereabouts.'

Why didn't I feel any better?

'Well, that is all. I bid you a good evening, Sofie.'

He gave a brief bow and then turned.

Still holding the gun, I glanced down at where Muffy sat calmly, not a bark or a growl in sight.

'Hey,' I said, edging toward the hall.

But Vlad had vanished.

I shuddered and slammed my door...

* * *

Back at the agency the following morning, I wasn't feeling up to par. If it had anything to do with the fact that I hadn't gotten much sleep the night before, I wasn't admitting it. Because to do so would be to tell Rosie about my late night visit by the neighborhood vampire's creepy nephew and my semi-armed response to him (I wasn't really armed, was I? Because I wasn't all that convinced that bullets would have done one bit of good). And there was no way in hell I was doing that.

At least I hadn't invited him in.

The thought looped around in my mind and back again.

What I had done was immediately pull Pamela off tailing him. She was good, the best the agency had. If he could give her the slip, well, there really was no reason to put her – or me – at further risk.

But it hadn't aided me in falling asleep. Every gust of wind had been the flap of a bat's wing; every creak in the building had been Vlad or one of his vampire guards walking across my apartment floor.

After making my third frappé in two hours, I took notes from my desk and headed back toward my uncle's office.

'Oh,' I said to Rosie, 'If Pete calls in or comes by, can you ask him to see me?'

'Why?'

I gave a small eye roll. The feisty office manager seemed to be asking the question a lot lately, not unlike a small child that had been spooked and was now looking for answers from every direction.

'I have something I'd like him to look into.'

'What?'

'Just do it, OK?'

'Fine! Be that way then.'

I hated to be that way, but she was giving me little choice. At any rate, I figured she'd get over it soon enough. We all would. Once this damned killer was finally caught, which is what I had redoubled my efforts towards doing the moment I came in.

I considered the mess on my uncle's desk: the multicolored words and names and places on the white board. The answer was here somewhere, I knew it. Buried and waiting to be found like a long lost treasure.

I just lacked the right equipment to find it.

The scanner was on low in the desk, Rosie's actually louder in the other room. I reached and switched it off.

'You wanted to see me?'

I hadn't heard the cowbell over the front door clang so I jumped when my cousin Pete said the words from the office doorway.

'Um, yeah. Hi.' I waved him in.

He stepped next to the board, looking it over much the same way I had, as if considering it from a different angle might offer up different information.

I leaned against the front of the desk and crossed my arms over my chest. 'I wasn't sure you were going to come in today.'

His frown went deeper than the surface

expression. 'What else am I going to do? My single case is now officially closed.' He rubbed his hand over his face, still wearing his brown suede jacket that didn't look any warmer than my black leather. 'They don't get any more closed than that.'

'No. I guess they don't.'

He sighed and sat down. 'There is one angle I've been working.'

'Same case?'

'Yeah. Some of Roula's friends say there was another girl with her the night she disappeared.'

'Sara Jeziorski.'

'That would be her. Anyway, since she doesn't have any family outside her mother – who appears more concerned with taking care of her new husband and family than the disappearance of her daughter – I did a little further checking on her. In the beginning it was because of her connection to Roula—'

'But now that Roula's gone, you'd like to continue?'

He nodded. 'Funny, isn't it? No one really knew either one of these girls. But whereas Roula's face was featured in nearly every Queens storefront, Sara was never even mentioned. Almost like she never existed.'

I rounded the desk and sat down. 'Unfortunately if her fate ends up the same as Roula's, it might be as if she never did.'

We shared a silence and in that moment I knew he felt the unfairness of the situation as deeply as I did.

'Funeral's on Friday,' I said.

He nodded. 'I heard.' After a few more moments, he asked, 'So what did you want to see me about?'

In light of our conversation, I'd nearly forgotten. I felt around on top of the desk until I found the file I was looking for. 'I thought that since you're in people-finder mode, you might want to look into these two.'

I handed him the file on the missing twins. He flipped it open and then got up.

'Got it.'

I decided there was something satisfying about assigning work and being confident that it would not only be done, but done well.

# TWENTY-FIVE

The next item on my agenda was one I'd been putting off, but I knew I'd have to do eventually. While my phone call to the non-Romanoff-connected blood bank with which Dr Westervelt had been associated netted some answers, I couldn't help feeling an in person look around would be the only way to jog all the information around that currently crammed my head.

Since I couldn't seem to reach the PR person again for a one-on-one, I drove to the bank and parked, figuring that if I absolutely had to, I'd give blood.

I shuddered as I walked to the entrance. Giving blood wasn't anywhere near my Top One Hundred Things To do In This Lifetime List. Up until a few years ago, I nearly passed out merely having samples drawn for regular tests. And I'd never actually given blood.

And the idea of doing so now, with everything going on, made the thought doubly unappealing.

I drew a deep breath and looked around the clean reception area. Well, there was a first time for everything.

After talking to the nurse at the front desk, I was asked to fill in a few medical forms and then led to a room where what looked like dentists' chairs ringed a large area. A few chairs were taken, with people sitting squeezing Styrofoam balls while bags sat near their feet next to them, a clear hose ferrying their blood from their arms to the bags.

My stomach lurched, ushering in second thoughts.

'I see you have never given blood before,' the nurse commented.

I nodded, incapable of words even though I'd come here with the intention of milking anyone there for answers, even if it meant letting them milk me in a manner of speaking.

Get a grip, Sofie, I ordered myself. Look, these people are doing this without any risk. One of them even appeared half asleep, he was so relaxed.

I swallowed hard and sat down where she requested, nodding at the woman next to me.

'Someone will be right with you,' I was promised.

'Tell them to take their time.'

She smiled and left the room.

'First time?' the woman next to me asked. She was hooked up to one of those bags and was busy squeezing her ball, well into the process that the unknown person who would insert the needle and drain a pint of liquid from my body required to operate.

'Yeah,' I said. 'You?'

'Nah. I come every fifty-six days. Been a shortage lately.'

Tell me about it, I said silently.

'It's good for the body,' she said.

'Oh?'

'Yes, encourages it to react and create fresh blood.'

I squinted at her.

'Aside from the good deed you do.'

I twisted my lips, thinking she wouldn't be looking for the money they offered.

She was about my age, maybe younger, blonde and pretty.

I took a deep breath and looked around, trying to orientate myself. I figured the more comfortable I became with my surroundings, the more my body would start pumping some of the blood they were about to take from me to my brain so I could ask questions.

There was a woman's scream from the other room. I nearly leapt out of the chair as I looked to my neighbor for confirmation she'd heard it as well.

So much for becoming more comfortable.

A tall male in a white smock entered the room, smiling. I tried to detect any sign that he was anxious or that there wasn't something serious going on outside that room, but he looked relaxed and open enough.

'Nothing to worry about,' he assured everyone as he approached the woman next to me.

'Very good,' he said. I watched as he pressed a cotton ball against where the needle was inserted into her inner arm and then glued a bandage over it. 'Let me get you a cookie and a glass of juice.'

He came back and served her on a small tray next to the chair and then collected the bag and walked from the room.

I knew a moment of relief that he hadn't moved directly to me.

'That's it?' I asked her.

She smiled as she drank her orange juice. 'That's it.'

Well, that didn't seem too horribly difficult.

Of course, I was forcing myself not to think of the mammoth needle that was least twenty times thicker than normal ones.

'Hey, is anyone going to take care of me?' the older gentleman who had appeared to be sleeping asked loudly.

A female nurse came in looking harried. Now she didn't appear relaxed and open at all. 'I'm sorry, sir. There's been an emergency in the other room.'

My hands tightened on the chair arms. Emergency?

She freed him and served him a cookie and juice. 'You can get your check from the front desk on your way out,' she said.

She turned to the woman next to me. 'I'll be with you in a moment.' She appeared momentarily confused. 'Where's your bag?'

The girl and I exchanged glances.

'A male nurse just came and took care of me.'

Her brows knit together. 'There is no male nurse on duty today, miss.'

I couldn't have gotten out of that chair fast enough.

So much for giving blood. At this rate, I might never ever enter another blood bank again in my natural lifetime.

* * *

The unsettling residue left by my blood bank experience followed me for the rest of the day.
There had to be some mistake. Of course there had been a male nurse on duty that day.
Still, I'd pressed the issue and within minutes the police had been called, staff questioned, and it was determined that the man had, indeed, not been associated with the bank.
Upon questioning, a couple of the nurses reported that there had been similar instances in the past week, where blood had been collected by someone but had never been logged in.
Talk about creepy.
I reported the incident to Pino, who in return said he'd pass it on to Gina.
I was surprised later that afternoon by a call from Gina while I was at the agency.
'I wanted to thank you for passing on the information about the missing blood earlier,' she'd said.
'Does that mean I get points?'
She hadn't laughed but I was pretty sure I could hear her smile. 'Indeed, it does. You remember asking me if any of the victims had hepatitis C?'
'I do.'
'Well, it turns out one of them did.'
She'd gone on to tell me that the lab results on the body recovered last Thursday had come in and showed a positive result for the liver ailment.
'Now, are you going to tell me why you wanted the information?' Gina had asked.
'Give me until tomorrow,' I'd requested.

Then I called around until I finally tracked down the doctor. He agreed to meet me at his offices downtown.

# TWENTY-SIX

There was something to be said for holidays. Even in a city as big and bustling as New York, no matter how busy you were in the days preceding and following, or how preoccupied, getting up on Thanksgiving Day to find it quiet, as if everyone had exhaled as one, permeating the air with a sense of profound gratitude for the break, was hard to ignore.

I opened the window for Muffy and then leaned against the glass, staring out at the street below. No traffic. No one out rushing to be somewhere else. A sense of peace and serenity reigned; at least until it was time to go to wherever the family was scheduled to gather for dinner, and a completely different kind of chaos ensued.

I whistled for Muffy and then shivered, pulling my dressy sweater jacket closer over the clingy white top I had on underneath. Black jeans and boots completed the outfit. Hey, it was as dressed up as I usually got.

I heard Muffy's footsteps on the fire escape and stepped back to allow him to jump in.

'Yeah, who's my boy?' I asked him, running my hands over his coarse fur and scratching him under the chin.

He tolerated me for a whole two seconds with animated tail-wagging before sticking his snout into the air and escaping my attentions.

I'd like to take him with me to my parents, but with so many people scheduled to be there, I wasn't sure it was such a good idea; Yiayia might get ideas.

As usual, I was going empty-handed. I'd asked my mother if she wanted me to bring anything and she'd offered me the verbal equivalent of the head pat I'd just given Muffy and told me not to worry, she and Yiayia had everything under control. I had enough on my plate looking for Roula's killer.

I shrugged into my leather jacket that felt a bit snug with both my shirt and sweater and opened the door in time to catch Mrs Nebitz walking out of her apartment across the hall on her grandson Seth's arm. She was decked out in her Shabbat best, complete with hat.

'Happy Thanksgiving, Mrs Nebitz,' I said, giving her a brief hug and a kiss on both cheeks.

It wasn't something I normally did, but it seemed appropriate considering the day.

'Happy Thanksgiving, dear,' she murmured, the pinkness of her face revealing she'd enjoyed the little extra attention. 'You remember my grandson Seth, don't you?'

'Of course. Happy Thanksgiving.'

How could I forget Seth? Hadn't it been him who had broken Rosie's heart last month and left me picking up the jagged pieces that refused to fit back in her petite chest?

He seemed to pick up on the direction of my

thoughts and had the good sense to look away.

'How's Rosie?' he asked, surprising me.

I lifted my brows, as did Mrs Nebitz, who had been adamantly against her good, Jewish grandson dating the feisty Puerto Rican from the moment she found out until he finally broke it off.

'She's fine. Celebrating at home with her family. Her sister had the baby. It's a boy.'

He looked pleased, until I think Mrs Nebitz discreetly knocked his leg with her cane and he visibly winced.

'Well, we must be going, Sofie,' she said, effectively nipping any further discussion in the bud.

Or so I thought.

'Do you think it would be all right if I called her?' Seth asked.

I considered him. 'I don't know. Do you think it would be all right?'

I looked pointedly at Mrs Nebitz who was too concentrated on her grandson's face to register my expression.

'Why don't you go down first, Sofie?' she suggested. 'You know how long it takes me to get downstairs. I wouldn't want to hold you up.'

'That's OK,' I said. 'I'm early anyway.'

'I insist!' she almost snapped.

OK...

'Very well. Happy Thanksgiving, then.'

'Happy Thanksgiving to you, too, dear. Give your family my best.'

'The same with yours.'

Once in my car, I sat for long moments letting

the engine warm up, my breath like phantom icicles that melted with my next intake of air. But aside from vigorously rubbing my hands against my jeans, I paid the cold little attention as I watched Seth hand Mrs Nebitz into a waiting taxi.

I understood the old woman's objections to her grandson getting too cozy with a girl whose background and cultural traditions were so different from hers. Coming from a Greek family, I understood all too well. But it didn't mean I had to agree with it. And I didn't like that it painted her in a color I didn't find very becoming.

I watched the taxi drive past, giving them a small wave.

All I knew is that Rosie had been broken beyond repair when Seth had severed their ties.

And, if I wasn't mistaken, Seth hadn't escaped completely unscathed either. Or else he wouldn't have asked about her, indicated a desire to call.

I sighed, noticing my breath wasn't quite as white. Didn't I have enough going on in my own love life without going around poking into others? Of course, when it came to others, my eyesight was better than 20/20. My own? Well, I was beginning to fear there wasn't a magnifying glass thick enough to ferret out much needed clues.

I put Lucille into gear and began to pull away from the curb, only to step on the brakes as a police squad car sped by, lights flashing, siren noticeably silent.

I stared after it.

Oh, no. That wasn't allowed. Not on Thanksgiving.

Another squad car sped by.

Great.

I reached over and took the police scanner out from where I'd stashed it under the seat and switched it on. I still wasn't clear on codes, but I could follow addresses. And this one was near Sunnyside.

Fine. I was early enough I could make the crime scene and still get to my parents' in time for dinner.

I listened to police chatter as I drove in the same path the cars ahead of me probably had. Where I'd taken joy in there being no traffic earlier, now I only noted that it made my progress quicker.

I was on the scene in no time and getting out of the car.

And there was Pino along with Detective DellaFlora, both of them looking like they did on any other day.

'Another one?' I asked an officer closer to me.

'Hey, Metro,' he greeted. 'Happy Thanksgiving.'

'Yeah. Happy Thanksgiving,' I returned, wondering how all these guys knew who I was, yet glad I didn't need introduction and wasn't being blocked out. 'Is it?'

He nodded toward the scene in question. 'Looks like it. Call came in ten minutes ago. Jogger came across the body.'

He pushed his cap back and scratched his head.

Pino spotted me and began walking toward me. I couldn't tell if it was to chase me away or to share.

'Happy Thanksgiving,' I said, mimicking the officer's approach.

'Yeah. *Chronia Polla*,' he gave me the general Greek greeting appropriate for all holidays. 'Looks like we've got another one.'

'I kind of figured that out for myself.'

'Did you figure out that there's something off with this one?'

I squinted at him. 'How so?'

'For one, she has ID.'

The previous victims had little in terms of personal possessions outside the clothes they wore. Identification had taken a while. 'Oh? Can you give me the name?'

'Wendy Newberger.'

I frowned, unfamiliar with it. 'Is it on the list of missing?'

'Good eye. No, it isn't.'

That was odd. Why break with tradition now? 'You think this might be a copycat?'

'Possible.'

Gina stepped over without my realizing it. 'Hey,' she said.

'Happy Thanksgiving,' I returned.

'Not for that girl over there.' She looked at Pino, her stressed expression instantly relaxing. 'Did you tell her?'

'I shared the name on the ID and she put together that she's not on the list.'

I was happy for this new open cooperation, yet a little suspicious of it, as well. Did it stem from a result of Holiday good cheer? Or was there something else at play here?

'And her blood?'

'Another anomaly,' Gina said. 'There's an open wound on her inner thigh, and it appears she's been drained, but it's not with the neatness and clinical precision of the previous victims.'

'So we are dealing with a copycat then?' I asked.

'It's a possibility.'

An officer called out for Gina and she left.

Something played around the fringes of my mind that I couldn't quite get a handle on.

'You having dinner at your parents'?' Pino asked.

I nodded. 'You?'

'My mom is making something light.'

I looked at him. 'And Detective DellaFlora?'

He looked down and then away. 'She's on duty all day.'

My guess was that he had extended an invitation and she had rejected it. Not ready to meet 'Mom' yet? Seemed like a good guess.

My cell phone vibrated in my pocket. I checked the display. Speaking of mothers...

I ignored the call and shoved my hands in my coat pockets.

'Hell of a time for this to happen,' I said.

'Yeah, well, when you've been a cop for as long as I have, you learn that Holiday don't mean a moratorium on crime. Especially violent ones. If anything, they spike upward.'

'Which means no holiday for you.'

He met my gaze. 'Something like that.'

I bounced a little and looked around, not realizing that I was hoping to see Jake's truck until I didn't see it.

'I guess I better get going,' I said. 'My mother will call 911 if I'm too late for dinner.'

He nodded toward the police turnout and gave me a small smile. 'She wouldn't get very far.'

'You don't know my mother.'

# TWENTY-SEVEN

I felt considerably different about the day by the time I parked outside my parents' house only a couple blocks up from my own place. My mother had called twice more, which meant she must be between preparing dishes and had a little time on her hands.

It also probably meant Dino had already arrived.

Oh, yeah, I remembered that she'd told me she'd invited him. Of course, I'd called the other day to tell her that I'd also invited someone: Eugene. And by the looks of the twenty-year-old gold Cadillac parked crookedly right in front of the house, he was already there.

Which is probably why my mother was calling me.

I smiled to myself, trying to shake off the residue that remained from the morning's action. But the thought that I was familiar with the name of the girl wouldn't leave me, and wouldn't until I figured out how I knew her.

Of course, it could be any one of a number of ways. We had clients coming in and out of the agency all the time. And then there were old classmates, kids from the neighborhood, even people I'd seen on the news.

It could be anything.

I took a deep breath and opened the front door to my parents' house, prepared for both the best and the worst.

And that's exactly what I got.

All in all, it wasn't a bad beginning and everyone appeared to be in good spirits, despite the fact that tomorrow was the day of Roula's funeral. My mother couldn't stop staring at Eugene whose non-stop energy, it seemed, extended to his down time and holidays. He stood next to my grandfather's and father's chairs and cheered on the Jets, clapping his hands loudly at good play and making his displeasure known when it wasn't.

'Now ain't that some shit?' he said to my grandfather, who grinned at him while my father grimaced.

Thankfully, Eugene didn't seem to notice anything awry.

I could make out Efi's footsteps upstairs. Apparently her boyfriend would be coming for dessert later. My brother Kosmos sat on the couch reading instead of watching the game. And two of Grandpa Kosmos' oldest friends – also widowers – were seated on folding chairs closer to him, both appearing happy to be included in the day's festivities.

Dino had yet to arrive. And I wasn't sure how I felt about that.

I stretched the good linen over the dining room table, surprised when my mother grasped my arm and pulled me into the kitchen, pulling the door closed behind us.

'What?' I asked.

'You didn't tell me he was black.'

I smiled. No, I hadn't. On purpose. The expression on her face now was worth the price of admission.

'And that's important ... how?' I asked.

'It's important because...'

I wasn't helping her out on this one.

Of course, I had known what her reaction was going to be. While Astoria was racially and ethnically diverse, the Greeks tended to stick pretty much to themselves. Hell, there were enough of them on Long Island that they could go their entire lives without making a non-Greek friend. And even though one of Thalia's best friends had been Bangladeshi, Mrs Kapoor hadn't ever come to holiday dinners. My mother had said it was because of their religious differences. I'd always secretly wondered if she'd ever invited her.

Then again, Mrs Kapoor had never invited us to any of her feasts, either, so I couldn't be too hard on my mom.

'Well,' Thalia said. 'I don't know what kind of food he eats.'

I suppressed an eye roll. 'He eats the same food we do, Mama.'

She smiled, and then laughed, finally seeing the humor in the situation. 'That was kind of stupid, wasn't it?'

'Yeah, I'd say on the dumbest things ever said scale, you rated a solid "four".'

'And that's from...?'

'One to ten. Ten being the dumbest.'

'You won't tell him?'

'Of course I won't.' I drifted over to the stove and began lifting lids, Yiayia safely at the sink cleaning some type of vegetable or other.

The wooden spoon stung my wrist. 'Ow.'

OK, I thought she'd been safely at the sink. I should have known better.

'So...' my mother said at my other elbow, stirring something that didn't appear to need stirring with another wooden spoon. I managed to pop a *keftedaki* – a small, Greek meatball – into my mouth without incident. 'What happened with Dino?'

I nearly choked. Thalia soundly patted me on the back until I could breathe again.

'What do you mean, what happened?'

Thalia returned her attention to the pan. 'I just noticed that he's not here yet. I thought that maybe—'

This time I did give an eye roll. 'You thought maybe I had something to do with that?'

She shrugged again.

'So you know about our date then,' I said.

She smiled at me, unable to conceal her delight. 'I know.'

'Yeah, well, do you also know that I don't have any plans to go on a date with him again anytime soon?'

I hated to see the smile vanish, but I was starting to itch at the attention too many people paid to my love life.

I reached for another *keftedaki* and Yiayia whacked my hand again.

'Here,' my mother said, holding out a relish tray.

I happily popped a black Kalamata olive into my mouth and then accepted the tray.

'Take it out to the guys.'

'Are you sure they'll eat it?'

She gave me a warning glance. I laughed and walked out to the other room.

'Oh, and answer the door if anyone comes!' she called after me.

Unnecessarily, because I knew that if anyone came to the door, no one else would answer; they'd all sit transfixed, or with their nose in a book, as if I was the only one with ears.

Well, except maybe for Eugene. Probably he would answer the door. And probably he would scare away whoever was on the other side, make them think they had the wrong address.

I smiled as I held the tray in front of him.

He held up his hands. 'Oh, no. My mama didn't raise no fool. First pickings always goes to the man of the house.'

We both looked at my father who also raised his hands. 'In our house, guests eat first.'

Eugene smiled and rocked back on to his heels. 'Thank you. You don't have to tell this guest twice. This looks good!'

His hand hovered over the tray and then he took a *dolmathaki* – a stuffed grape leaf – and munched on it. I then offered my brother something and placed the tray on the table that had been positioned in front of the men's chairs. They seemed to hesitate for a moment and then all leapt on the tray at once.

I stood next to Eugene for a few moments, enjoying a few plays of the game, before turning to finish setting the table. I got two steps before the doorbell rang.

As I expected, no one but Eugene moved to answer it.

'That's all right,' I told him. 'I've got it.'

He gave me a thumbs up and shouted at the referees on the television.

I shook my head.

Of course, I knew there was only one thing missing from the gathering; and somewhere in the back of my mind I was actually looking forward to seeing him. But for reasons I was incapable of exploring just then, being face-to-face with Dino always did interesting things to my stomach.

'Hi,' he said, grinning.

'Hi.'

That's it. Nothing more. No Happy Thanksgiving. Or 'nice to see you.' All I could utter was the one word.

'Can I come in?'

It took me a moment to register his words. 'Oh. Oh!' I stood back from the door and allowed him entrance, trying not to take a deep breath of his tangy cologne but failing. I just hoped my leaning in wasn't too obvious to anyone watching.

He turned just inside and we nearly bumped noses, both laughing awkwardly ... until I looked into his eyes.

Damn.

'I, um, brought this,' he said, his gaze attaching to my mouth. I involuntarily licked my lips, watching his pupils widen.

'Dino!'

My mother. Of course.

I stepped back and took the box I just now realized he held. I couldn't resist opening it. A chocolate torte.

Our gazes met again, and I got the significance of his bringing the same thing that had culminated in our first tryst on top of my kitchen table together eating said torte off of each other.

'Thank you,' I whispered.

My mother advanced on him, hugging him and kissing him loudly, saying the general *'Chronia Polla.'*

I ducked out of the way and headed for the kitchen. Eugene leaned in closer to me as I passed.

'Hey, man, is that my competition?'

I laughed so loudly even my brother looked up from his book.

Then I cleared my throat, sure from Eugene's grin that he was joking, and continued on to the kitchen.

Roughly a half hour later, everyone was seated at the table, which bulged with an abundance of food, both Greek and American; everything I'd spent what seemed like forever going without and had begun to dream about. There was the requisite turkey that sat in front of my father so he could carve it. Closer to me was a crown of veal cutlets with wild rice in the middle. *Tiropites* and spanakopita overflowed serving plates, and mashed potatoes, stuffing and fresh artichokes smothered in a Greek yogurt sauce along with at least a dozen other offerings that would fill my refrigerator for at least the next week.

Thank God!

Of course, my mother had made sure I was well taken care of in the company department. Where normally I was seated between my sister and brother, now I had Dino at my left elbow, Eugene at my right. With both of them trying to get my attention: Eugene with overt questions and comments about how delicious everything looked and how he hadn't had a home-cooked meal since he couldn't remember when; Dino with his thigh pressing against mine so that my knee jerked, causing the silverware on the table to clatter and my grandfather to reach for his squat wine glass to steady it.

Eugene cleared his throat loudly.

Everyone looked at him.

'If you don't mind, I'd like to lead grace,' he said just as Yiayia and my Grandpa Kosmos began their traditional, silent Greek Orthodox signing of the cross. 'My way of showing my respect to you and your family for inviting me for this meal.'

'Grace?' my mother repeated.

'The prayer,' I said quietly.

'The prayer ... oh, yes! Right.'

Eugene took my hand, then reached for my sister's to his right, bowing his head and waiting as everyone else got with the program and did the same.

'Dearly beloved, we are gathered here...'

Out of the corner of my eye I watched him grimace.

'Sorry ... wrong prayer. Ain't nobody getting married.'

My knee hit the underside of the table again and I smothered a groan of pain.

'Lord, bless this awesome family for sharing your bounty with me on this fine and important day...'

I looked at everyone from under my lashes.

'I know that I haven't always been the best person I can be, but these good people, your people, make me believe there's hope that tomorrow's a better day...'

Were my mother's eyes watering?

'Things have been tough in the city lately, and we've all been experiencing some great pain...'

I looked at him again.

'But we take peace in knowing that it's all part of your plan, Good Lord in heaven...'

A sniffle from somewhere but I couldn't pinpoint exactly where.

'So, thank you.'

Eugene released my hand and rubbed his own together. 'Now, you going to carve that bad boy, or should I just pull off a piece?'

# TWENTY-EIGHT

Eugene's enthusiasm helped set the upbeat tone for the meal. There was more laughter than I expected, and zeal for the food that was indeed as delicious as my mother had ever made. The original hurry to dig in was followed by a mellow picking an hour later, helped by a slight wine buzz.

Eugene sat back and patted his neon green and white polyester covered belly, which was indeed noticeably rounder than it had been when he arrived. Of course, he was also puffing it out.

'I am fuller than that stuffed turkey over there,' he moaned. 'I couldn't possibly eat another bite.'

My mother rose slightly from her chair and picked up serving platters one by one, sliding even more food on to his plate. 'Eat, eat! You're too skinny.'

I smiled to myself as I tried to ignore that Dino's leg had remained flush against mine throughout the entire meal, making it almost impossible to concentrate. At one point, he'd even reached his hand underneath and run his fingers up from my knee until I gasped.

Grandpa Kosmos' eyes sparkled knowingly across from me and I couldn't help but smile when normally I would have grimaced.

The wine, I surmised, coupled with the relaxed and enjoyable atmosphere at the table.

'So, are you guys going shopping tomorrow?' Efi asked from the other side of Eugene, her gaze on my mother.

I watched as the color drained from Thalia's face and said to my sister, 'The ... funeral is tomorrow.'

I'd been hoping to get through the day without mention of that; tomorrow would come soon enough and we all needed the break from the reality of the tragic situation. Me, especially, considering what I'd seen just that morning.

'Oh. Right,' Efi said, not looking apologetic in the least. Which was par for the course for my sister. The way she'd view it is that we always went shopping on Black Friday, another uniquely American tradition the Greeks had wholeheartedly adopted.

'But that's not going to take the entire day, surely,' Efi added, this time earning a stare from me.

'What?' she asked. 'I just wanted to say I wouldn't be going. Jeremy's taking me to see *Wicked* on Broadway tomorrow.'

'You're not going to the funeral?'

I barely caught my sister's eye roll as she went on to say that she hadn't even known the girl and that while, yeah, it was awful what had happened to her, she didn't see why she should cancel plans that had been weeks in the making.

Wicked...

My mind caught on the name of the play. Well,

not so much the name as the mention of a play and Broadway, and refused to budge.

Then I realized why.

I got up so quickly from the table, I startled everyone.

'Pardon me...'

I paced back and forth in the kitchen, my cell phone pressed to my ear as I waited for Pino to answer.

My call went through to his voicemail.

'Shit.'

I disconnected and pressed redial, doing this two additional times before he finally picked up.

'What is it, Metro?' he muttered, and I thought he was trying to be quiet.

'It just occurred to me why the dead girl's name is familiar to me,' I said.

'Right now I have bigger fish to fry.'

I squinted and stopped pacing. Bigger fish? What was bigger than possibly solving a murder case?

'Another missing girl showed up,' he said.

'What?' I barely breathed aloud. 'Two bodies in one day?'

'No. This one's alive.'

I'd left Eugene happily with my family, running into Efi's boyfriend, Jeremy, on my way out of the house; but the image that stayed with me was Dino's questioning gaze. I felt bad about leaving him hanging like that, and while the news I had was good – relatively speaking – I didn't want to distract the table from their meal.

'I'll be back in an hour,' I'd said.

'Sofie!' my mother objected.

I'd stopped near her and bent to kiss her cheek. 'Sorry. It can't be helped.'

I left the room quickly to bypass further questions and ten minutes later was at Elmhurst Hospital. Unfortunately I wasn't the first one there.

I grimaced at the throng of media, the television news crews the most obtrusive, where they crowded on Broadway, blocking traffic. A squad car bleated its siren, apparently just arriving to try to control the situation.

Great. How long ago had this happened? I hadn't thought to ask Pino during our call. I merely asked where the girl was and left the house.

I skated past the throng, murmuring, 'Excuse me,' and gained entrance without problem. Once inside, I flipped open my phone and dialed Pino again.

'Which floor?'

'Third.'

I closed it again, heading for the elevators. Since it appeared reporters weren't limited to taking over the outside, but were also hassling hospital personnel, I easily got inside the elevator and punched the button for the third floor, nodding at a young doctor in scrubs that entered after me, pressing the button for the fourth.

The doors opened and I exited, looking up and down the hall for what I was sure would be a conference of uniformed officers.

All I saw was Pino.

I started in his direction.

'Miss, you can't go down there!' a nurse called from behind a counter.

I ignored her.

'What's up?' I asked Pino before he saw me.

He turned, his frown apparent. 'What are you doing here, Metro?'

'Where would you have me be?'

'At home enjoying Thanksgiving dinner.'

I looked around him at the closed door to a room, seeing through the narrow glass the form of a sleeping Allyson Piszchala.

'What have you got?' I asked.

He'd already told me that Allyson had been identified by her mother and that she was one of the twins that had come up missing. Her sister Laylyn was still unaccounted for.

'What do you mean what have I got? I got nothing.'

I stared at him.

'If you'd have stayed on the phone long enough, I could have explained that.' He drew in a deep breath and let it out. 'Hell, if I'd known you'd come down here, I would have called you back to tell you.'

I looked around. 'Where's Gina?'

'Gone.'

'Christ, when did all this happen?'

'Call came in right after you left the crime scene this morning.'

A good three hours.

'So what didn't you have a chance to tell me?'

'That she was discovered a victim of a hit and

run on Queens Boulevard in Forest Hills. She was out cold and still is.'

'Hit and run?' Queens Boulevard was better known as the Boulevard of Death by natives. The multi-lane street was a main artery and a great many Long Islanders used it daily.

'Mmm. Eye witness said she was wandering in the street, trying to flag cars down ... . He said he couldn't be sure, but he thought she was crying for help.'

I absently rubbed the bridge of my nose, staring at the still figure in the hospital room. 'What's the prognosis?'

'Broken collar bone, fractured hip, multiple head contusions.'

'When does the doctor say she might regain consciousness?'

'That's just it. He says there's no clear reason for her to be comatose, that it may be a psychosomatic condition. So she may come around in ten minutes or never.'

'Well, that can't be good.'

'Tell me about it.' He started to hike up the waist of his pants, caught himself, and then put his hands on his hips instead. 'Gina just went to get us some sandwiches.'

The side of my mouth twitched in the beginnings of a smile. 'Hoping to be here when she wakes up, huh?'

His eyes shone at me in acknowledgement, but he said no more.

I held up my hands. 'I guess I'll just be on my way then.'

I wished him a Happy Thanksgiving and

turned toward the elevator.

'Oh,' I said, swiveling back around even as I walked backward. 'What was she dressed in when she was found?'

'I was wondering if you were going to ask.' He smiled. 'A green hospital gown...' We both watched as a patient was aided back to a nearby room by a nurse. 'Not unlike those found here.'

'And, had she been ... drained?'

'Two puncture wounds found in the same place as the other victims. But while the doc says she's down a few pints, she was nowhere near drained.'

'Drugged?'

'Still waiting on tox reports, but the doctor says it doesn't appear so. It does look like she was restrained though. Ligature marks on her wrists and ankles.'

I'd stopped moving and was actively digesting the information. 'When will the results be in?'

'We've put a rush on them, but it is Thanksgiving.'

'OK. I'll call you tomorrow.'

'Sof...'

I smiled and waved. 'Don't work too hard!'

'Wait a minute: what's the info on this morning's victim you wanted to share with me?'

That made me hesitate. Did I tell him? And what? Risk looking like an idiot?

'Oh, that,' I said, not breaking my stride. 'I'll share it once you've shared the toxicology results.'

He said something I couldn't make out and I smiled.

At this point, I had something else in mind when it came to the latest victim and the one I suspected was responsible for her death.

As the elevator doors closed on me, I swallowed hard; the cubicle gave me the uncomfortable sensation of being closed in a coffin. I could only hope that what I had in mind wouldn't end up with me in one.

# TWENTY-NINE

As I stood outside Ivan Romanoff's house just up the street from my parents' place, I questioned my sanity. Probably I should have told Pino what I knew, no matter how bizarre it sounded. Because right now, I didn't like the thought that it was just after dark, and I was alone.

Probably I should just go back to my parents' house where they were likely even now having dessert.

I thought of that yummy chocolate torte that Dino had brought, along with yummy Dino himself, and thought that was a very good idea. Much better than the one I was currently contemplating.

Contemplating? I was standing on the guy's porch. Couldn't get much more decisive than that.

Of course, there was nothing to stop me from climbing back down those stairs and getting back into my car. Nothing at all. I hadn't knocked. Besides, I wasn't even sure the old vampire ... I mean man, was back from whatever trip he'd taken yet anyway.

Which was a good reason to go ahead and knock. When no one answered, I could soothe myself with the knowledge that I'd tried.

A particularly frigid gust of wind blew through me as I lifted my hand and knocked, so lightly that not even I heard it, much less anyone who might be inside.

Unable to excuse myself, I knocked again, this time louder than I anticipated. Knocks like that one usually came complete with, 'Open up! It's the police!'

I shuddered and wrapped my leather jacket a little more tightly around my body.

I released the breath I hadn't been aware I was holding. There. See. That wasn't so hard, was it? Now I could go on about my business without feeling guilty about not doing something about my realization—

The door hinges squeaked.

Shit!

'Sofie? Is that you?'

Ivan Romanoff.

'Um, yes,' I said. 'Hi.'

The screen door groaned outward. 'Please, please. Do come in.'

I looked behind me. The street was empty, not a solitary person in sight. No one knew I was there or where I had gone.

I saw Lucille parked right out front and relaxed slightly even as another cold wind gust seemed to propel me directly inside the house.

'Thank you,' I said, shivering at the sudden warmth while he closed the door after me. 'I wasn't sure if you'd returned from your trip yet.'

He was dressed in simple dark slacks, a starched white shirt and a green and black checked sweater vest. 'Yes, I returned early this morning, yes.'

'Did you have a good trip?'

Stupid question. Not because his trip couldn't have been bad, but because for some reason I got the impression that he didn't travel by plane, train or automobile, despite the old Lincoln out front.

'It was ... fruitful, yes. Thank you for asking.'

I stuffed my hands deep into my jacket pockets and looked around. The place hadn't changed much from the last time I'd seen it. All the furniture looked to be circa 1955, no personal mementos anywhere. Somewhere a clock ticked. I figured that was probably the most important piece in the entire house. Vital for a vampire to be aware of the hour at all times.

'I'm glad,' I said absently. 'I wasn't sure if you celebrated Thanksgiving...' I cringed away from the mental image of Wendy Newberger's body in the middle of a dining table rather than the traditional turkey. 'But I wanted to wish you a happy holiday.'

His smile was indulgent. 'Yes, yes. Thank you.'

'Do you?'

'Pardon me?'

'Do you celebrate the holiday?'

'I am American, no? So I celebrate it.'

'With family?'

I'd always wondered whether the link between him and Vlad was a real blood link ... or a real blood link.

I scrunched up my face, beyond even making

sense to myself at this point.

'With family, yes.'

If I was hoping he'd offer more, I was sadly mistaken.

'And Vlad? Did he join in the festivities?'

'My nephew? No. He stayed behind to look after business.' He clasped his hands behind his back. 'But you already know this. I told you myself.'

'Yes. Of course you did.'

'Is something the matter? Something you're reluctant to discuss with me?' He looked me over. 'You have not come again to try to return my money, have you?'

No, but I should have thought of that. 'No, I...'

Go on, spit it out.

'Look, Mr Romanoff, I don't want to ruin your holiday, but there's this concern I have.'

'Go on.'

'Well, do you remember the other night when you stopped by the agency?'

'Of course. It was not that long ago.'

'Do you recall the girl your nephew was with?'

'Yes. Becoming a young woman.'

'Not any more.'

'I'm not sure I understand.'

'That woman was found dead. This morning.'

'Oh.' He looked crestfallen. 'I am very sorry to hear that. She was so full of life.'

And of blood.

At least until Vlad got a hold of her.

I tilted my head until I'd regained his attention after it wandered to the floor. 'Do you remember what I said when you originally tried to hire me, Mr Romanoff?'

'Please. Refresh my memory.'

'I asked if the crimes might have ... could have ... if it were plausible that they were committed by someone within your ... family...'

Why was I having such a hard time getting to the point?

At any rate, there it was. Finally.

'Yes. I do recall your suggesting that.'

'And do you remember your answer?'

'Of course. It is the same one I have now.'

'That no one within your family could be responsible.'

'Yes. Of course.'

I absently wondered where the button was to get him to respond in another way.

'And if I told you I'm convinced that someone is responsible?'

He didn't answer for a long moment. 'Then I would be very interested in hearing that.'

I bet.

'Look, Mr Romanoff, if we're going to get anywhere here, then you're going to have to be honest with me.'

'I am honest with you always, Miss Metropolis. It pains me to think you believe otherwise.'

'The police already think that Wendy Newberger's murder was a copycat.'

'So it is not linked with the others then?'

'No. It doesn't appear so.'

'And your interest in this is...'

'My interest in this is that your nephew, Vlad,

killed the girl.'

His expression was a cross between disbelief and anger. 'And you've come to this conclusion how, exactly?'

'Isn't the fact that she was with your nephew the night she was killed enough?'

'You'll have to excuse me, but no. It is not enough.'

'So you're telling me it's a coincidence that someone in your family just happened to be dating a murder victim – who had also been drained of blood, by the way – the night she was killed ... especially in light of the suspicion that has been thrown your way regarding the other killings.'

'I thought you said this young woman's unfortunate demise was unlike the others...'

'Yes.'

'The circumstances sound similar to me.'

'Not similar enough.'

'I see.'

I heard a sound and my scalp tingled as if I was being watched.

'Are you alone, Mr Romanoff?'

Christ. You'd think that should have been the first question I asked before even setting foot in the door.

'No, indeed, I am not. My nephew is in the next room.'

As if on cue, Vlad walked around the corner, his grin wide and extra creepy.

I nearly fainted dead away.

# THIRTY

Vlad stepped up to stand next to his uncle, as if claiming first rights, setting me back on my heels, as well as compelling me to gauge the distance between me and the door even as my palm itched to hold my Glock.

'Good evening, Sofie,' he said in that way that unnerved me before, but now downright terrified me. 'Would you care for something to drink? Perhaps something to ... warm you?'

I squinted at him. 'Are you serious?'

His smile was decidedly mocking. 'Quite.'

'No.'

Ivan looked concerned. 'Perhaps there is something I'm not understanding here,' he said. 'I'm sensing all is not right between the two of you.'

'You sense correctly,' I agreed.

He looked at Vlad. 'You assured me all was well while I was away.'

'And I stand by that statement.'

I raised my brows. 'Oh? Did you share your need to visit my home with your goons in tow?'

'Goons?'

'Miss Metropolis is mistaken, Uncle. I merely stopped by as a courtesy call.'

'With two of your bodyguards.'

'I did not know you had bodyguards.'

'They're my friends,' Vlad tried to clarify.

'Yes, well-paid friends,' I said. 'And you didn't stop by for a courtesy call; you visited me to warn me away from my investigation of you.'

Ivan blinked at me. 'You are investigating my nephew?'

Oops.

I had to get a handle on that emotion thing. Got me into more trouble, I swear.

'Not investigating, per se...' I cleared my throat. 'Merely exploring all angles.'

'But how is investigating my nephew going to stop the police from believing I am not responsible either directly or indirectly for these gruesome murders?'

How, indeed?

'Actually, Mr Romanoff, I believe that thanks to the efforts of your nephew here, that job is now doubly difficult. I have not spoken to the police about my suspicions of Vlad's involvement in Wendy Newberger's murder, but if you insist on passivity, I will be forced to...'

Was it me or had the room just gotten noticeably colder?

The lights flickered and I gasped, certain I'd seen a flash of Vlad's teeth.

'I, um, think I'd better be going,' I said quietly, backing toward the door. 'I've said my piece. I leave the rest up to you.' I swallowed with difficulty. Probably because my throat was too busy being afraid of having Vlad's teeth buried in it.

'I will be contacting you tomorrow to learn of your decision.'

'Very well,' Ivan said, appearing suddenly at my side and causing me to jump. I was relieved when he reached around me to open the door. 'Thank you for stopping by.'

I didn't buy the common courtesy for a minute, but I wasn't going to look this particular gift vampire in the mouth. I just needed to get out of there ... now!

I stepped out on to the porch, shuddering from the wind and cold. I turned to say a final good night, but the door was already closed.

OK. I'd never known Vladimir to be rude.

Flap ... flap...

I ducked away from the sudden sound even though I still stood on the porch, the roof above me.

The wind...

Flap ... flap...

Jiminy Christmas!

I reached for my Glock, sliding it out and holding it at the ready. Oh, I knew that bullets weren't any good against vampires ... but when they were in bat form, a round could do a helluva lot more damage than when they were in human shape.

Of course, the challenge lay in being able to hit such a small, moving target. Especially since I still had trouble hitting a large, stationary one.

OK...

Vladimir. It had to be. I had no idea how he had gotten outside without my seeing him, but it had to be him.

Or one of his goons...

Neither choice emerged any better than the

other.

I continued to hold the gun out with my right hand and reached for my cell phone with the other. Scrolling through my numbers, I pressed one and put the phone to my ear.

'Having trouble, Sof?' Jake's voice instantly filled my senses.

'You could say that. You still following me?'

'Yup.'

I looked around up and down the street and caught where he flicked his lights on and off a couple of doors up.

'Good.'

I closed the phone and put it away, and then slid my Glock back into its holster. For whatever godforsaken reason, I was convinced that nothing could happen so long as Jake was watching out after me.

Still, I couldn't have moved faster toward my car, trying like hell to ignore the flapping of wings all around me...

I was never so glad to see the sun rise on Friday morning. You never realize the importance of something so mundane that you take for granted every day until you have a murderous vampire flapping his bat wings above you. Of course, I was still kicking myself for thinking I could accomplish anything on my own in that regard. Probably I would have been better passing the information on to Pino and letting him deal with it.

But no. I had to go over to Romanoff's myself and suggest he might want to do some in-house cleaning ... and possibly not only put myself on Vlad's next victim list, but bump myself right up to the top spot.

At the very least, Pino could have questioned him. He was a real man with a real residence, even if it was in Manhattan. Vlad need never know who had let the police know about his connection to the woman. I'm sure others had seen the two out together. There was even the possibility that Wendy Newberger had told a friend or two, and they could have contacted the police once the news of her murder hit the newspapers.

Right...

Wasn't I the one who had someone following him? Wasn't I the one who'd shown up at his apartment in the middle of the night and sipped cognac one minute, and woken up in her cold car with Jake Porter the next?

Of course, he could have just killed me then...

But then he hadn't killed her yet...

Boy oh boy, what kind of trouble had I gotten myself into this time?

At any rate, I was glad that Jake was good to his word. Not only had he been parked outside my apartment building when I got up (did the guy never sleep? Then again, I could do with a nice night of uninterrupted, peaceful sleep myself), he was outside the agency now, leaning against his truck and smoking a butt.

Of course, I didn't want to think about what happened afterward when I'd finally returned to my parents' house. Dessert had long since been served and everyone but Eugene had left; the shoulder my mother had given me had been so cold that I'd wanted to put my coat back on.

'Dino left,' she'd told me.

'I see.'

'He was disappointed.'

'Did he say that?'

'No. I'm saying that.'

'It couldn't be helped.'

She'd thawed slightly then. 'Did you find Roula's killer?'

'Not yet.'

'Then it could have been helped.'

I'd shared the news on the girl that had escaped, but she hadn't seemed as thrilled as I'd thought she'd be. Instead, she'd pointed out that since she'd been unconscious anyway, it could have waited another day and I could have remained with the family.

I'd given her an eye roll and fully expected to feel the paper she'd pretended to read against the side of my head.

I could laugh about it now, but I hadn't been as amused then.

Of course, anything short of a marriage announcement would probably have left her in the same mood.

So I'd woken Eugene up from where he'd fallen asleep on the couch, my father and grandfather also sawing some major logs in their nearby recliners, and I'd left ... without food.

Following a sleepless night that left me alternately shifting restlessly in bed, and pacing to the windows to look for flapping shadows and Jake's truck – at some point even Muffy had grown weary of my fidgeting and left the bed to take up residence on his Barcalounger – I came into the agency early to find out what I was missing to link everything together.

At around nine, I'd called Pete to ask him to come in, but thankfully he'd already been on the way. He'd seen the news on the girl who'd gotten away and was eager to learn more.

I had to give it my cousin; on a day when others might complain about coming in to work, he was doing so voluntarily.

'Sofie?'

I looked over my shoulder at where the cousin in question sat with his chair turned toward the white board. Only I'd turned it to the cork side where I'd put up a map of King and Queens counties a couple of days ago.

'You OK?' he asked.

I rubbed my forehead with the heel of my hand. 'Yeah. Sorry. Operating on little sleep, I'm afraid.'

He got up and took the container of flag tacks from me. 'Here, let me do this. You go sit down. Before you fall down.'

'Actually, I need another frappé. You want one?'

He shook his head. 'In the winter I prefer my coffee hot.'

'Nes, then?'

He smiled. 'Love one.'

I traded the brightness of the office for the dimness of the front. I'd switched on all the lights earlier, but after a customer had come knocking at around ten looking to retain us for a cheating spouse case, I'd shut them off lest the next visitor be a missing pet case.

There was enough light coming in from the street despite it being darkly overcast to make my way around heating up some water for Pete's cup of Nescafé and making my frappé. As I shook my sealed travel cup I stepped toward the windows. Jake's truck was no longer parked across the street. I frowned. Guess he figured I no longer needed his help.

But how would he know that unless he knew about the vampires?

'Sof?'

I jumped at the sound of Pete's voice behind me.

'Boy, you really must be tired.' He chuckled and I glared at him.

'Yeah, well, just be happy I didn't spill my frappé, or else you'd be in real trouble.'

He held up his hands. 'Sorry. Didn't mean to scare you.'

But I got the distinct impression that he was glad he had.

'Where was the girl yesterday morning found?'

I told him.

'But don't add her.'

'Why?'

I vigorously shook my cup to work up the froth to a smooth cream. 'Trust me. It's a copy-cat.'

'You can't know that.'

'I can and I do.'

I stepped over to take his water off the single

burner and then handed him his cup, the Nescafé and sugar already measured out. 'Here. Make yourself useful and hit your own coffee.'

By hit I meant to vigorously stir the mixture with a bit of water and the spoon, making sure to 'hit' it against the side. You knew it was ready for the water when it turned a smooth, light shade with no specks of coffee crystals visible. I reached into the refrigerator and took out the can of condensed milk there.

'Are you going to tell me how you know the last victim was a copycat?'

'Nope.'

He chuckled.

From inside the office my cell phone rang. I sighed, deciding to let it roll over to voicemail.

'Trust me, you really don't want to know. But if it helps, you can call Pino and he can confirm my suspicions.'

'That's OK. I'll pass. But I still think we should add her. Maybe with a different colored flag.'

I sighed as I opened the travel cup, added ice-cold water and milk and then stirred the frappé with a straw. 'Fine.'

Respective coffees ready, we walked back into the office and spent the next half hour trying to find a pattern in the pins on the map. The biggest clue was the location of Allyson's hit and run on Queens Boulevard in Forest Hills. The problem there was that it was such a highly populated residential area, she could have been kept anywhere. Any door-to-door knocking would yield nothing but a pair of aching feet.

I squinted at the board from my seat behind the desk.

'Wait. Where does Allyson live?'

Pete reached for the file on the desk between us – a file I could have as easily picked up – and opened it.

'Forest Hills.'

I got up and went to stand in front of the map, my finger on the location she'd been found on the north side of the road traveling west.

'Address?'

He read it. 'It's a house. She and her sister lived ... live with their parents.'

The house was still a good mile up the road from where she'd been found.

Was it possible she'd been trying to walk the distance? In this cold? In nothing but a hospital gown?

I traced a line back down the Boulevard of Death. How long could she have withstood the journey? You had to take into consideration that she was probably pretty pumped with adrenalin from her escape, and likely more than a little confused after her ordeal. A lot going on there emotionally.

'What are you thinking?'

'Huh?' I glanced over my shoulder at my cousin. 'I'm thinking that we should be looking somewhere around ... here.'

'And your reasoning?'

I told him.

'A guesstimate at best,' he said.

'You're right. But at this point, a guesstimate is better than a big, fat zero. I should call Pino and find out where they're looking.'

I picked up my cell phone, but before I could press the call button, it rang.

Pete chuckled yet again when I started. I glared at him.

My mother, of course.

I was ready to press the button to send her call to voicemail when it hit me: Roula's funeral was today and I'd promised to go with her.

Shit.

After yesterday, I didn't dare renege. Not if I hoped ever to see a plate of leftovers again.

As I took the call I wondered whether maybe I could talk her into putting together a plate or two or three for me to take home when I picked her up.

'Hi, Mom,' I greeted in my sweetest daughter voice. 'I was just thinking I should leave the agency now. Pick you up in an hour?'

'Make it a half hour.'

'Forty-five minutes.'

'Fine.'

'Oh, and Mom? Do me a favor and wrap up some of those leftovers for me.'

# THIRTY-ONE

It occurred to me as I went through the funeral motions with my mother that many of the attendees weren't so much grieving the loss of a young woman most of them had never known, but rather mortality as a whole. I mean, we were all going to die. It was just a matter of when and where and the circumstances. I'd come close enough to finalizing all three of those details over the past six months that I could identify with their fear.

Let's face it, we usually didn't think about dying on a daily basis. Which was a good thing, or else we might not know how to smile. Then again, perhaps we would appreciate the value of that simple gesture more than we normally did.

I frowned. Probably I just needed a good night's sleep.

'You liked Dino in the beginning, no?'

I blinked at where my mother sat in the car next to me, nearly forgetting for a moment that I was dropping her off after a particularly somber service, that was probably made doubly so when you factored in my exhaustion quotient.

'What?'

'Dino,' she repeated. 'You—'

I raised my hand, wishing we were already at the house instead of five minutes away. My mother could do a lot of damage in five minutes. 'I heard what you said; I just wish you wouldn't.'

She shifted in her seat and rearranged the straps of her purse in her lap. 'I'm merely pointing out that long before you knew of my matchmaking attempts, you were attracted to him, that's all.'

'Sure it is.'

'There's nothing wrong with a mother wanting to see her daughter happy.'

I ground my back teeth together. 'I am happy.'

The contradiction wasn't lost on me as I forced myself to relax.

'He's a good boy.'

I nodded. 'On that, we can agree.'

He was a very good boy. And not just in the traditional sense. He was a good chef, and good in bed and good in every way that counted.

But there was no way I was telling Thalia that. Especially about the bed part.

'Then what's the problem?'

'The problem is that you both want me to get married tomorrow,' I said.

She nearly turned completely in her seat to face me. I knew immediately that I'd made a big mistake. Huge. Monumental.

I gnashed my teeth together again. Two more minutes. I couldn't have kept my mouth shut for two more minutes.

'He asked you to marry him?'

I'd have been more pissed if she'd looked a little less joyful. 'No, Mom. He didn't propose. Not with a ring on a bended knee. But—'

But, what?

He hadn't proposed.

The realization hit me like an oncoming vehicle. I sat up a little straighter. OK, yes, he'd asked how I felt about marriage and kids. But that was just your normal, run-of-the-mill date stuff, wasn't it?

Of course, it hadn't occurred to me at the time. Truth was, it had been a long, long time since I'd been out on a *date* date. My ex Thomas-the-Toad Chalikis and I had been a couple for ... well, for forever. I couldn't even remember what we'd talked about on our first date, outside his telling me how hot I was, and my liking that he found me hot.

That should have been warning flag Number One.

And that dinner with Dino had been a first date, hadn't it? Never mind that we'd already indulged in hot, sweaty monkey sex – and a lot of it – it was the first time we'd sat face-to-face and conversed like two adults.

I inwardly winced. Of course, I hadn't behaved much like an adult, had I?

I could place part of the blame on Jake; it hadn't helped that he was sitting outside the restaurant at the time. But the fact remained that I'd reacted like a complete imbecile. As if Thalia had been sitting right next to Dino prompting the questions he was asking.

And, I guess, in a way she had been. But his

conversation hadn't come from her; it had come from him. He'd genuinely wanted to know more about me.

And I had soundly thrown it back in his face.

Yikes!

'You know,' my mother said, and I braced myself for whatever boulder-sized pearl of wisdom she was about to drop on my head. 'You should always trust your first instinct. It's been proven that you know everything you need to within the first thirty seconds of meeting someone.'

'I read the book,' I said.

'What?'

'Never mind.' I suppressed an eye roll. Not because she didn't deserve one, but because I connected her words together with ones I'd said the night before.

I'd been facing Ivan Romanoff and asked him if he remembered what I'd told him straight off the bat.

I'd believed the murderer had most certainly come from within his ranks.

And somewhere down the line, I'd deviated from that rationale. Even when it was obvious that at least one murder was directly linked to his nephew.

Who's to say that the copycat hadn't been a red herring? Or perhaps something had happened to her that made her different from the others? A mistake made, but the killer the same?

Could Ivan Romanoff be responsible for all of the killings? Could he be the infamous Bleeder?

'Sofie?'

I didn't answer.

'You missed the turn.'

'I meant to do that,' I said.

She made a face at me. 'Can you do at least one favor for me, please?'

I stared at her, promising nothing.

'Go out with him again when he asks.'

'He's not going to ask.'

'Yes, he is.'

'Great. So you've returned to full match-making mode.'

She reached over and patted my knee. 'Only because this time I know I've got it right.'

After a quick stop at the agency to find Pete long gone, and to pick up a few necessary items, I called Eugene and asked if he could do me a favor. I was happy when he told me that after yesterday, he owed me big time.

I'd considered calling Rosie, but the last time I'd relied on her to do anything with any connection to vampires, she'd bailed on me like a shrieking banshee, leaving me flying solo.

The flying reference made me shudder and I leaned forward to look through the windshield, happy that Lucille's engine was too loud to make out any ominous flapping sounds.

I'd tried calling Pete, but he wasn't picking up his cell. It was Friday, so maybe he had another date.

I sighed. Probably I should be considering another date with Dino, as my mother had suggested, rather than seeing through any part of this stupid idea that had popped into my mind.

So my last resort had been Eugene. Not that I thought he'd be much help, but at least I wouldn't be alone. Besides, he couldn't be any worse than Rosie. Nobody could be worse than that.

I pulled up to the corner Eugene had given me the directions to in Jackson Heights. He was back in full pimp mode, complete with black fedora bearing a neon orange band. He got into the car, careful not to damage the feather.

'You want me to put the top down?' I asked him.

'Girl, you crazy? It's colder than a mother fucker out there.' He gave a little shimmy. 'Hell, ain't much warmer in here. Turn on the heat already.'

'It's on.'

'Then turn it up.'

Between the time I'd originally made the decision and now dusk had started to settle until now it was pitch black out.

Great. Why was it when I made a stupid decision it had to be dark?

'So where we going?' Eugene wanted to know.

He made a sniffing sound as I pulled away from the curb. 'Just driving around,' I said.

'That's it? We ain't going nowhere in particular?' He sniffed again. 'Is that food I smell?'

I gave an eye roll as I pointed Lucille in the direction of Queens Boulevard. 'No.'

But he was already looking in the back seat where my mother had put a bag stacked high with plates of Thanksgiving leftovers.

'Oh, yeah! I ain't had a thing to eat since

lunch. You mind if I have a nibble?'

Since he was already peeling back tinfoil and popping leftover turkey into his mouth, I didn't think it mattered what I said. 'Please, be my guest. Go on ahead.'

'Damn, but your mama's a good cook. Reminds me a lot of my mama, bless her soul.'

He made the sign of a cross with his turkey-covered fingers and then dug in again.

'Ow.'

Since I hadn't hit him, like I wanted, I looked to see what had caused the reaction. He shifted on the seat, reached behind him, and pulled something out.

'What in the hell is this?' he asked.

I took the wooden stake from his hand and stashed it on the floor behind my seat. Rosie would be majorly miffed if she found out I'd borrowed her vampire arsenal. But I figured I was safe until Monday when she returned to work.

I patted the front of my leather jacket, feeling the sharpened pencils I'd stuck in the pocket. At least three times, I'd nearly stabbed myself with them as I shifted gears.

'Nothing.'

Eugene stared at me for a couple of moments and then shrugged, easily satisfied.

'Hell, if all we're doing is riding around, then this should be a piece of cake, shouldn't it?' He looked in the back seat again. 'Speaking of cake, do you have any of that kick-ass chocolate stuff your boyfriend brought you yesterday?'

'No!' I swatted at his hand.

He tsked loudly. 'Damn, girl, you don't have to get physical. I was just aksing.'

'No you were just taking.'

He made a ceremony out of sitting to face forward, careful not to get any of the plate's contents on his orange polyester suit that had to date back to the 70s.

'Excuse the hell all out of a brother and everything...'

He made loud smacking noises as he ate. I shook my head, wondering where in the hell he put all the food he ate.

'Damn, a great big ole orange Slurpee would sure wash this down real nice,' he said.

'I'm not stopping.'

He tsked again and this time I got an eye roll. 'All right, all right. I get it. It's that time of the month. I can roll with that.'

'It is not that time of the month!'

If it were possible to blow somebody's hair back with the power of words alone, I was pretty sure that Eugene's Afro would be flat against his head just then.

I wondered if it was too late to turn the car around and drop him off where I found him.

'Damn, woman. Put a brother's eye out with spittle already.'

I squeezed the steering wheel and concentrated on the street, stretching my neck out as I did so. 'Sorry.'

'It's OK.' He looked around. 'So where we doing this driving around? Maybe I can get some business done, you know, while we're out and about and all.'

'Eugene?'
More smacking noises.
'Eugene?'
'What?!'
'Shut up.'

# THIRTY-TWO

I drove to the location where Allyson Piszchala was struck by a hit-and-run driver on Queens Boulevard, my direction west. Eugene had stayed quiet for all of a minute – probably out of shock – then continued his chatter while he took great pleasure out of eating the turkey in his lap. But now that I'd reached the area of interest, I found it easy to tune him out.

Traffic was unusually heavy, filled with those either returning to the city or leaving it after the holiday, as well as locals doing their level best to make Black Friday as dark as possible. Which meant I got more than my fair share of horns honked at me as I slowed down to take in my surroundings.

After the fifth blast and an angry traveler moving to pass me, Eugene perked up and flipped him the bird.

'Fuck you, mother fucker! Who you think you're messing with? Gonna honk your goddamn horn at me.'

I stifled a laugh, ignoring the other driver who returned the vulgar gesture and looked to be shouting the same thing at us.

'Why you driving so damn slow anyway?' Eugene asked, switching his irritation to me.

'Don't this piece of shit go no faster?'

'Don't call Lucille a piece of shit,' I told him. 'She's a classic.'

'Yeah, classic piece of shit, maybe. Bitch can't even heat a body up properly.'

I sighed, nothing I was seeing jumping out at me. Of course, Allyson could have come from either the north or the south side of the street, which left a lot of ground to cover. I turned on my blinker and took the next right.

'Thank God,' Eugene mumbled.

'I think you've been indulging in a little too much of that green stuff. Just shush and eat your turkey.'

He was only too happy to oblige on the latter part of my request. 'Hey, don't come between a man and his weed.'

I absently wondered how long it was going to take him to polish it off and start on the rest. Probably I should just take him back to his car.

Then again, no. The surrounding neighborhood was darker compared to the brightly lit main drag. Let him eat everything so long as I didn't have to be alone.

'What we looking for? You got an old boyfriend or something that live around here?'

'What?' I squinted at him. 'No.'

'Well, you're looking for something.'

'This is the area I'm thinking that girl who escaped The Bleeder might have been held.'

His eyes widened, the whites overly pronounced against his dark skin. 'No shit.'

'No shit.'

He looked around for something with which to

wipe his hands.

'Glove box,' I told him.

He took out a napkin, his gaze instantly turning to look at the surrounding neighborhood as I made a left and headed back toward Queens Boulevard.

'Who you think doing this fucked up shit, anyway?'

I shrugged. 'I don't know.'

He swung his head toward me. 'You don't think it got anything to do with that bat-turning son-a-bitch you had me following downtown, do you? 'Cause I'm telling you right now, if it do, I want you to let me out at the next corner.'

I looked at him. 'I don't know.'

'Oh, hell no.' He put the empty plate on the floor and wiped imaginary crumbs from the front of his suit.

After the next block, I said, 'Look, odds are stacked way against us finding anything just driving around. I'm sure the police have already been all over here, doing the same thing we are.'

He appeared to relax somewhat. 'But you're hoping different.'

'I'm hoping different,' I agreed.

'Yeah, well, you see anything, you let me know, OK?' He took his cell phone out of his inside jacket pocket. 'I got some calls to make.'

'Thanks,' I muttered.

Not that he heard me. He'd already turned his attention toward talking to whomever he'd dialed first, talking as if I wasn't in the car. And the more I heard, the more I wished I weren't.

After a half an hour of driving up and down

both sides of Queens Boulevard, and listening to a half dozen of Eugene's phone conversations, I was ready to throw in the towel. This was worse than looking for a needle in a haystack; this was akin to seeking a particular spot of blood in a pool of it.

She could have been held anywhere. One of the most innocent of personal residences with a picket fence, to the second floor of an auto parts shop.

If she didn't regain consciousness soon, the guy could easily close up shop and move somewhere else, taking her sister with him.

I was on the south side of the boulevard now, systematically making my way further west. I was reaching the point where it was impossible for her to have made it that long in nothing more than a hospital gown in this cold.

Of course, it would probably have been a better idea to come in the daylight hours, when I could at least see.

Eugene finished his latest conversation.

'Yeah, man, I should be done with this soon. Holler at ya when I'm back home.'

I wondered if the person on the other end knew that 'home' was his car.

'We finished yet?' he asked me as he put his phone back in his pocket.

I drew in a deep breath. 'Yeah.'

'Thank God. My ass is starting to fall asleep.'

I looked at him. 'How in the hell do you handle the long stretches when a cheating spouse is in a motel room?'

'I get out and walk around. Hang with the

motel people. Get something to eat. What? Do you just sit there in the car?'

I just sat there in the car.

I guess that explained why I occasionally had trouble getting into my jeans while he could put away an entire Thanksgiving meal in two bites and remain toothpick thin.

Skinny wasn't a state of mind; it was a way of life.

Yeah, well, apparently I didn't want to be skinny badly enough.

I looked to my left at a stretch of residential properties, some strung with Christmas lights, one family decorating a tree in the front window. I thought of what I'd be doing then if I weren't sitting in the car driving around on some fruitless mission, and realized I, as well, would likely be at my parents', helping my mother prepare for the coming holidays. Or going through what we would have bought that day on our own Black Friday excursion.

I looked to my right at what looked like an abandoned manufacturing facility. The squat building wasn't that large, maybe fifty yards across, and the short parking lot was cracked, shoulder-high dead weeds waving in the cold breeze.

Done. There was nothing left to see—

I stepped on the brakes.

'Jesus Christ, girl, give a guy a warning before you go and do some damn fool thing like that,' Eugene protested, standing his hands against the dashboard.

I barely heard him as my heart beat heavily in

my chest.

An old white van was parked to the side of the abandoned building. I made out what looked like faded writing on the side. My gut feeling told me it would spell out 'Flow...'

'What? What you see?'

Eugene looked around and then leaned forward to stare upward through the windshield.

I slid my arm across the top of his seat and backed up to an empty parking spot. Only it wasn't really empty, it was somebody's driveway.

Damn.

I parked there anyway and pulled up the emergency brake.

'Stay here. If you see the cops, or if the homeowners complain, move the car.'

'What are you going to do?'

I gestured toward the building. 'I'm going in for a closer look.'

I got out of the car and pulled my leather coat closer, still wearing my funeral best of all black. I reached behind the driver's seat, but couldn't find what I wanted.

'Eugene, can you see if you can find that stake I put back there?' I asked.

'Steak? You got steak in here?'

'S-T-A-K-E.'

He still wasn't following me.

'The piece of wood.'

'Oh. Well why didn't you say so in the first place?'

He found what I was looking for and slapped it into my outstretched hand.

'You, um, ain't expecting to find the thing that will kill, are you?' he asked, pulling his own coat closer even though he was inside the relative warmth of the car.

'If you hear me scream, come rescue me.'

He laughed so hard not even me slamming the door was capable of completely drowning it out.

OK.

I stood in the middle of the street, considering the building in front of me. I experienced a moment of déjà vu. It wasn't all that long ago that I'd found myself outside a landscaper's yard, wondering how I was going to bust the lock to get inside for a look see.

Only there was no lock on the gate here. In fact, there was no gate at all. Only a fence that stretched on either side of the open driveway.

I swallowed hard and then tucked the stake inside my jacket. On one side was my Glock, the other the stake. Then there were all those pencils that were probably going to give me lead poisoning and the bottle of holy water in my jacket pocket. Hey, I figured I was pretty well prepared for whatever came my way.

A strong gust of wind had me ducking.

'What? What is it?' I heard Eugene call from the open window of the car.

I waved to indicate everything was OK.

And hoped I was right.

I took a deep breath and stepped forward, working my way into the shadows, which wasn't too terribly difficult considering there were no lights coming from the abandoned property. I made my way into the lot, dodging the waving weeds and suppressing the sudden desire to sneeze. I rubbed my nose with the back of my hand and ducked off to the left, in the direction I'd seen the van.

Movement.

Christ!

With no options available to me short of flattening myself on the cold cement, I froze, not daring to breathe. About thirty feet ahead of me, a dark figure was moving something toward the back of the van. I ducked slightly, squinting. Whatever he was hauling, it was heavy.

I snapped upright. Of course it was heavy. It was a body.

I backed up a step, determined to get back to the safety of the car and place a call to Detective DellaFlora. Instead, I dashed forward toward the business front, out of sight of the van owner, and slid my cell from my pocket. I was upwind and hoped that he wouldn't hear my quiet plea to the female detective.

'Whatever you do, don't do anything!' she told me.

She didn't have to worry about that. I wasn't moving a muscle.

I slid the phone back into my pocket just as a door slammed. I jumped, having little doubt it was the van owner.

Great. Now what was I supposed to do?

# THIRTY-THREE

Good crap almighty, he was going to leave.

And just then I couldn't think of anything to do about that but stand by and let him.

Hey, I'd learned my lesson with the murderous landscaper with a thing for wood-chippers. Or at least I thought I had. If that were true, then I wouldn't be standing where I was right now wondering how in the hell I was going to conceal myself so he wouldn't see me and add me to whatever pile of people or bodies or both he had in the back of that van.

I palmed my Glock and looked both ways. The wall I leaned against was flat, no place for me to seek shelter. If he drove past, he was certain to see me.

The van started up.

Shit!

Something swooped low over my head, mussing my hair. At first I thought it was the wind, but where I stood there was none.

Another swoop accompanied by an ominous flap flap.

A woman screamed and I immediately crouched lower, holding my gun out in front of me.

Only it wasn't a woman. It was Eugene.

Apparently he'd wanted to wake up his sleeping ass and had gotten out of the car. I watched as what looked like two crows dive-bombed him, pecking at his hat. He ran back to Lucille, wildly waving his hands. I knew he was packing, but I guess he was too distracted to think to draw his weapon.

Something grabbed at my hair again and I swatted it away.

A bat.

A big, nasty, tattered-wing-flapping bat.

Even as I defended myself, I saw Eugene's hat lift from his head and disappear into the air before dropping down beside him.

He made it to the car, not the passenger's side, but the driver's.

In an effort to fight off my own winged attacker, I moved away from the side of the building and jerked upright. A perfect target for the van's headlights as it backed up and drove toward the street; me directly in its path.

I instinctively pointed the Glock and squeezed off a round, my target not so much the driver, but the van. The bullet hit the windshield dead in the middle. The van swerved to the right, ramming into the fence and driving partially over it.

The bat pulled at my hair and I aimed the gun at it, squeezing off a second round.

It shrieked and dove away, vanishing into the dark night sky.

Good. I hope I hit the sucker.

I was torn between keeping my eyes on the van and its driver and Eugene, until my fearless partner for the night took the decision out of my hands. Suddenly the tires on my Mustang squealed loudly and the car sped down the street, Eugene at the wheel.

I stared, speechless, reminded of the way Rosie had abandoned me a few months earlier.

Only she hadn't taken my car with her.

The van's engine revved. I looked back to find the driver trying to dislodge the front tires from where they were caught on the downed fence. Checking to make sure I had another ammo cartridge in my jacket pocket, I held my gun out in front of me and advanced on him.

'Get out!' I shouted, questioning whether or not I could be heard over the engine. 'Get out of the goddamn van now!'

I thought of everything that had happened over the past two weeks. Of bats flying outside my apartment window, of pale bodies drained of blood, of my vivid nightmares and lack of sleep; and I planted my feet and squared my shoulders, determined to put an end to this once and for all.

A bullet whizzed by my right ear even as all three bats targeted me for attack. I dropped to a crouched position and wondered if it were physically possible for my heart to beat straight out of my chest.

The van driver had rolled down his window and just used his own weapon to shoot at me.

And the bats seemed dead set on separating my hair from my head without the benefit of scissors.

I jerked my hand to ward one off where it flew straight in my face and accidentally squeezed off another round. It went wild, hitting Lord only knew what. I was rewarded with another report from the direction of the van. Cement exploded next to me, spraying me with debris.

Damn!

Thankfully, the bats lifted off, scared off by the gunfire perhaps. Their absence allowed me to regain my bearings as I rolled to my left, away from where the round had hit. I planted my feet back under me and prepared to shoot again when I realized the bats hadn't so much left me as switched targets. I stared in amazement as they attacked the van driver through the open window.

Rather than rolling up the window, as I would have done – or at least would like to believe I would have done – the driver got out instead, swiping at them.

Wait a minute ... I knew this guy: it was the creepy nurse from the blood bank that had done the disappearing act.

My stomach dropped to my feet. Had I really been that close to the Bleeder without realizing it?

My skin crawled and nearly dropped clean off when one of the bats hightailed it back to attack me.

I stumbled, which put me in the light of a street lamp where I got a better look at the flying menace trying to bite me. Was it me, or did it look ... partially burned?

I remembered Eugene bringing the bat to the office and its flying through the open door and out into the sunlight ... then the other night the sight of Vlad's goon.

Oh, yeah, this guy, this bat rather, had a

vendetta. And I was the object of it.

Even as I tried to swat him away with my gun, I reached inside my jacket with my other hand, grabbing for a sharpened pencil. Hey, I'd seen the move in a Quentin Tarantino flick; it was worth a try.

I came out with three.

Instead of trying to drop the other two, I lowered the gun to the ground and grabbed at the wing of the blasted bat. Got it! I slammed it – or him – to the ground and then stabbed him ... all three pencils hitting him right in the middle.

His screech was such that I lifted my hands to my ears to block the sound. A wing flap ... then another ... and then he stopped moving altogether, his little bat head listing to the side.

Jackpot!

The cry must have alerted the other two, because they switched targets again ... which meant the van driver was now free once more, while I contemplated how I was going to do to the other two what I'd done to their friend.

But I didn't have to. Instead of flying for me, one of them seemed to stop mid-air, its shape no more than a blur in the heavy shadows. When it appeared again, it wasn't a bat but rather none other than Vlad himself.

I swallowed hard and backed up, vaguely aware that The Bleeder had returned to the van.

Oh, God. I was dead now for sure.

Details of my nightmare came back to me ... I could hear the whisper of my name ... feel the coldness of the cement beneath my partially naked body...

'I'm ... I'm...'

I was what?

'Sorry,' I said lamely.

The other bat alit on the downed one, as if trying to pull out the pencils.

The enraged expression on Vlad's face scared me more than anything he might potentially do to me.

He stretched his neck one way and then the next and fixed a stare on me that made my blood beat cold.

'It was self defense,' I whispered.

The stake. I still had it here somewhere. I patted my jacket anxiously ... only to discover it must have fallen out.

Damn. I was going to die for sure.

Sirens sounded in the distance.

I knew a relief so profound my knees nearly gave out from under me.

Detective DellaFlora. It had to be. And if I wasn't mistaken, Pino would probably be with her...

Vlad stepped forward. The question was whether or not they'd be able to reach me in time...

For every footstep he took, I took one backward. But instead of smiting me in one fell swoop, he picked up the dead bat instead. He removed the pencils.

Was it possible it could come back to life?

Then he was gone.

I blinked, sure I was seeing things. I scanned the parking lot, but Vlad was nowhere to be seen. And, thankfully, neither was the other bat.

Silence. I looked to see the van driver had finally given up. He got out of the van a second time, grabbed something from inside, and started running.

'Stop!' I yelled after him, scrambling for my gun.

He got into the street and turned, aiming his own firearm at me.

Shit!

I dove for cover ... but there wasn't any cover to be had.

I swore I could see directly into the barrel of his weapon and imagined the bullet with my name on it waiting inside.

I braced myself for impact.

But before he could squeeze the trigger and release the round, my Mustang appeared from out of nowhere at full speed, hitting The Bleeder head on.

# THIRTY-FOUR

Within seconds, half the borough's police force descended on the scene. I lifted myself from the pavement, blinking at the flashing lights that made it look like daylight. There was a sharp pain in my side. Had I gotten shot anyway? I opened my jacket to find my black blouse slightly wet. I looked at my fingers: blood.

Pulling my blouse from the waist of my pants, I took note of a hole ... then spotted the sharpened piece of wood on the ground I must have landed on.

Great. I'd stabbed myself with my own stake.

'Hey, Metro,' Pino called from the street. 'You OK?'

'Nothing a good frappé or two can't take care of,' I said to myself as I walked across the lot to join the growing group of officers and civilians alike gathered around the body in the street.

The car had hit him with such force, it had thrown him fifty feet away. I couldn't tell if he was dead or alive. All I knew was that he no longer held the gun he'd pointed at me and would never be a threat to anyone else again.

'Man, you should have seen it!' Eugene's excited voice filled my ears. 'There he was, standing in the middle of the goddamn street, about to bust a cap at this pretty young woman here and I knew I had to do something. So – bam! – I hit him with my car.'

I finally glanced at him. I could ask him a million questions, beginning with 'Where in the hell did you go with my car?' but I voiced none of them. Truth was, whatever his reasons, in the end he'd come through.

'OK, everyone!' a uniformed officer finally said. 'You've looked your fill. Party's over. Move on!'

We all seemed to do so as one, slowly backing up, our gazes locked on the man in the street.

Paramedics worked their way through the crowd. A female dropped to her knees beside him and pressed her fingers against his neck. 'I got a pulse, people!'

A pulse. After what this guy had done, he didn't deserve to have a pulse. Then again, maybe there was a reason he was still alive.

I glanced over my shoulder at where Gina was in the parking lot, looking into the back of the van. I walked over, staying far enough away to not be in the way, but close enough to get a handle on the situation.

There appeared to be seven people there, all bound with plastic ties at the wrists and ankles, all wearing hospital gowns like Allyson had been found in. Gina motioned for help, and three officers joined her even as more paramedics pulled up. Each of the victims were helped out, freed of their restraints and then led to the paramedics' truck.

Gina was busy taking notes as she came to

stand next to me. 'It looks like the gang's all here.'

In the moment Eugene had hit The Bleeder and I heard him hit the cement, I knew both relief and fear; what if he'd already begun moving the victims to another location? If he were dead, we might not ever know where that other place lay, meaning they would suffer the same fate as their captor.

A uniformed officer came from the direction of the building.

'DellaFlora, you're not going to believe what's in there. It looks like a scene from one of those freakin' horror movies. Stephen King kind of shit.'

'Thanks, Frank. Cordon it off and make sure no one else gets in to contaminate the scene before forensics gets here.'

'Done.'

I admired Gina's direct effectiveness. I might have expected some antagonism from her male colleagues, but from what I could tell, they treated her with respect and perhaps even a little of the admiration I was experiencing.

'You got here fast,' I said.

She grimaced and looked at me directly. 'Yeah, well, looks like we were both doing the same thing; riding around the area hoping to catch a break.'

A break. That's exactly what had happened.

She took a deep breath and then released it. For the first time I saw the circles under her eyes and the paleness of her skin. Probably she'd gotten as much sleep as I had in recent nights, which was precious little.

Perhaps now we could both go home and climb into bed knowing a killer was off the streets.

The difference lay in that tomorrow I could return to life as usual ... while Gina would probably be presented with another killer to find.

Of course, my own track record of late indicated differently, but I wasn't going to focus on that now.

Another matter I chose to ignore was that of Vladimir Romanoff and what I'd seen ... or thought I'd seen, tonight.

'You want to have a look?' she asked me, nodding toward the building.

A part of me wanted to say yes. But I resisted it. I figured that it must look similar to the set up at the blood bank but with some variations that allowed for unwilling volunteers.

'Nah. I'll pass,' I said.

'Hey, you all right?' she asked.

'Me? Sure. Why do you ask?'

She indicated where I was holding my side.

'Oh. Yeah. I think I accidentally stabbed myself with a stake.'

She squinted at me. 'You should have the paramedics take a look at it just to be on the safe side.'

She called one over and despite my protests, I found myself being led to sit on the bumper of the vehicle next to one of the victims, my wound being tended to.

The woman was closer to my sister Efi's age than mine and she shivered despite the heavy wool blanket she'd been given. Probably it didn't help that she'd been bled for Lord only knew how long so that some older woman panicking at the ticking of the clock might gain a few minutes of extra life ... or feel like she had.

'You could probably use a couple of stitches,' the male paramedic said as he examined, treated and slapped a bandage on my side.

'Thanks.'

Gina had already moved on, going inside the building to have a look around. I followed the sound of Eugene's voice, which was still high with excitement as he told anyone who would listen of his latest adventure. As I walked toward my car, I had to move out of the way while a stretcher carrying The Bleeder was wheeled by. I took note that he was cuffed and shackled ... much the way he'd kept his victims.

Poetic justice?

The two police officers accompanying him told me he wouldn't be going anywhere again soon.

Pino was standing with Eugene in front of my Mustang.

'Man, you should have heard the sound! Pop!'

I moved him aside so I could make a damage assessment. The front bumper along with the radiator was dented inward. The engine was still running, but wheezed as if it had something caught in its throat it couldn't quite cough out.

I stared at Eugene.

'What?' he asked, standing peacock straight. 'I saved your life.'

Yeah, that he did.

Pino pushed back his cap and scratched the top of his head. 'Forensics is going to have to take the car in. You know, to examine it for evidence.'

'I expected as much.' I crossed my arms. 'It doesn't look like I'm going to be able to drive it until it's repaired anyway.'

'I can give you a ride home,' Pino offered.

'Naw, man, she don't need no ride. She already got one,' Eugene said.

A horn honked and we all looked over the hood of my Mustang, beyond the flashing lights of squad cars, to where a pimped out white Lincoln Escalade had just pulled up, the bass-heavy music vibrating the street below us.

Pino mumbled something under his breath and I silently agreed. You'd think with so many police officers in the immediate vicinity, the new additions would at least have enough common sense to turn the music down.

Then again, it was obvious everyone was busy with something else. Everyone except, of course, Pino, who looked ready to advance on the Lincoln and request license and registration.

I touched his arm and gave a subtle head shake. He grimaced in return.

'Just let me get some things out of the car first,' I said.

'I don't know if I should allow you to do that.'

'Well, then, you're going to have to physically stop me.'

There was no way I was letting him have my police scanner. And then there was the food in the back. Lord knows how long forensics would have it, and then there was the matter of repairs after that.

I reached in, shut off the engine, took my house and agency keys off the chain, gathered my purse, the scanner and a couple of other personal items before pushing the driver's seat up and collecting the two bags of food.

Sensing that they felt awfully light, I looked inside each: correction, two bags of empty plates.

I straightened and leveled another stare at Eugene.

'What? You said I could have some.'

I collected the garbage and slammed the door. 'Some. The key word in that sentence, Eugene, is *some*.'

He tsked. 'Ain't that some shit? Save a woman's life, and she still ain't happy...'

# THIRTY-FIVE

Last night's news was abuzz with reports The Bleeder had been caught. Per my request, my involvement in the case was being reported as simply 'an unnamed civilian,' so thankfully I was being left in peace. My uncle Spyros might tell me I was being silly; that any kind of publicity was good publicity.

Then again, maybe he wouldn't. I seemed to recall a high profile case or two in which he'd been involved for which he hadn't taken credit.

The realization caused me a moment of pause where I stood in his office taking down the items on the bulletin board early the next morning.

Despite my best attempts, I hadn't managed to get much sleep last night. Aside from the phone calls from Pete, Rosie and my mother, there was that other matter that still gaped wide open.

So rather than roll over and pull the pillow over my head when I lay wide awake at six this morning, I got up instead and came into the office on a Saturday morning. I was to pick my mother up at eight for a day long shopping marathon, hitting all those places with sales she had mapped out and finally buying myself a warm winter coat.

Until then, I had time to fill and I figured I could clean up a bit around the office.

I piled the photos and the diagrams and maps on top of the desk and then slid them into a large accordion file. There was something about closing a case like this that was deeply satisfying. Of course, when I turned back to the board I was reminded of that other little bit of unfinished business. The photo of Wendy Newberger I'd asked Pete not to put up sat smack dab in the middle of the otherwise empty board.

A loud rap on the outside door.

I frowned at the picture, leaving it where it was as I went to go see who could be knocking at this early hour. Especially since I hadn't turned on the lights except in the office.

I shouldn't have been surprised to find Ivan Romanoff's cadaverous driver on the sidewalk in the still dark, pre-dawn hour, but I was.

I unlocked the agency door and he went to open the back of the old Lincoln.

'Good morning, Sofie,' Ivan said.

'Good morning.' I wrapped my coatless arms around myself.

'I was hoping I might see you here this morning.' He nodded toward Lurch, who took a white envelope out of his pocket and extended his hand to me. 'It appears our business has been successfully concluded.'

I didn't take the envelope. 'Is it? Because there is one matter I think is still very much at issue.'

His frown looked bone deep. 'Ah, yes. I feel the need to apologize for my nephew's actions last night. His ... friend ... paid me a visit shortly thereafter. He shared with me everything.'

'Everything?'

'Yes,' he said with a somber nod as he squared his shoulders. 'Rest assured, Vladimir will be of no more worry to you.'

I narrowed my eyes. 'Oh? And how's that?'

'He's ... how shall I put this? He's been reassigned.'

Reassigned. 'As in retired?'

He smiled briefly. 'No. He is to fill a post in Eastern Europe for the time being, with no plans to be in the area again in the immediate future.'

Eastern Europe. Ouch. That had to hurt the man who had recently learned to enjoy the New York City high life.

I took a deep breath, wondering how wise it would be to mention that there was still the matter of Wendy Newberger's death to address.

I thought of the girl's picture on the bulletin board and absently fingered the cross Grandpa Kosmos had given me that still hung around my neck.

'I assure you, Sofie. Punishment is being imposed that is equal to the crime.'

Vampire prison?

The quirk of his lips made me wonder if he really could read minds.

'I see,' I said.

Ivan took the envelope from Lurch and pressed it into my hand. 'I cannot thank you enough for the work you have done.'

He then kissed both of my cheeks and began to turn away.

'I've got a question for you,' I said without

realizing I wanted to say anything. 'Are you ... real?'

He didn't blink. 'Yes, Sofie. I am real. I have the same needs you do: love, nourishment and connection.'

Then he turned and got back into the car.

I stood frozen to the spot, watching sightlessly.

Had he really just kissed me?

I resisted the urge to wipe whatever residue might have remained on my cheeks (was vampirism transferable through bodily fluids? Like zombieism?).

Long after the car had disappeared, I lifted the envelope, weighing the significant thickness of bills, and went back inside. I wasn't altogether certain I wanted to accept the offering.

Talk about blood money; was it possible to get more literal than that?

I tossed the envelope into my top drawer and then locked it, figuring I could decide soon enough what to do with it ... if anything.

I walked back into the office and stood staring at the board. Despite what had just happened, it didn't feel right to take the picture down. I flipped the board to the other side where I'd already wiped it clean and left it there, then took the file containing all case information and put it on Rosie's desk alongside the stake I'd returned bearing my own blood.

Boy, she was going to have a field day when she came across that on Monday.

But now with The Bleeder in custody, maybe she wouldn't be so unreasonable.

I moved to make myself my second frappé of

the day, only to discover there weren't enough Nescafé granules to get a full cup.

I wondered what had happened between Vlad and Wendy Newberger. Had rough sex gotten too wild? Had he accidentally bitten her when he hadn't intended to? Or was something darker to blame? Since there didn't appear to be an over-population of vampires – read: no reports of dead bodies coming back to life – I presumed they had their own way of dealing with pro-creation.

I grimaced, finding the term icky when applied to their breed.

At any rate, I was reasonably reassured that whatever happened, it wouldn't be happening again anytime soon.

I was also reasonably convinced that neither of the Romanoffs was connected to The Bleeder, beyond the latter's activities shining an unwel-come light on the formers' normally discreet activities.

As for The Bleeder himself, I spoke to Pino late last night, to make sure all the bases were covered, and he'd told me DellaFlora was busy running the show, not yet allowing the down time she claimed to crave. Despite the late hour, she'd managed to verify the name of The Bleed-er as Daniel Cleaver, a former, disgruntled em-ployee of the very blood bank I'd visited. She'd even managed to get a copy of his photo to Dr Westervelt, who verified Cleaver was the one from whom he'd procured his blood.

From what we were all able to piece together, Westervelt had been limited in his ability to acquire the increasing supply of blood he needed via legal channels without explaining its intended use. And since he couldn't report that it was for the questionable and highly illegal procedure of blood infusions for which his clients clamored – well, when Cleaver approached him with a deal, the 'good' doctor had every reason to expect the product would come from the bank with which Cleaver worked; he'd had no idea that his supplier had been dismissed ... or that he'd instituted new and deadly methods for obtaining the blood. A resource already in low supply in the city, for which he could ask a high price, and get it.

DellaFlora planned to check into the possibility that other high-end doctors specializing in catering to those in an endless search for the Fountain of Youth had also been customers of the sick, new-age entrepreneur. And one of her first stops was going to be to my client, actress Jane Creek.

I called Jane, as well, last night to let her know of the detective's impending visit. I don't know what I'd expected, but I'd been amused by her apparent pleasure. Probably she had contacted her press agent the instant I disconnected to spin the information and earn her another day or two of news coverage.

I shook my head, wondering if I'd ever understand how her mind worked ... even as I was partly thankful that I didn't.

The irony that vampirism was the ultimate cure for mortality wasn't lost on me. Hey, all one would be required to do was drink blood and avoid the sun. Probably a minor sacrifice for some.

Of course, I still wasn't entirely convinced there was any such thing as vampires.

Another paradox was that even now The Bleeder was down the hall from Allyson Piszchala at the hospital, although he was still unconscious, his prognosis grim. I guess Eugene had hit him harder than we all realized, which made my being without my car for the time being, and stuck with a rental, well worth it.

As for Allyson's twin sister, she was also in the same hospital, sharing the room with her. Allyson had regained consciousness last night. Pino told me that her mother had been watching the news on the capture of The Bleeder on the hospital room TV and she had opened her eyes, as if knowing her and her sister's ordeal was finally over.

I rubbed the back of my neck. What was I doing? Oh, yeah: frappé.

Of course, there was the perfect place to get a fresh frappé that I knew would be open this early on a Saturday morning...

I smiled to myself, closed up my uncle's office, shrugged into my coat and locked up the agency after myself. I glanced up at the sky, taking in the purple fingers of the coming dawn. Surprise of surprises, it looked as if the sun was going to shine today.

I waited for traffic and then crossed the street to my rental car. Subcompact, was what the agent had told me my insurance covered. I wondered what could possibly be smaller than compact. I found out. The car I had was little bigger than a bread box and handled probably just as well.

I inserted the key in the lock when bass-pounding music made me turn my head. A familiar gold Cadillac pulled up next to me and the passenger window rolled down, letting out a cloud of smoke that had nothing to do with cigarettes.

'Hey, Sofie girl, how goes it, babe?'

'Morning, Eugene.'

'Morning? I ain't gone to bed yet, so it's still night to me.' He held up a white plastic bag bulging with something. 'I wanted to bring you this. You know, as an apology for eating all your food last night.'

I accepted the bag and looked inside at the various Styrofoam containers.

'It's food from my favorite soul food place. Best damn barbecue in the entire city.'

'Where'd you get soul food this early?'

'I got it last night. Hey, leftovers for leftovers, right?'

I laughed. 'I appreciate the thought.'

He looked behind him where he was holding up a couple of travelers. But since they had yet to beep, he wasn't making any effort to move. 'Hey, you need a car?'

'Why? You offering to lend me yours?'

He tsked. 'No, girl. Not even my woman is allowed to drive my baby.' He caressed the steering wheel. 'Speaking of which, with all my hero work last night, guess who's back in the house?'

'You mean you have an actual address again?'

'That's right. I'm going there now: you know, to let her show me some appreciation.'

I quickly held up my hand. 'T.M.I.' I said, not needing that particular information.

'Anyway, you need a car, I can get one for you.'

'Hmm ... why does that sound like it might be stolen?'

He grinned, flashing his gold tooth at me. 'They won't even know it's gone for at least a week.'

'No, but thanks.' I gestured to the subcompact. 'I got a rental. Now you want to talk piece of shit.'

He considered the blue bread box. 'Yeah, but I bet it got heat.'

I gave an eye roll even as one of the drivers behind him finally laid on the horn.

'Well, I gotta go,' he said.

'Thanks for the food, Eugene ... and for everything else.'

'You know, there's a way you can show me some appreciation.'

I gaped at him, open-mouthed.

'Naw, girl, I got all I can handle at home. I'm talking 'bout my paycheck.'

Somehow I'd never seen a guy like Eugene Waters growing on me. But he was.

'We'll see,' I said with a smile.

With a final wave, the window and the volume on his music went up, and the car rolled down the street.

I shook my head and got into my own temporary vehicle, taking a moment to adjust to the foreign surroundings and toying with the seat positioning again. One thing was nice; it did have heat.

I turned it on and reveled in the sweet feel. I'd have to make sure to tell the mechanic to fix Lucille's heater when forensics finally released it.

I pulled from the curb and drove the few blocks to my destination, looking in my mirrors the whole way. I didn't have to wonder who I was half-expecting to spot; what I did wonder was why I hadn't spotted him lately.

Where was Jake?

I thought about calling him, but decided against it. Right now I had another male securely in my sights. And I wasn't going to stop until I got a second shot at that date thing; and maybe some more great sex.

I pulled up outside Dino's *zaharoplastio* and parked. The sky was beginning to brighten quickly, but without cloud cover the air was colder than ever. As I walked to the bakery front, I took a deep breath of the fresh air, hoping to detect the aroma of all things baking. Strangely, nothing but cold cement filled my nose.

I shrugged. Maybe the wind was blowing in the opposite direction.

I grasped the front door handle and met resistance.

Hunh. That was odd.

Dino usually opened his doors at six every morning.

Cupping my hand against the glass, I peered inside the dark interior. The display cases appeared empty and there was no movement at all.

I drew back, puzzled, staring at the Closed sign.

'Hey, you know the guy that owns the place?' an older man who was sweeping his own pawn store sidewalk asked.

'Yeah. You know where he is?'

'Sure. I.N.S. came by yesterday. Heard them say they were deporting him.'

I squinted at him, certain he had to be mistaken. 'What?'

'That's right. Guy across the street thinks it's because he's Arab.'

'He's Greek.'

'That's what I told him.' He shrugged. 'Hey, if you happen to talk to him, let him know that my offer to buy the place still stands.'

I slowly backed away from the shop, my mind racing a million miles a minute.

Dino was being deported...

I couldn't seem to wrap my head around the idea. The possibility never occurred to me before. As far as I knew, he'd entered the country legally. Hell, post 9-11 you couldn't get in anymore without going through extensive checks and mounds of paperwork.

Why, then, would the Immigration and Naturalization Service want to deport him?

My thoughts wandered to the other man in my life...

Jake Porter.

I squinted at nothing and everything, remembering the past couple of weeks ... Of Jake following me ... Of his popping up at Dino's shop...

No ... It wasn't possible...

Could Jake have arranged to have his competition removed from the picture?

'Hey, you'll tell him, won't you?' the sweeper asked.

I waved vaguely at him as I headed for my car, my destination being one mysterious, hotly handsome and endlessly frustrating Australian...